AN ANTISEMITE

AN ANTISEMITE

Alan Dent

PENNILESS PRESS PUBLICATIONS
Website: www.pennilesspress.co.uk

Published by

Penniless Press Publications 2021

ISBN 978-1-913144-28-9

Even though Israel has the most sophisticated army in the region and possesses an advanced atomic capability, it continues to regard itself in terms of the Holocaust, as the victim of an unconquerable, bloodthirsty enemy. Thus, whatever Israelis do, whatever means we employ to guard our gains or to increase them, we justify as last-ditch self-defense. We can, therefore, do no wrong.

Simha Flapan

SUSPENSION

"What've you been doing?" said the secretary as Bill George arrived at his Labour Party meeting.

He was at the bar ordering the first of four or five pints of lager. At intervals during the business, he would wriggle out of his bench-seat puffing:

"I'll just get to the bar while you read that," or "I'll be back in a minute while you think about that."

Bill, who didn't drink, stopped a few metres from him.

"Me?"

The secretary dipped into his trouser pocket for change. The barmaid smiled at Bill while she waited and he had the odd but obviously absurd feeling that she was in on what Nigel knew. A swig of the pint reduced it to nearly half.

"Aye. I've had a letter."

He rummaged among his papers for a minute and extracted a sheet. Bill put on his glasses.

"I'm not supposed to show you, but there, read that."

"Does that mean I'm not allowed in the meeting?"

"Aye. Haven't you been informed?"

"No."

"According to this you have."

"Well, I haven't."

"I'm sorry."

It was a short and relatively pleasant walk home. The July evening was still light and the trees along Royal Avenue were in friendly leaf. There was that summer-dusk odour in the air reminiscent of childhood games in the street. Of course, there were no children playing *Farmer, Farmer* or *Queenie-O-Coco* . The main road through the suburb was relatively quiet, the evening rush hour over, so he was able to cross without using the pelican. As he turned into Edgehill Rd, from the humped railway bridge, a lad on a bike swerved to avoid him.

"Sorry," said the kid.

"You're all right."

7

The incident summoned a swift memory: a clash of bikes at the curve of a no cycling ginnel, Bill's apology and the older lad's threat that next time he'd have something to regret.

Mad yapping told him the Kennedy's Staffordshire was in the garden, no doubt harrying the skateboard which set off its barking. He paused at the black iron gates whose spears were tipped gold.

"Hello, Bob. Come on, boy."

Letting go of the board, the squat, muscular animal trotted to the gate, sniffed and wagged its tail for thirty seconds before going back to its activity. Bill was no great dog lover but the Kennedy's animals had been known to bite, the postman had refused to enter: familiarity was safety.

He flicked the kettle's switch, though he wasn't particularly thirsty. The small kitchen had recently been redecorated by his sister who enjoyed painting and making things smart. He'd neglected it for nearly a decade. The cupboard tops were greasy, there were condensation streaks down the walls, the paint by the window had flaked leaving a patch of plaster reminiscent of a bear. The living-room too was showing signs of weariness. He sat in the corner of the sofa whose arm had turned black and shiny and thought for the hundredth time he should investigate a new one. His reassuring little pile of books and papers was at his feet. He picked up the remotes and connected the tv to Radio 3, reached for the well-worn copy of *Nostromo* and began to read.

Occasionally, his concentration was broken when the ideas running behind his conscious effort became too intrusive. He put the opened book down on the cushion. He'd been carefully polite in the letters and e-mails he'd sent and he'd stuck to uncontroversial facts. The murder of Lord Moyne, for example. He couldn't recall verbatim the quotation he'd culled. He went to the loaded, untidy bureau in the dining-room. He used to sit and work at it, now it was too jammed. He used the dining-table his sister had passed onto him, much to her disdain. Buried, he found an envelope, sealed but not addressed. He tore it open and found the letter, Four paragraphs in was the quote:

"If a comparison is to be made with the Nazis it is surely those who wish to force an imported regime on the Arab popula-

tion…the proposal that the Arabs should be subjugated by force
to a Jewish regime is inconsistent with the Atlantic Charter, and
that ought to be told to America."

Was that it? How could he know?

He went back to Conrad. There was no sense trying to
think about the other matter as he had no substance to grasp. Until
he was properly informed, there was nothing he could do.

An e-mail arrived ten days later. Apparently, a letter had
been sent snail mail. He was CN-2539. The text explained the
administrative suspension. There followed advice about contact-
ing his GP, the Samaritans or Citizens' Advice. He got up from
the table, pulled open the patio door he'd repaired with off-cuts
and putty from the shed. He'd pushed the mower the day before
so the grass was shorn. He didn't care too much about the state of
the lawn, what he liked was the flower bed beneath the kitchen
window. It was a small patch which sloped towards the back
fence beyond which the trains ran. He liked the lines of yellow
and orange marigolds above all. There were foxgloves, lupins,
geraniums, a dahlia, two small fuschias. He stepped along the flat
stones which made a half-hearted path by the window. The day
was warm and there was a gentle breeze. He was tempted to go
back indoors, shut down the computer and forget it. His GP? The
Samaritans? Maybe there were people who were hit badly by the
kind of letter he'd received but his overall response was disdain.
He walked the few yards to the front gate to take a look at
Edeghill Road. The little boy from next door was pestering his
dad who was cutting timber on his workmate.

"Hello, Kyle," said Bill. "Helpin' your daddy?"

"No, he isn't," said Malc, looking up from his work. "Are
you? Can't get a thing done for his chatterin'."

"How's it coming?"

"Oh, nearly there. Got to get it finished before I'm back
to work on Monday."

"Busman's holiday, eh Keith?"

"Aye. No, Kyle, leave that alone. I've told you."

"Hey," said Bill, " come and have a look at this, Kyle."

The lad followed him to his shed from which Bill pulled
an old wooden trolley made of throwaway planks and fitted with

9

pram wheels. Its steering device was a rope threaded through holes drilled in the thick, square axel.

"What d'you think? Shall we ask your dad if you can have it?"

"Dad," shouted the boy, running off "Dad, look what Bill's got."

Bill pulled it by the rope, remembering when he'd nailed it together for his son, perhaps a year or two older than Kyle at the time.

"It's an old thing I made for my lad," he said. "He can have it if he wants, though it'll cost you in iodine and plasters."

"Aye," said his neighbour, inspecting. "Aye, never mind him, I'll be havin' a go."

"How d'you do it?" called the boy.

"Get your knee on it," said his dad, "hold the rope to steer and scoot with the other foot."

The youngster had a go and careered along the pavement.

"Don't go on the road," shouted his father.

"He'll get the hang of it," said Bill.

Back at his laptop he read the set of questions he was asked to answer within seven days so the matter could be dispensed with *in a timely manner.* Apparently when his answers were received, he'd be informed of the *progress of the investigation.* Each of the ten questions began: *Please can you...Please can you explain why you said "there is a long history of Zionist anti-Semitism"; Please can you explain why you mentioned that Folke Bernadotte was assassinated by Jewish terrorists...*Finally came: *Do you regret sending this material* and *do you intend to send similar material in the future?* Well, he said to himself, I could hardly intend to send it in the past.

The stupidity of the questions made him think he should forget it. Let them expel him if they like. He shut down, put on his shoes, grabbed the Conrad and went out for his daily walk and coffee.

Slowly, he'd developed a lingering disgust for his town. It was one of those places brought into existence by the industrial revolution; a sleepy market town of a few thousand surrounded by gentle hills, woods and with a tidal river running on its southern flank transformed by the cotton industry. In the 1960s the heart was torn out of the place. It had been hit hard by Thatcher's anti-industry policies and the recent austerity had stripped out much of what kept it from shabbiness. Then there were the years he'd spent teaching in one of its schools. Every day he liked to escape. It was a short bus ride to the coast and now he had the pass he could escape for a coffee, a read and a walk by the sea. There was a little, Italian café which looked out on the square where they set out tables in summer. Crowded as always when the sun shone, he went inside. Unusually, he saw someone he knew.

On her table she'd spread out papers and was writing in a thick book. He wondered if he should avoid disturbing her but she looked and smiled.

"All right, Barbara. You look very industrious."

" Campaign to save the library."

"Ah, good. Are you winning?"

"We had a meeting last night. Thirty people turned up."

"Wherever one or two are gathered together."

"Are you sitting down."

He hooked his coat on the back of the chair.

"Morning, Bill," called the waitress who was already making his coffee, "okay?"

"Fine, thanks. How are you?"

"Busy."

"You like to be busy."

"I do, it makes the day pass quickly."

Barbara had been an English teacher in a big comprehensive where she'd run into the usual trouble: in her mid-fifties the SLT (Sycophancy Lettuce and Tomato as Bill liked to call them) had begun to find fault with her lessons. She'd taught for over three decades, seen hundreds of pupils through O Level, GCSE and A Level, watched her protegés progress to university, been promoted to second in department, passed through the threshold, moved on to UPS 2, yet all at once her teaching was less than adequate. If the pace of her lesson was good, there was too little peer assessment; if the peer assessment was fine, the pace was too slow; if the behaviour for learning was without fault, the planning

11

was less than perfect; if the planning was impeccable, the behaviour for learning was below par. The risible circus in which one of the hierarchy appeared with a clipboard, loitered at the back of the room for twenty minutes and delivered the inevitable verdict began to make her physically and psychically sick. The counsel of perfection she was expected to fulfil was an Orwellian dishonesty. She would have preferred it if the Head had said bluntly: "Look, you're fifty-four, you're expensive, you know your own mind and you're experienced. I want young, cheap, compliant teachers. I want to please OFSTED. Let's strike a deal."

For eight weeks she was observed. Of the sixteen lessons, fifteen were deemed good. For the last, the county adviser arrived. A little, thin woman with thick glasses from behind which she looked at the world as if it failed to meet her requirements, she'd taught for two years in a girls' private school before seizing her opportunity to escape the rigours of the classroom (even a classroom populated by the dutiful daughters of the conformist middle and upper classes of Surrey) for the less demanding territory of educational administration where she could earn a living telling others why they weren't as accomplished as her. With the creation of OFSTED, the establishment of league table and high-stakes testing, all the paraphernalia of a regime of persistent pressure and humiliation whose aim to destroy the comprehensive system was poorly disguised by a flimsy rhetoric of raising standards, she came into her own. The satisfaction she gained from having teachers driven from their jobs was exquisite. She would glide home in her red Saab convertible feeling thoroughly justified in having removed another inadequacy . It was in the best interests of the children. She convinced herself she was a selfless devotee of standards. The children must not be let down. Every lesson must be perfect. She'd reached the point where a lesson she couldn't find fault with shook her confidence. Little by little, she'd convinced herself it didn't exist. Every lesson was inadequate, to some degree. Did all teachers then deserve to be dismissed? Yes, it was unfortunately true. Teachers were the enemy. She and the SLTs were charged with the sacred duty of imposing adequacy. If she permitted a teacher to remain in the profession, it was only because practicality made the sacking of the entire teaching force impossible. Yet she was convinced, like her political masters, that such surgery was necessary. She agreed the profession was The Blob.

Barbara's sixteenth lesson was judged unsatisfactory because her planning didn't perfectly match the delivery. Ms Collins insisted on formal support (a Kafkaesque misnomer in which a process of sustained undermining was considered a prop). There were another eight observations. The Head closed in. Ms Collins goaded him. Barbara collapsed under the strain. The union case worker mocked Ms Collins's report: how could the planning match delivery when the pupils had been delayed by ten minutes in assembly? Any rational person could see Barbara had to adjust to their late arrival. Ms Collins glared at him through her bottle thick glasses. There were many other faults. I hope not as many as in your report, retorted the irreverent trade unionist.

It was hopeless. The Head had done the arithmetic: she was earning forty-two thousand; he could replace her with an NQT on twenty-one. She arrived at eight-thirty and left at four. She refused to undertake a lunchtime duty. She questioned every initiative and was heard to say often: "I've been doing this for years and I know what works." The Head wasn't going to miss this opportunity.

The union man advised her to get signed off. He could secure six months on full pay and a deal: sixteen weeks pay, no tax or national insurance, a neutral reference. She complied.

For a year after her forced exit, she worked for the union in a two-day a week role in London. She enjoyed the train journey on Monday morning, the overnight in Hackney with her old friend from university, new colleagues, a walk in the capital's streets at lunchtime, and she felt valued and useful again. The year over, she devoted herself to local campaigns and to her work for the Lib Dems who she supported partly because in her neck of the woods people would no more vote Labour than dance naked in the streets.

"What's the book?" said Barbara.

"Conrad."

"Which one?"

"*Nostromo.*"

13

"I don't know that," she said. "I've read the one about the Congo."

"*Heart of Darkness.*"

"Yes. Bit depressing."

"Oh, I don't know," said Bill. "Nothing is quite so depressing as optimism."

Barbara gave a little laugh and looked at him obliquely.

"What are you doing with yourself, anyway. Still active in the union."

"No," he said. "All that business."

"Yes, I know."

"What about you?"

"I go the meetings. Keith is treasurer. He keeps us on the ball."

"Yes, I bet."

"He's doing a lot for the Labour Party."

"And the Trades Council still?"

"Yes, he can't wind down. I knew he wouldn't."

"Why should he when he's still energetic? And I guess he has to show his brother he can match him."

Keith's brother was a leading figure in the Institute of Directors. Apparently at opposite end of the political spectrum, they met almost in the middle where Keith's socialism blended into social democracy and Brian's free tradeism tempered into Mac-Millanite pragmatism.

"Are you still active in the Party?" asked Barbara as the waitress arrived with the coffee.

Seeing the papers and hearing the question the employee blenched from serious discussion.

"Politics doesn't agree with me," she said. "It gives me a headache."

"You're lucky," said Bill, "it gives most people a pain somewhere else."

"What you reading today, Bill?" and she leaned over him to spy the volume.

She read the title aloud.

"I've never heard of it. What's it about?"

"The pursuit of wealth at all costs."

"Who's that on the front cover?"

"That's the man himself. Fine moustache he has isn't it? Fidanza he's called."

"Is he the hero?"

"You might say so. You might also say he's a villain. He ends up dead because he can't resist the lure of silver. It's a cautionary tale."

"Mmm," she said, "enjoy."

Bill dipped his spoon in the cappuccino and ran it round the edge, taking the little heap of foamed milk into his mouth. He'd picked up the habit of reading in cafes in Paris where, at fourteen on a school trip, he'd seen for the first time, men and women at pavement tables sipping exprès while intent on a newspaper or book. Later, as a student, he'd developed the habit so that now his day didn't seem complete if he hadn't spent an hour at a table with a volume or journal. It seemed extremely civilised and when he'd discovered the history of Parisian cafes and their associations with political, artistic and philosophical movements, he wanted to make it part of his life. There was a café in town established by an Italian which had retained its 1930's décor and attracted a coterie of would-be bohemians – aspiring actors who never appeared on stage, poets who never published a word, musicians who recorded their compositions on tapes stored in great dusty piles in their bedrooms – where he became an habitué, reading *Le Neveu de Rameau* or *Le Rouge et Le Noir* amongst weary shoppers who came for an egg roll, a vanilla and a nice cup of tea.

All the same, he couldn't resist trying to bring the atmosphere of the *Quartier Latin* to his northern town, or perhaps couldn't live with the idea he'd left it behind.

"No," he said, "as a matter of fact, I'm suspended."

"What for?"

"Anti-Semitism, apparently."

"What?"

"Mmm."

"How did that come about?"

"I'm not allowed to say, on pain of expulsion. Not the details anyway. But I sent an e-mail to someone who appeared on the *Panorama* programme."

15

"Oh, that."

"Did you see it?"

"Yes. I wasn't convinced."

"I'm glad to hear it."

"There must be some anti-Semitism in the Labour Party. I mean, it's in society so you'd expect there to be."

"So there must be some in the Lib Dems?"

"Of course not," she laughed.

"It's transparent, Barbara. Corbyn wants to ban arms sales to Israel. He supports the Palestinians. He's not prepared to continue Labour's cowardly submission to the State of Israel. It's a set-up."

"But even Corbyn says there's a problem."

"He's caught off balance. He should come out fighting."

"He has to deal with the anti-Semites though."

"Like me."

She laughed again.

"No, they've got it wrong in your case."

"Then maybe all cases."

"Well, that Chris Williamson, he looks a bit of nasty character."

"Really?"

"Didn't he refuse to apologise?"

"Did you hear what he said?"

"I saw something on the news."

"What he said, you can find it on Youtube, was that Labour shouldn't apologise for its record on racism. That it has proud record of standing up to prejudice. As a matter of fact, I disagree with him."

Bill picked up the big cup and took two sips of the lovely coffee whose exquisite bitterness was filtered through the mild and slightly sweet whipped-up milk. What was it that gave the sweet edge? Lactose? What was lactose anyway? How did it differ from glucose or sucrose? He drank it without caffeine because he was prone to palpitations. The G.P. had given him a tip:

"How long do they last?"

" A few seconds."

16

"Nothing to worry about. If they last twenty minutes call an ambulance. This is what you can do. Stimulate the vagus. Here," and the charming, clever Asian ran his finger down his neck from just below his ear to just above his clavicle, "it runs all the way down, you see. That's why it's called the vagus, the wanderer. Stimulate it and it slows the heart rate. When you get a palpitation, do that. It'll calm it. And if it lasts a few seconds, its nothing. We all get them. Ectopics. Mostly we don't notice them."

In spite of doing without caffeine, Bill still felt a lift after his daily cup. Maybe it was auto-suggestion, but it worked. He felt more lively for forty-five minutes.

"You think there is anti-Semitism, then?"

"No, I think Labour has a sordid record. It has connived in colonialism in Africa and Asia, given hardly a peep when nearly a million Palestinians were ethnically cleansed and look at its attitude to Ireland."

"Sounds like you should be glad they've suspended you."

"It's simply the subversion of democracy. You're free to vote for what you like, unless it's socialism."

"Won't get people to vote for socialism round here."

"Not allowed to vote for it anywhere."

"People can vote for Corbyn if they like."

"Yes, Barbara, but look at the triumph of media distortion. Probably the most active anti-racist in the country is accused of anti-Semitism by whom? By a bunch of benighted Zionists who keep two million people imprisoned in the Gaza Strip because they're Arabs, and he's the racist. It's stunning. Orwell would be agape."

She laughed again, raising her head in the way which always made him think of a horse.

"No smoke without fire, people think."

"People are kept deliberately ignorant."

"Now, now. You're not allowed to say that. The people are sacrosanct in a democracy."

"I'm sure they are in a democracy."

"Oh, we are Mr Cynicism today."

17

The coffee had cooled enough for him to drink it without pause. Its lovely, aromatic bitterness filled his mouth. The final act was to scoop the remaining froth onto the shiny little spoon, bit by bit, and close his lips around it. When nothing remained, he set the cup on its saucer, the spoon leaning idly against its rim, like a tired workman on his spade.

Had he not met Barbara, he would have been reading. Twenty or thirty minutes of Conrad and he'd head off to the shore. She began to tell him about the library campaign. Austerity had forced the closure. They'd mounted a petition. Thousands had signed, in the post office, the heritage centre, the Oxfam shop, some of the cafes. Even Tories, who had voted for the administration had joined in. Bill nodded. Presumably they'd imagined austerity would be someone else's.

Barbara was busy in the right directions. What she gave her time and effort to was worthy; but he was bored and, though he didn't like to admit it, felt above her level. Not that he wouldn't have done his bit. He'd spent enough of his life, after all, pushing leaflets through letter-boxes or handing them out in town centres on Saturday mornings. It was necessary, low-level, grassroots work. Yet it was petty and ironic. There would be no need for Barbara's campaign if people had done the simple thing of voting against what they were now signing a petition to try to reverse. No one in this well-heeled, bourgeois little place (he noted how anachronistic the latter adjective seemed) wanted the library to close. It was a neat, cosy building, welcoming and calm. Old folk nipped in for an hour or two during the day in winter, sure to meet someone they knew. There were newspapers. Children came, in spite of the internet, looking for books to help with school projects. The staff were well-known: they couldn't walk a hundred metres down the street for a sandwich without ten people saying hello. The pre-school corner was a gathering place for young mothers or grandparents needing relief from intensity. And the cost was minimal.

He nodded, smiled and tried to look and sound interested, but he was thinking about the sea.

There was a wind from the west, strong but warm. He went down the concrete steps to the pebbly shore. The tide was lapping a metre from his boots. He anticipated that further on it might be smashing against the sea wall. Crows came flapping, floating from the green and in the distance, he saw the kestrel hovering. He strode to get the feel of his legs and, as usual, when he'd sat for a while, felt the odd surge of his heart as he gathered pace. Probably, that would kill him, in the long run. For the time being, he hoped the G.P. was right. Across the estuary, Southport was sharply visible. The early morning clouds had dissipated and the sky was almost entirely stark blue. The boat which had been anchored in the same spot all through last winter was submerged to half-mast. Another, a small rower was tugging on its rope like a dog eager to be free, while at the foot of the wall he passed the small fishing vessel whose cabin had been cracked and battered by the Christmas storms.

A spaniel came haring down the next flight. Bill was familiar and looked up for its master, a young, thin man with red hair and glasses who was here with the dog at about the same time every day. The animal ran to him as if it would jump up to greet him, but scooted past, five centimetres from his legs. A Labrador galloped in pursuit, its female owner calling it back impotently.

"He's off," said Bill as he passed her.

"She's impossible today," said the woman, smiling, catching his eye and hurrying.

On the driftwood bench at the top of the slipway the alcoholic and his partner sat smoking. At his feet was a green, nearly empty bottle. He was a dark-haired, handsome man of thirty-five or so, always belligerent in his speech and she a mild blonde with a noticeably fine figure and a little girl's face and demeanour. Most people who passed would say hello. It was the way of walkers, of people spending the time of day pleasantly, unlike the alienated culture of the city where others were so numerous they began to lose their human signature. He wondered if this time he should nod and speak but a glance told him the drunk was well gone. He climbed the little slope. The men were still at work building the new defences. The fenced-off promenade meant a detour along the road and the rough sandy path behind the houses whose backs faced the sea. They were large, splendid places with

19

expansive gardens ending at the six foot wall with a gate for each one.

He always wondered who the occupants were. How did they earn their livings? It was no petty income could provide such space and comfort. His trajectory as a teacher had taken him from the starting salary of six thousand to thirty-five across thirty-two years. His naivety seemed to be carried in on the wind. Gulls drifted overhead enjoying being carried on the swirl. What we evolved for we enjoy. His legs were tiring already. He wondered how the gulls experienced wing-tiredness. Did they keep going or settle? Did old gulls falter, unable any more to cover the distances? Or did they battle on against their aching muscles till one day they fell from the sky and were washed out to sea to be guzzled by a shark? As he'd imagined a teacher's pay would let him live well, so he'd thought his legs would always carry him easily over meagre distances. What was three and half or four miles? How far did a gull fly in a day?

The lake, man-made for boating, was agitated by the breeze. Ducks and swans were close to the sloping edge. A spaniel on a lead lurched for one of the big, white birds as its owner yanked it back and scolded. Bill nodded and said hello and the younger man replied. It was odd how even the slightest, passing human contact was sustaining. He recalled some sentimental formulation he'd seen somewhere, on a greetings card or a poster maybe: a stranger is only someone you haven't yet got to know. The world was composed of strangers. The truth was, only those close to you engaged your emotions and attention, the rest were just passing through. Yet those passing through also defined your life. The man he'd just spoken to wasn't one of the dog-walkers he saw frequently. Maybe he'd never see him again. How odd, to say hello to someone you knew nothing about and who you'd have no further contact with. Yet the mere fact of his humanity made him significant. To exist was to engage the destiny of others and most of those others were strangers.

His mind ran on quickly to the thought that once all social distinctions were stripped away, what was left was identity. Every person on the planet, now, in the past, and in the future was identical to every other in their human essence. When he was a stu-

dent it was called "the human condition". There was no distinction between people anything like as powerful as their species
identity. Yet obsession with distinction was everywhere. To his
left was the estuary, ancient, given, part of the world which existed long before we arrived. The sense of contingency was lovely.
It was far more awe-inspiring to imagine that, had some minor
change happened in the far past, we might never have been here,
than to be burdened with the notion that we were placed by some
omniscient puppet-master whose intentions we must, every minute of the day, try to guess.

The final stretch at the seaward side of the sand dunes
was along the path beyond which was the bed of grasses, water-
logged and waving in the wind, and then onto the beach with the
grey sea lapping a metre from his feet. His leg muscles tightened
as he pushed up the steps to the prom. In the little chalets to the
right families were camped for the day, sitting in folding chairs
with plates of salad, or for the kiddies, chicken nuggets and chips
on their knees, slender glasses of prosecco in their hands. He
glanced into the neat buildings, like dolls' houses. People had
brought blankets and books, bottles and bags of goodies: such
was the charm, still, of a simple day at the seaside on the Lanca-
shire coast. Rounding the boating-pool he bumped into Jimmy
Villiers, a councillor from his home town.

"All right, Jimmy?"

"Eh up, Bill. What you doin' 'ere?"

"Just havin' a walk. "

"Yeah, I come to blow away the cobwebs. You get stale
sitting in council meetings."

"Isn't that the idea?"

"Bugger off."

"I've just had a nice coffee, but I'll buy you another if
you like."

"I'd rather have a pint."

"Okay, you can pay."

In the *Lord Derby* they found a corner as far away from
the musak as possible.

"So you're off the booze?"

"Doctor's orders."

"What you got?"

"Nothing."

"Is your doctor mad?"

"Prophylaxis, Jimmy."

"Is it fatal?"

"Prevention. Slightly raised blood sugar."

"A drop of beer won't harm that."

"No, but they tell me to keep my weight down and booze is calories. I drank like a sparrow anyway, so reduction meant elimination."

"When are you going to stand, anyway?"

"Impossible now, Jimmy."

"Why? Bankrupt?"

"Does that disqualify you? No, suspended."

"Eh?"

Bill nodded.

"What for?"

"Anti-Semitism, apparently."

"Fuck off."

Bill laughed. He wondered whether Jimmy's disbelief suggested he couldn't credit anyone would think him a racist or his unwillingness to accept his Party could be so daft.

"True. Watch your back, Jimmy. Put a poster of Netanyahu on your wall or you'll be suspect."

"What did you do, say Hitler was a Zionist?"

"Livingstone was wrong about that but right about the Havaara Transfer Agreement. Hitler didn't know about it at the time."

"You're well informed."

"I've been reading."

"Aye. What's it all about then?"

"Not allowed to tell you the details or I'll be expelled, unless I can trust you not to say a word."

"Be in the *Post* tomorrow."

"I sent an e-mail."

"Who to? John Mann?"

" Chap called Cash."

"The Tory?"

"No, not him. This one's a Zionist. Runs an outfit called the People's Protection Association."

"Which people?"

"Jews."

"Protection from what?"

"The likes of you and me."

"Socialists."

"Aye, socialists who have the neck to say Israel has something to answer for."

"I hope you didn't insult Rabbi Sacks."

"You know me, Jimmy, I wouldn't insult organised religion."

"So what did you say? Golda Meir was a lesbian?"

"Was she?"

"Who cares?"

"Well, Cash has a theory, I'm sure he's very proud of it, though it's hardly original. It's warmed over New-Antisemitism, which would give anyone the runs. All people on the Left, that's you and me, Jimmy, are racists without knowing it and the proof is we oppose racism. Remember when we stood outside the football ground handing out Anti-Nazi League flyers, in the February freeze, and the NF thugs turned up?"

"Charming evening, I recorded it for posterity in my journal."

"That proves we're anti-Semites. Because we're anti-racists, and not just in our words but on the streets, we think we can't be racists, and because we think we can't, we are. So the infallible proof that a person is an anti-Semite is they are actively engaged in anti-racism."

"Did he get a Phd for that?"

"Probably."

"You told him it's a bag of shite."

"My considered intellectual judgement. I also pointed out that Zionism is guilty of atrocious anti-Semitism and told him to clean his own pigsty first."

"Good advice. I need another pint."

"Slow down. Heather'll blame me if you stagger home."

"Just one more. A single pint is no good to anyone."

Bill took a glance at the punters. How odd it was to be sitting here talking about his suspension on specious grounds in a pub in one of the most resolutely Tory places in the country. What chance would he have of explaining to these people? They knew as much about Israel and Palestine as about the topography of the depths of the ocean. How could he know? It was an assumption and maybe one too far: people could be surprising. Yet it was unlikely any of the people he was looking at had taken the trouble to find out. Why would they? And if they relied on what was fed them, what did they know? Israel was a beleaguered democracy. Arabs couldn't be trusted. They were terrorists. Yasser Arafat had wanted to destroy Israel. All Arabs want to destroy Israel. It was a matter of security for Israel to control Gaza and the West Bank. Israel had been invaded by the Arabs. When? Oh, sometime or other. The Arabs would continue the Nazi genocide given the chance. As for the fighting, Arabs and Jews just did that. Like the Catholics and Protestants in Northern Ireland. They liked fighting. Nothing to be done about it.

Was it egregious arrogance to believe the people were so benighted? Once he'd had faith. The image of his dad reading *The Daily Herald* came to him. When he was a kid in the late fifties and early sixties, the common folk could get their ideas from such a paper or from what their unions produced and on the tv everyday were trade union leaders entering or leaving Downing St. Of course, the press was in the hands of the rich, the BBC was conformist beneath its putative impartiality, and the schools, the churches, the universities, the judiciary, the civil service, the armed forces promoted a conventional view which to challenge was heresy. All the same, there had been a space in which questioning could flourish. How had that come about? His mind searched for some easy explanation but complexity wouldn't resolve. No doubt partly it was to do with men like his dad who'd come back from the war determined to see change. They'd fought against fascism so weren't impressed by authoritarian rhetoric and had engaged in a collective effort so were comfortable with collective solutions to social problems. There must have been millions of blokes like his dad and women like his mum who

24

wouldn't have blinked at the nationalisation of the banks or the introduction of workplace democracy.

What had happened?

Jimmy placed his third coffee in front of him.

"Good job you don't have the caffeine, you'd be jumpy as cat with piles."

"Do cats get piles?"

"Ask your vet."

"I don't have a cat."

"Dog?"

"No."

"Get one, they're great company."

"You've got a wife for company."

"I've got a wife."

"Can't have a conversation with your mutt, Jimmy."

"Exactly. Just a nice walk and no complaints."

"What's she complaining about?"

"Today? The front gate."

"What's wrong with it?"

"I painted it."

"What's wrong with that?"

"The colour."

"Bright yellow?"

"Brown."

"She doesn't like brown?"

"Not on front gates."

"Where does she like it?"

"Anywhere I don't choose it."

"Some would say you're a sexist, Jimmy."

"Others would avoid cliches. Anyway, you were saying."

"Not much else to tell. I pointed him to Herzl's anti-Semitic ranting, and Arieh Altman's assertion that anti-Semitism must be at the core of Zionism."

"So where's the anti-Semitism?"

"You tell me. They've quoted the bringing-the-Party-into-disrepute rule."

"Tony Blair did that."

"Bombing the poor of Iraq is good for the Party's reputation, Jimmy."

"Aye. How do you extricate yourself?"

"I have to answer a set of questions…"

"Are you now or have you ever been…"

"Not far off. 'Could you please explain what you meant by…" I'm surprised they didn't ask me 'Could you please explain what you meant by Dear Mr Cash."

"Answer'em and have done."

"Think it'll be that easy?"

"They can't keep you suspended if there's no case to answer."

"But there is, Jimmy. For what I've just told you, I could be expelled."

"It'll play itself out."

"Think so?"

"Corbyn isn't in favour. If he wins next time, he'll put an end to it."

"More likely they'll put an end to him."

"He can pull it off. Not a Labour majority, but the Tory majority done for. Labour, SNP, Plaid Cymru, the SDLP and Caroline Lucas in conjunction and throw down the gauntlet to the Lib Dumbs. He could get a lot of his programme through."

"The leaving Europe business will scupper him. That and the manufactured anti-Semitism.

"Second referendum. There's a lot of support."

"And a lot of opposition. People have been bamboozled, Jimmy. Forty years of persistent propaganda. Them against us. The Evil Empire of the EU dictating to doughty little Britain, the beacon of freedom adrift in the Irish Sea. Most raging anti-Europeans haven't a clue how the EU works. Most people who voted to leave have probably never considered that the European Parliament has voted for every piece of EU legislation, and our MEPs have had the right to speak and raise their hands."

"We're always up against the media. Didn't stop us winning in '45."

"They've learnt since then. It isn't just the media. Look at popular culture. Every bit of it is organised to reinforce a conservative view. It's isn't accidental."

"You can't attack popular culture, Bill. Our supporters love it."

"Exactly. That's the triumph of the Right. Hook the masses on pop music, soaps, vacuous tv and make their beloved stars multi-millionaires and you've got a propaganda machine Goebbels couldn't have dreamed of."

"The people need their pleasures, Bill."

"And those pleasures are easy to exploit."

"That starts to sound like snobbery."

"Perfect isn't it? You criticise the entertainment peddled to the masses like cocaine and you're a snob. Not even Shakespeare is beyond criticism, Jimmy. *Love's Labour's Lost* is a lousy play."

"I wouldn't know."

"Don't bother reading it. But don't miss *Hamlet*."

"Our supporters aren't intellectuals."

"Does that mean they don't deserve the best?"

"They make their choices."

"Do they? Maybe they're force fed. You know why there's so much so-called reality tv?"

"It's cheap."

"You wouldn't want the folk in your ward to get second-rate medical care. Why third-rate culture?"

"You don't have to be a cardiologist to be prescribed statins."

"But a cardiologist who prescribed smoking would be crazy. That's how culture works."

"People like it, they pay for it."

"You've become a Thatcherite, Jimmy. You know what her Minister for the Arts said way back in the 80s?"

"You can't have any money."

"Worse. If they'd just pulled the money they would have been condemned as philistines. They cut the money and said this: 'the only test of our ability to succeed is whether we can attract enough customers.' Beethoven's fifth was unpopular when it was

27

first performed. So were the Impressionists. No one understood Ibsen. Jane Austen sold hardly any books in her lifetime. Culture isn't about winning audiences, it's about saying what has to be said, however unpopular."

"That's your hobby horse, Bill. But people like *Holby City*."

"Yeah, they'd like Hugh Quarshie's salary too."

"Watch it, you'll be accused of racism."

"Again?"

"It's dodgy territory, Bill. A man of colour who does all right for himself."

"That's the racism, Jimmy."

"What is?"

"That you put your socialist belief in equality aside when a coloured person is rich."

"He's rich, but he's not a capitalist. It's the capitalists we've got to go after."

"These people are capitalists, Jimmy. What do you think they do with their money? People who pull in four hundred grand a year for acting in a soap. D' you think they donate it to the Palestine Solidarity Campaign? They invest it. They buy property and cars and paintings and jewellery. That's the trick. They're the people's heroes and heroines, and they're rich. The people love them, the people love the rich. That's your socialism knackered."

"People don't see soap stars as bosses."

"No, but they accept huge disparities of wealth and that's what makes socialism necessary."

"We can argue for higher taxes."

"Sure, but who will Cliff Richard fans side with if he says he pays enough?"

"A few filthy rich celebs, Bill. Who cares? It's the employers, the bankers, the City people we have to go after. Our people understand they have too much."

Bill shook his head.

"The Left is all at sea over this, Jimmy. You can find people who will spout the cliches of Marxism in every meeting, but no one has thought through where we are. This isn't 1848.

The healthy promise of a democratic culture has become the sickly nightmare of manufactured masscult."

"How do you make that a campaigning issue? Tell Man U fans their players are overpaid?"

"If we're going to have equality, that's what we're going to have to do."

This time Jimmy shook his head.

"I need another pint," he said.

At home, Bill settled at his laptop to begin answering the questions. He was tempted to begin: "Yes, I have stopped beating my wife." The phone rang. It was his ex asking if she could borrow five grand.

"Five grand? I'm not bloody George Clooney, Caroline."

"Don't condescend to me."

"What?"

"You always call me by my name when you're being patronising."

"Okay. What shall I call you? Doris?"

"I'll let you have it back within six months."

"What's it for?"

"I've just spent a bit too much on my credit cards."

"How much too much?"

"That's none of your business."

"But you want five grand."

"A loan."

He would have refused except he knew it would send her to Liam or Jessica. He wouldn't have borrowed from his children unless he was destitute. Niether, he knew, would turn her down if they had a bit to spare, struggling though they were with the high costs of life in the capital.

"Okay. But I want it back at a thousand a month."

"Five hundred."

"You can afford a thousand."

"Ten months, Bill. That's not long."

"This is the last time, Caroline."

"Fine. Put it in my account today."

"What's the number."

"You've got the number."

"Somewhere, just tell me."

Once again, Caroline had his arm up his back. She'd repay, at length. That he'd be reimbursed in six months he doubted. It was true, of course, if he lost the five thousand he'd be fine. He'd accumulated, slowly, frugally, a buffer of a hundred thousand. His retirement lump sum he'd put away. His mother's bungalow had sold for eighty thousand and he'd got twenty. His pension was fifteen hundred a month. Most days he spent nothing. The weekly food bill was sixty. He used the central heating only on the coldest days. Most months he saved between five and seven hundred. He was pleased to have reached his hundred grand target. He owned his little terrace, did without a car, didn't bother with a mobile phone. He laughed thinking of what he'd been talking about to Jimmy. What would David Beckham think of a hundred grand in the bank? Such was the way the culture mocked thrift and responsibility.

He had to dispel thoughts of Caroline and her curious ways with debt. It had occurred to him long ago, when they were bringing up the children and she secretly notched up tens of thousands that some part of her, oddly, treated debt as a kind of emotional bond. Of course, it was. Being bound to a creditor was at least some kind of connection, however humiliating and distorted. Yet she seemed to rush for it, to relish it. He knew, of course, there was also imitation. The powerful, the successful, the interesting spent money lavishly. Acting out could make you feel you were like them. How odd it was to see millions living as-if lives. He recalled the pupils he'd taught, twelve and thirteen year-olds behaving as if they were multi-millionaire stars, incubating wild ambitions while reality offered them dull employment.

These thoughts sank away as he began to write. He realised the questions were a trap. To answer them briefly was to admit guilt. Yes, he had stopped beating his wife. There was no alternative but to reject the questions by writing answers which challenged what was concealed in their form.

The bureaucrats had asked for a response within seven days so the matter could be dealt with *in a timely manner*. He worked at it for three days and hit ten thousand words. Re-reading he was somewhat sickened by his style; but time was against him.

If he failed to meet the deadline, how would the bureaucrats respond? Maybe they'd expel him claiming he'd been given a chance and had failed to take it. To send his reply promptly was to remove one of their weapons. He looked through the section he'd headed AROUND BALFOUR:

You will be aware Balfour was an anti-Semite. In 1905 he refused entry to Britain to Jews fleeing the Russian pogrom on the grounds of the "undoubted evils" that had fallen on Britain because of its Jewish population. The British government was assisted in its finessing of the Declaration by Lord Rothschild and Chaim Weizmann. The latter wanted the Declaration to refer not to the "Jewish people" but the "Jewish race"....

Who was he lecturing? It seemed ludicrous, the stuff of a university seminar. There was something strained and pompous in what he'd written which made him want to cast it in flippant, jokey terms. Why couldn't he make a joke of it? After all, it was absurd. There was a simple way out: to not bother. They'd treat that as contempt or admission of guilt and kick him out. What would he lose? Hours spent in tedious meetings. Delivering leaflets in the rain. Having mad German Shepherds come galloping down driveways to defend their territory as soon as he touched the gate. It would be a liberation. It wasn't as if he was short of things to do. If the Party choose to send him to Siberia he might as well enjoy the snow.

To be free of politics offered the hedonism he'd always favoured. Life was full of pleasure: getting up in the morning and standing under a hot shower; toast and honey; a bike ride over the hills of the Trough of Bowland; a pint and a chat in a lively pub; fish chips and mushy peas; a Georges Brassens song; falling asleep on the sofa; re-reading *The Great Gatsby*. He hadn't got involved in politics because he was twiddling his thumbs or for the fun of it. Though he cringed at the thought, it was out of a sense of responsibility. Was that just arrogant and self-serving? The definition of himself he liked was hedonistic. How to enjoy the next half hour was life's most important question. Yet, there it was, the cage of politics which descended and locked because the rich asserted their right to great wealth, the world was armed like a drunken psychopath, the ecosystem was out of balance, and

31

worst of all, the air was thick with lies and distortion to keep the madness in place.

Once he'd believed he'd find a niche. The word had the right connotations: a nest, a home, comfort, ease, belonging. Does a bird in the nest worry about where trees came from? There'd been a moment when he'd thought it possible. There must be some spot where he could lodge himself and live out his life while the *pacts and sects of great ones* went about their ludicrous business. The thought of *Lear* made him laugh. When illusions collapse, what are you left with?

To hell with it. He hit the return key to send his dissertation speeding along the fibre optics. What would happen now? Maybe they'd deem it anti-Semitic in every syllable and consign him to the outer darkness. In any case, he'd done what they'd asked and all he could.

A bit of fresh air and to get his heart going. It had rained for half an hour but the clouds had dispersed and the early evening sun was strong enough to make a shirt and a light jumper enough. He went by the river which was rushing out to sea, a wide, brown band driven as if by purpose, by intelligence. Over the rocks by the old, cobbled bridge it gurgled and foamed. He went on briskly to the park where the path was busy with dog walkers, runners, cyclists. Hedonists. But maybe not. There was something a little too close to work in the application of some of the walkers, expensively equipped, lightweight Nordic poles attached to their hands. In any case, he could stride with hands in his pockets and whistle as he went which took his mind back to one of his first jobs.

The urgency of getting out of school was compounded of boredom, exasperation, disappointment but above all the desire to find a way into the adult world, to know how it worked, to belong to it, to grow up. It seemed ridiculous, impatient, petulant and short-term now. His sixty-eight year-old self admonished the sixteen year-old: a bit more effort, a couple more years and then on to university; but at the same time he consented to the charm of his youth's kicking against the pricks. School, after all, had been organised boredom and systematic punishment. Whatever an employer could do, it didn't include bending you over and thrashing your backside; and employees fought back. In those days, trade unionists were on the telly every day. Rodney Bickerstaff, Alan Fisher, Jack Cooper, Clive Jenkins, Jack Jones, these were men who could take on employers and governments because they had the power of organised workers behind them. As an employee, he'd be part of that. He'd join a union. That would be better than sitting in a classroom in a tie and blazer and getting in trouble for failing to do your homework, or *prep* as the grammar boys ridiculously called it.

He watched a cormorant dive under the water and waited for it to reappear. The break in his thought made the fifty-year-old past recede for a few hundred yards but when he started whistling again he saw himself in the grill room of the *King's Head*. It was the first job he applied for. Working in a hotel seemed a decent prospect. People are in a good mood after all when they're out enjoying themselves and the manager held out all sorts of interesting possibilities of advancement. Not that he had any particular desire to climb. He was more interested in horizontal movement: following what was interesting was more intelligent than shining up the money lamppost. The manager's name wouldn't come back to him, but he pictured him vividly: thin, balding, his nose long and his lips pressed together as if he was forever on the verge of an emotional outburst. He wore grey suits and highly polished shoes and waistcoats which hugged his slight frame. His voice was thin and rasping, as if it was forced though some tiny pipe lined with sandpaper. It was when Bill was leaving at the end of a shift he stopped him in the dining-room.

"Take your hands out of your pockets and don't whistle. It disturbs the residents."

The peremptory tone recalled the high-handed ways of teachers: Naylor, the PE man who barked orders, grabbed boys by their sideburns and whacked them with whatever was to hand. It was to escape such arbitrary authority he'd left, and now the boss was telling him not to whistle. No detention. No lines. No whacking. But sacking. It was worth being dismissed to defy the stupidity.

The following day he arrived with his hands in his pockets and whistled his way to the grill room. The manager called him into his office. It was clean and neat to the point of sterility. The grill room kitchen was narrow. The waiters and the chef had to squeeze past one another. It was windowless and required an extractor to keep it from becoming a stifling crypt. The fridge door and the door from the grill room couldn't be opened simultaneously. The floor was sometimes slippy and Bill had to steady himself to save from ditching a plate of apple pie and cream.

"Need to get the floor wiped, chef."

"Wipe the floor, I'ant got time to wipe me bloody arse."

When the manager asked Bill if he'd forgotten what he'd told him the day before, he could have been back in school. He was urged to say:

"Of course I haven't. What do you think I am, gaga?"

There was that odd air of regret about the man, the sentimental hypocrisy of the powerful who delight in lying to themselves about how they enjoy being imperative. He was saying something about professionalism and how it was an expectation of the guests that the staff would serve their needs, be unobtrusive and blend into the background. Bill was listening and processing but at the centre of his attention was his disdain for everything the boss represented. What was he after all but the servile agent of some faceless conglomerate? The *King's Head* was but one of hundreds of hotels owned by the business, run in the interests of its shareholders. He was a mere instrument, and he submitted. He even convinced himself he liked being used. Of course, he got a fat salary, a nice house in the suburbs a Jag, holidays in the sun, a private pension, but as Bill surveyed him he thought he wouldn't give up whistling for that and more. A man who couldn't whistle if he felt like it was a slave. The manager was no chattel. He was a free man in the labour market. Yet being a free person in such circumstances was being bound hand and foot.

"So, William," he said. "do I trust there'll be no more whistling or standing with your hands in your pockets?"

"No."

"You mean, no, there won't be any more?"

"No, I mean yes, there will be."

He was told to collect his things and not come back. His mother was distraught and worried.

"Don't bother, mum," he said. "I'll get another job to-morrow."

And he did. A building supplies business was looking for a clerk. The office manager was Cliff, a harassed little man of fifty who smoked endlessly, lost his glasses, spoke in a growling undertone Bill couldn't understand and lusted over Lilian, the eighteen-year-old receptionist. Bill's job was to keep track of the invoices and do the accounts. Cliff "trained" him in his haphazard ways.

"Are you a qualified accountant?" said Bill as he sat by him watching him scribble figures.

Cliff turned to him, his eyes narrowed by the smoke;

"The only qualification you need is that you don't get caught out."

The job lasted nine charming months, graced by the warm and thrilling attentions of the slim and nonchalant Lilian. One of those girls who left school at fifteen with the intention of having a good time for five years before marrying and starting a family, she treated life with a carefree levity which cheered Bill up.

"Tell you what," she said.

"What?"

"We could go to the pub at lunchtime."

"Could we?"

"*The Plough*. They do sandwiches."

"What about pies?"

"Sandwiches are healthier."

"I'm perfectly healthy."

"That's what I was hoping."

When Cliff discovered their lunchtime assignations, he staggered their breaks.

"I told him to his face," she said.

"Did you?"

"You're just jealous, you dirty old man."

Lilian's parents lived in a modest semi near the football ground. When her mother and father went to bed, they would make the best of the cosy living-room where the gas fire hummed. One evening, she across his knees, they were idly watching the news.

"It gives me a headache," she said.

"Why?"

"I can't understand it."

"There's nothing to it. The rich rule the world."

"You're bonkers, you are," she said sitting up and straightening her black hair.

"Well, it's true. What influence does your dad have? He works hard but no one pays any attention to him."

"He doesn't want anyone to. He just wants to go fishing and to the pub."

"But he has to go to work."

"Everyone has to go to work, you nit."

"Yeah, but not for a boss."

There was an item about the UN.

"Turn it over."

"Just a second."

"Why?"

"It's interesting."

"What is?"

"They've passed a resolution about the Palestinians."

"Who are they when they're at home?"

"You know, the war."

"What war?"

"A few months ago."

"I don't remember a war."

"In the Middle East."

"What's that to do with me?"

"Everything's to do with you," he said, putting his arm round her shoulders and kissing her.

"War isn't. I think it's stupid."

"You're right," he said, "jumping to his feet. And we go now to Harewood Road where our correspondent is talking to Lilian Marshall. Miss Marshall, can you tell us about your new theory of war which is making such a stir across the globe."

"You're not right in the 'ead."

36

"And there you have it, from the horse's mouth. War is not right in the 'ead."

"Stop it, you'll wake me mother."

He looked to the ceiling and put his finger to his lips.

"Hear anything?"

"Honestly, stop it, Bill."

On the doorstep, he put his hands on her waist and she lifted herself on her tiptoes to kiss him.

"I'll explain it tomorrow," he said.

"What?"

"The Six-Day War."

"Six days? It was hardly worth the bother."

"That's what Nasser said."

"Who's he when he's got his socks off?"

TWO FUNDAMENTALISMS

He was trying to recall how things with Lilian ended. There was no row, they never rowed because she was so easy to tease and ready to laugh. Nor could he remember any decision. Somehow, it just faded. For a moment he let his mind drift into the fantasy of having married her. They would haven been okay. She was lovely in her affectionate responsiveness and they rubbed along without friction; but it wouldn't have worked. She was one of those girls who accepted her position: she was working-class; she knew her place; she knew what wasn't for her, and it was most of the things which preoccupied him. He could never have talked to her about Kafka or Flaubert. There wasn't an ounce of maliciousness in her and if she'd understood the corruption and cynicism of the world's leaders, she would have been outraged; but that was all for other people . She existed in her restricted arena. She liked to shop for nice clothes, have a night out, she wanted a good house and holidays in the sun. What had happened to her? It came back to him that she'd married a footballer. Who'd told him that? He had no idea but he was glad. He liked the thought of her being comfortable and enjoying it, though footballers were absurdly paid.

A black Labrador came running across the grass. It seemed to be making a bee-line for him. More curious than alarmed he stood still, assuming the dog would lose interest if he wasn't walking, but it approached, its tail wagging, and nuzzled his legs. He spoke to it in a calm and friendly tone and wondering where its owner might be looked up to see a woman rounding the bushes by the side of the path. She was smallish and wore a long, cotton top of Indian style, embroidered with red and green, a skirt to her ankles, sandals and sun glasses. Her brown hair was tied back from her pale face. She came smiling, no doubt because of the dog.

"Hello, Bill," she said. "He recognises you."

For a second, he couldn't place her but when she took off her glasses he recognised her at once.

"Tina. It was the glasses."

"Yes, I'm incognito."

"Hiding from the police?"

"No, pupils."

"Not many of 'em around here, are there?"

"I've moved on. I'm at St Mary's."

"Picture of the Pope on your mantlepiece?"

"I'm not a convert. It was the money not the doctrine."

"The devil and the deep blue sea."

"How are you, anyway?" she said, kissing him on the cheek.

"I'm fine. I'm retired. OFSTED can't touch me and boys in black blazers pass me on the street and have no idea who I am."

The dog scurried down the bank towards the water where two swans were gliding. She stepped to the top of the slope and called him back, bending to click on his lead. Bill noticed how slim she'd remained and felt a prod of desire and a twinge of regret. She turned to him smiling.

"Where are you going, anyway?"

"Oh, just a little twenty-five mile stroll to make me sleep better."

"You won't want a coffee then."

"Unless it's decaff. The other stuff makes my heart go pit-a-pat, like tobacco does to Pozzo."

"Who?"

"Never mind. Where are you taking me?"

"The Pagoda's open."

"This late?"

"Didn't you know?"

"I'm no longer a gadfly."

"It's hardly the high-life. A cup of coffee and a slice of carrot cake."

"Oh, that's far too risky for me. Got to keep my blood sugar down."

"Are you diabetic?"

"Pre. It's in the family."

"Well, no sugar then?"

The dog lapped the water in the metal bowl by the door.

"That's enough, Sam," she said. "He'll drink the lot."

She chose a table by the window which looked out over the pleasant expanse of the park, donated by a nineteenth century capitalist. While she went to the ladies and to order and the dog settled itself at his feet, he reflected that their successors were less generous. Where were the endowments from today's wealthy? It occurred to him it might be an opening gambit; it was the kind of thing he liked to talk about and once the thought got going there was plenty of room for expansion; but it wasn't Tina's arena.

Emotionally, he was on her wavelength. There was a dissatisfied current to her feeling which matched his own radical malcontentedness. Who could be content in such circumstances? Who was? The strutting of the rich and powerful was no indication of ease; rather a neurotic need to continually bolster a failing self-worth; but intellectually they were distinct. He couldn't engage her in tense debate about his preoccupations because, like most people, she attended to the news.

A memory came back to him. Maybe it had been about 2010 when it was acceptable to see the Iraq war as a mistake.

"At the time," she'd said to him, "I thought it was for the best."

"How can the most powerful military the world has known, raining terror on a poor country be for the best?" he'd said.

The conversation had frozen.

The grass and the trees were lovely. You could almost believe they'd been created for human delight, rather than human delight having been created to respond. It was a happy moment. His life had been full of them. Nearly seventy years of happy moments sunk in a sludge of dissatisfaction.

"There we are," she said, "decaff, no chocolat, no sugar."

"A virtuous coffee."

"But there'll still be cakes and ale," she said.

"Very good," he laughed.

"We went to see it, last week. First time we've been to the theatre in twenty years."

"All the more enjoyable then."

He would have asked if her husband enjoyed it if he could have remembered his name. What he did recall was what she'd told him about his behaviour: cameras around the house, strict rules about what she could spend money on, and then some odd comment she'd made to the effect that, "My husband leaves me alone." He'd taken it naively at first, thinking he was one of those men forever at work or playing cricket or something and expecting her to get along without company; but at length he'd twigged and the implications had stunned him.

"Yes, we hardly ever get out. Going to the city for a play, well.."

She was a dutiful teacher, but not in the way he liked. Not dutiful first to the material or the pupils , but to those in charge. He was always looking for a fellow-spirit when he was teaching, someone with a sense of mischief who was willing to cock-a-snook at the do-what-you're-supposed-to-do ethos, a nd when Tina had joined the staff, for a short time he thought he might have found one. He recalled how she'd laughed when he picked up the circular from the Subject Leader (a title he thought preten-tious and fascistic) reminding them not to forget the lunchtime meeting, and he'd torn it in half, dropped it in the bin and said:

"Fancy going to *The Crown* for lunch tomorrow?"

Her hair, which she'd unfastened in the ladies, hung onto her shoulders. He remarked how it caught the light from the win-dow and then had a curious thought about why she'd let it down. She cut into her carrot cake with her fork.

"Sure I can't tempt you?"

"Not with carrot cake."

She laughed in a quick, unleashed way which showed the white of her neck.

"What're you doing to keep busy?"

"Oh, plotting the overthrow of capitalism. Tedious stuff."

"Still involved in politics, then?"

The coffee was deliciously bitter and its froth warm and emollient. He didn't want to talk about serious things because the pleasantness of conversation, talking about nothing and com-municating more beyond words than in them, went well with the coffee and suited the occasion. He fixed her with an objective look for a second while her eyes were on the little plate. If he told her, there was a huge field of discussion before them. How much

41

did she know about Israel/Palestine? Like most people she read the papers or watched the broadcasts and knew next to nothing. How odd it was that to tell her about this significant event in his life would require touching on arcane events in the Middle East a hundred years ago.

Searching for some simple thing he could say which might bring essential understanding he imagined this:

"Did you hear the French have invaded Switzerland?"

"What?"

"Yes, they rolled their tanks in yesterday and began bulldozing chalets. Apparently, they've been reading the Bible and have discovered verses which suggest god gave the land to them three thousand years ago."

"They haven't."

The last chunk of rich, light brown cake went into her mouth. She set the fork across the plate and pushed it aside.

"Mmm. That was just what I needed."

"As a matter of fact, I've been suspended from the Labour Party."

"Why?"

"Anti-Semitism, apparently."

"What?"

She was looking at him with wide eyes.

"Don't look so surprised. It could happen to anyone."

"I can't believe it."

"Well, there it is. I'm one of those raving anti-Semites you hear about in the media."

"But what did you do?"

"I sent Netanyahu a copy of *The Fateful Triangle*."

"Stop teasing and tell me."

"In short, I sent an e-mail. An innocent enough event. I mean, how many millions get sent every day? But if you send one to someone who claims all people left of Trump are anti-Semites and tell him his argument lacks a little substance, you're a racist."

"But they can't believe you're a racist."

"Oh, they do."

"What will happen?"

"I should think I'll be sent to the gulag for re-education. They'll smash my glasses because intellectuals are impossibly dangerous. Then they'll feed Tony Blair's speeches into my ears while making me watch films of lambs gambolling in fields of succulent grass beneath a benign sun. After a week or two I'll be eager for shock and awe and will relish bombs dismembering kids in the Middle East."

"Surely you have a right to put your case."

"Done it. Ten thousand words. Like your undergrad dissertation really, though I'm not sure they'd've appreciated an essay on the imagery of ambient movement in *Madame Bovary*."

"Well, they'll realise they've made a mistake."

"But they haven't, Tina. They're absolutely right. I believe Jews have no more right to Palestine than the Arabs. In fact, I believe the Arabs have a greater right because they've lived there longer and *we were here first* is a universal principle."

"That doesn't make you a racist."

"It does if you're Nathan Perlmutter."

"Who?"

"Are you sure you want to hear this?"

"I do."

"We could have a stroll round the park. I'm sure the dog would love a run, and there's not a cloud."

"He's all run out. Look at him, he's ready to nod off. And I'm all walked out. Tell me."

"Well, if I were to say anti-Semitism to you, what would you think of?"

"Hitler."

"And what was Hitler."

"Bonkers."

"Correct. It's a perfectly good definition often employed in universities teaching youngsters about the gamut of political opinion and frequently confused with the more common designation of fascist."

"Don't tell me they think you're a fascist."

"No, that's the beauty of the theory. You see, traditionally that's where the threat to Jews comes from. The far-right. Though the Soviet Onion did a handy line in prejudice too, but

they were political fascists while being economic State capitalists..."

"I thought they were communists."

"So did they, but you know what thought did."

"Followed a muck cart..."

"Exactly. Well, the new theory dispenses with evidence,
which always gets in the way. Think of poor Darwin amassing all
those fossils. The time you save if you just say, god. So in spite of
the evidence that the greatest threat to the Jews has come from the
far-right and the liberal left has been consistently anti-racist, the
new theory is that the liberal left is racist because it's anti-racist."

"Some theory."

"Yeah, but it's cleverer than you think. Are you a racist?"

"Of course not."

"There, conclusive proof that you are because you are so
convinced you aren't , unconsciously you are. Thus, the more you
assert you aren't a racist, the clearer it is you must be. If you devoted all your free time to fighting racism, that would establish
that you are racist to the marrow."

"And what if I went about abusing coloured people?"

"Then obviously you're a racist."

"Then everybody's a racist."

"You've got it."

"But if everybody's a racist, nobody is."

"That's philosophically sophisticated. We could, after all,
be racist by nature, then we all would be, and a defining distinction wouldn't be necessary."

"But we aren't."

"Of course not. However, from the Israeli point of view,
the beauty of the theory is that the liberal left, which traditionally
supports rights for the Palestinians, is racist by definition because
it defines itself as non-racist."

"If the liberal left is racist why isn't it racist towards the
Palestinians?"

"It is, or it must be, by implication. It just thinks it isn't.
As it thinks it isn't racist towards the Jews but must be because it
thinks it isn't. There remains one test and one test only of someone not being a racist."

"They're dead?"

"Almost. They agree with everything which furthers the interests of the Israeli State."

"They might still be racist towards the Palestinians."

"Yes, but that doesn't matter."

"Why not?"

"Because the Palestinians didn't suffer The Holocaust."

"Nor did the original people of North America."

"Exactly."

"But they were victims of racism."

"Oh come, come, Tina. They were moved aside to make way for progress. That's not racism. Re-read Churchill. Racism is what happens to Zionists if they don't get their own way."

"No one can take such a theory seriously."

"Are you an anti-Semite?"

"No."

"Do you think Jews and Arabs should have equal rights."

"I think everybody should have equal rights."

"You're an anti-Semite, Tina."

"Because I believe in equal rights?"

"A core belief of liberals who are racist by definition, as just explained."

"My nerves'll be shredded if you carry on."

"That's the idea. It's why "gaslighting" has entered the vocabulary. The culture of deliberate confusion and contradiction. What day is it?"

"Wednesday."

"You're an anti-Semite."

"What?"

"It's Saturday. You say it's Wednesday to stop me going to the synagogue because you're an anti-Semite."

"But it is Wednesday."

"See how entrenched you are in your prejudice."

"That's absurd."

"It's mad, Tina. It's utterly wayward, but it's the way our culture works. The Israelis ethnically cleanse nearly a million Arabs from Palestine and accuse the Palestinians of trying to wipe out Israel. Arafat recognises Israel and agrees to peace, the Israelis invade Lebanon."

A child of six or seven came by and began stroking the dog which got to its feet, its tail wagging.

"Leave the poor dog in peace, Callum."

His mother, pushing a buggy where a baby slept, its sun-tinted legs dangling, took the boy's hand.

"It's all right," said Tina. "He's a real softie."

"Yes," said Bill, "that's what she told the postman when he asked for his fingers back."

"Stop it."

Still warm, the outside air was nevertheless beginning to import the river's cool.

"I'll walk to your car if you like."

"Okay. You can fight off the muggers."

"I'll leave that to the dog."

Smalltalk sweetened the half mile. When she took her keys from her pocket and clicked the doors open, she sighed and said:

"Well, home to the kids. Let's hope they haven't wrecked the house."

"Won't the man of the house have them tied and bound."

"The man of the house is in California."

It came back to him her husband was a management consultant, or some such embellishing definition, and was summoned to conferences in Tokyo and Madrid to explain the obvious. Had he dreamed she'd told him he was absent more than present? His memory was so vague it might have been one of those deceptive retentions which sometimes lead us into embarrassing error. Her demeanour suggested exasperation.

"Lucky him."

"Yes, he doesn't have children to keep in order."

"Give them a damn good thrashing and send them to bed with a bowl of thin gruel."

"They're not getting a Nando's that's for sure."

"Haven't you fed 'em? Neglectful mother."

"They can never be fed to satiety."

46

"Explain the caveman diet will keep them alive to a hundred and seven. When's the mighty hunter back from the land of guns and freedom?"

"Oh, tomorrow. He has to call in at the office in London. Or so he says."

The comment gave him a little abdominal shock as she threw a glance.

"Okay. Better get back to my budgie."

"Not your goldfish?"

"The cage won't hold water."

She gave a little toss of her head as she laughed and got into her BMW.

What did she make of that? At least the levity prevented it descending into ponderous gloom, but all the same he felt he'd intruded. He could have supressed the fact. What was it, after all but a triviality? An obscure man gets suspended from his political party on the basis of an overblown reaction to an e-mail. Maybe he should see it as a relief. If the process went as he expected and he was left dangling for months, he would no longer spend dull hours in tedious meetings attending to discussions about overhanging trees, cars on pavements or dog fouling; no more rick his back trying to push a soggy flyer through a two-inches-from-the-floor letter box at eight on a Sunday morning. He could be the hedonist he'd been at sixteen.

Dusk was falling. A teenager, he'd often used the park as a shortcut home. After the pubs shut on a Friday, at the end of a late-night film session at the *Odeon* where they'd mocked some cheap western or ghoulish thriller, he cut across the grass and under the trees without nervousness. The dark was as frightening for anyone as it might be for him and he was confident in his capacity to scoot away from trouble. He'd never encountered any but once he'd walked home a girl whose name he couldn't recall. It was fifty years ago. There was no shame in having forgotten. All the same, he experienced it as a loss. Was it Carol? Or Katherine? She'd been Keith Richard's girlfriend for a while. The rock guitarist's namesake was one of those lads he'd had a pint with now and again and who'd, once, invited him into his house for an after-the-pub beer.

The lass had asked him if he was walking back and if she could come with him. In the dark, she'd put her arm around his waist and in the middle of the lightless expanse of grass they'd kissed and sunk to the ground. Oddly, he remembered it with great fondness. He'd seen her only a handful of times subsequently and usually in Keith's company. No doubt if he'd got to know her there'd have been insuperable differences. He stopped himself. Caroline might have worn him down to cynicism, but there was no reason to make universal what was specific. Perhaps they'd have got on brilliantly. How odd life was. All that had happened which should have been avoided, all that might have which hadn't.

For some weeks he'd put off getting the train to London. His old university friend had invited him to Ealing for a few days. It was always a delight to make the most of the capital: theatres, concerts, galleries, parks, walks around the famous streets, cafes, and Steve was congenial company. What put him off was his wife. Judy had rediscovered Christianity some time after university and was deeply involved in Bible study. Bill had no objection to that. Life could be a tough business and boredom was one of its major challenges. Anything that kept someone busy and away from harm couldn't be objected to. If she'd been undertaking an in-depth analysis of characterisation in Agatha Christie, he'd have been equally neutral. People waste their time on all kinds of things but it's wasted only in an objective sense. If trying to prove the earth is flat keeps someone from addiction or suicide, its subjective value is enormous.

Being on a train lifted his mood, not that he was gloomy; but the sense of movement, and leaving the familiar behind, if only briefly was a boost. He'd intended to read and had stuck Flapan's *Birth of Israel* in his bag, but once underway had left it on the table, enjoying watching the landscape flash by and, more intriguing, the backs of houses which were always more interesting than the fronts. At the first stop he was joined by a big man with a mass of curly brown hair and a beard down to his chest. He was dressed in a khaki shirt open at the neck which revealed the profuse hair of his chest. Beside him he set a tightly packed, grey rucksack. He was one of those people who breathe loudly. Bill wondered idly if it was something to do with his bulk. He was a big man by nature but was clearly overweight.

Within a few minutes he'd taken out an oversized bag of crisps and was feeding them into his mouth like an addict coins into a betting machine.

"Are you a historian?" he said, out of nowhere, nodding towards the book.

"No, just interested."

"Flapan is wrong, of course."

Not sure how to respond to such conviction and intrusion, Bill said:

"Well, I'm about half way through, so I reserve judgement."

The big man shook his head.

"That book should be banned. It's anti-Semitic."

Had a fellow passenger expressed the opinion that women should be deprived of the vote, Bill couldn't have been more surprised. What kind of coincidence brought a bigot opposite him a few days after the Labour Party bureaucracy had suspended him for nothing?

"If you're right, I guess people will grasp that when they read it."

"You can't allow people to say those kind of things about Israel."

"What can you allow people to say?"

From the rucksack the big fellow lifted a full, litre, plastic bottle of Coke, twisted open the white cap with a fizz, put the neck to his lips and gulped.

"Nothing," he said, "which threatens the State of Israel."

"Well, who's going to decide what that might be?"

"We are."

Bill was tempted to ask him if he worked for Mossad but thought better of it. The sensible thing seemed to change the subject, as they were lurching towards entanglement in barbed wire.

"Off to London?"

His companion nodded.

"It's a matter of perception. If we perceive anti-Semitism, then it exists."

Bill smiled and looked out of the window thinking about the implications of perception being a proof. On that ground, Desdemona was guilty. Othello's perception of his wife made her an adulteress and nothing she could do could change it. Leontes was even more far-gone in demented perception: at least Othello deserved sympathy for the poisoning of his mind by the brilliant but evil Iago. Leontes needed no manipulator to turn him into a vicious tyrant. Nothing more than Hermione's persuasive powers condemned her. Yet both Othello and Leontes were convinced of what was most false and accused innocence out of their demented certainty. Literature was full of similar examples. It was almost its stock-in-trade. The way our subjectivity leads us astray was rehearsed over and again through the ages, which was part of what made literature so attractive. It was odd ,but it was pleasurable to be made aware of the unreliability of subjectivity. Poor Charles Bovary who was convinced his wife loved him and was happy. Poor her, who was equally convinced Rodolphe adored her and was going to transport her to realms where happiness grew like grass. In witnessing people made fools of by what they think most obvious, we are secured in our own sense of avoiding such folly.

"Is it an American edition?" said his unwelcome interlocutor.

"Yes. I don't think there is a UK one."

"Good. Did you buy it in America?"

"No, I've never been there. I don't fancy being shot."

He hoped his facial expression would soften his facetiousness.

"You should go. I have friends in America. We visit every year."

Bill was inclined to continue in the vein which kept him from opinionated ranting or arrogance. "And you get back alive?" he wanted to say but offered instead:

"That's nice. Your family like it?"

"My wife loves it. Her brother's a lawyer in New York."

"What's his field?"

"Crime?"

The easy rejoinder was, "No shortage of work, then."

"Very good."

"What d'you do?"

"Retired."

"From?"

"Shaping young minds, nurturing tender sensibilities in the paths of wisdom and truth. I worked in an exam factory."

"What subject?"

"Mod Langs."

"What're you doing reading Flapan?"

"Oh, you know, something light for a train journey. I'm surprised they don't flog it on station platforms along with Jo Nesbo and Ian Rankin. They could do a three for two offer: Flapan, *The Ethnic Cleansing of Palestine* and *Beyond Chutzpah*. Hot cakes."

"I'm Jewish," the big chap said, burping and filling the air with the sickly odour of *Coke*.

"I'd never've guessed," said Bill unable to restrain himself. "I had you down for a Presbyterian."

"I'm a member of the Labour Party. We've got a big problem with anti-Semites."

"So I believe."

"Corbyn is an anti-Semite. They've flooded into the Party."

"Really?"

"It's not a safe place for Jews."

"What about socialists?"

"Corbyn and his followers are anti-Israel."

"Wasn't Gandhi of a similar persuasion?"

"We have to kick them out. They're a sickness. Did you see the *Panorama* programme?"

"As a matter of fact, I did. It was that or the footie and you can have too much of a good thing, can't you?"

"What did you think?"

"Balanced, fair, intellectually rigorous, without a scintilla of prejudice or malice. Really a model of disinterested journalism."

"It proved its case. Forensically. I'm a solicitor. I have an instinct for a forensic argument."

"I believe Thomas Lowe made the same claim."

"Who?"

"He was an American lawyer who discovered a unique way to service his female clients."

"The problem is, you see, people start reading books like that, they get the wrong idea about Israel."

"I suppose when people start reading *Nineteen-Eighty-Four*, they get the wrong idea about democracy."

"Books like that make people anti-Semitic."

Bill became keenly aware of the man's bulk. Seventeen or eighteen stone. He'd always been slightly alarmed by physicality which overwhelmed his own. A slight featherweight dispossessed by natural selection of those characteristics usually considered most masculine, men of exorbitant muscularity and hirsuteness presented an unnerving spectacle; as did women graced in abundance with extravagant curves and fleshiness. Not that he imagined, inflamed by the sight of a modest paperback obtained on the internet for twenty-seven dollars, Netanyahu's bodyguard was going to launch himself across the table and strangle him as they entered a tunnel, or simply suffocate him beneath his gargantuan weight. All the same, it was true that no matter how capable of defending himself in argument, Bill was exposed and vulnerable physically, which, he reflected, was exactly how the world worked. The arguments against US capitalism were robust, but no one on earth could stand up to US armoury. He was protected by the law. In theory, so were the poorest countries in the world. International law, properly applied, made unwonted invasion impossible. In practice, the USA could trample into almost any country and slaughter at will. Physical strength was a bald fact. Women, on average, were at a disadvantage. Females weren't weaker in all species, of course. Some female spiders are vastly bigger and cannibalistic. But in species where males competed for mates, the females tended to be smaller.

He wouldn't have liked to have to tangle with the Coke swigger to find himself a partner. In fact, had it been necessary to fight at all, he'd probably have ended up solitary, unable to pass on his genes, such as they were. Was that where it came from, his odd sense of inferiority in the face of manly men, some atavistic neuron firing in the depths of his brain? The thought made him laugh inwardly. It was too ridiculous. Life was a ridiculous farce. He would have laughed his way through it but for the tragedy. In fact, he had laughed his way through it for the first thirteen or fourteen years, until girls and sex and reproduction and jobs and the whole serious business of life's essential demands, and the weighty megalith of politics descended and there was less energy for laughter as you had to prevent yourself being crushed, one way or another.

But there it was. The raw, absurd fact of physical size. A man like the crisp-muncher could have dispensed him in seconds. His hand round his throat and the delightful, warm flow of life was ended. What protected him was culture. The poor male spider, ten times smaller than his hungry mate, could make no appeal to law. There were no spider courts for endlessly murderous females; but for us, thankfully, force didn't prevail. What did? Reason. Natural selection had made us rational creatures. Behind the beard and the wild growth of hair was a lawyer, after all. Boring though it may be, the law was an example of our cultural creativity. Though he hated the book which lay on the table, the notary couldn't pick it up and tear it to pieces without being answerable to the law he practised. On the other hand, right now an Israeli bulldozer was no doubt razing a Palestinian home.

"Do you really think so?" he said, picking up the volume. "Wouldn't it rather turn people away from prejudice? Much of it is pretty routine history after all, not the kind of thing a ranting ideologue wants to digest."

"You don't understand anti-Semitism."

"You're right. It baffles me utterly, as does all irrational prejudice, or prejudice, irrationality being its intrinsic nature. Look, what a lovely day. Who could bother causing trouble?"

"The whole world wants to annihilate the Jews."

"Steady on. Think of the children. They're just worried about where the next gob-stopper is coming from. And the nonagenarians. The proximity of a coffin has a remarkably calming effect on the ambitions of the master race."

"Only the Jews can understand it. That's why we have the right to defend ourselves as we see fit. If I had my way, books like that would be banned."

"If I had my way the Palestinians would be treated as an endangered species."

"You make my point, your mind has been turned by reading that stuff."

"On the contrary, I read this stuff to confirm my ingrained bias in favour of equality. I like it because it makes life interesting. Inequality is so boring, don't you think?"

"Once it was the far-right we had to fear, but now the liberals are our enemies."

"So I've heard. The world is full of odd theories, isn't it?"

"All this talk of Palestinian rights. Who gives rights to terrorists?"

"Naturally, who would give rights to the Irgun, the Hagana, Lehi? They might end up creating a theocracy and engaging in ethnic cleansing."

They pulled into a station. A tall, African woman in an elegant blue suit boarded and inspecting her ticket said:

"I think you're in my seat."

Bill couldn't have been happier if she'd offered to share her bed with him.

"My apologies," he said, gathering his belongings into his bag. "Enjoy the rest of your journey," and he smiled broadly at the erstwhile conversationalist and went in search of a free seat.

Steve was waiting on the platform.

"Good journey?" he said, hugging.

"Lovely. I shared my table with Theodor Herzl. Amazing beard."

"Pint?"

"Two."

It was a wonder to Bill that whatever corner of London they happened to be in, Steve would know the best pubs.

"Have we been to Whitby?"

"That's a hell of a long way."

"No, Wapping. Come on, it's a great boozer."

The two tall glasses of light brown beer sat on the bar.

"Mine," said Bill, offering his card first to the barman whose moustache joined his sideburns in a fine, black line.

"How do you do that?" said Bill.

"What?"

"Shave so artistically."

"I'm an artist."

Though to a passing eye the two men in their sixties sitting opposite each other were enjoying the same cooling beer, Bill was savouring the non-alcoholic *Meisel's Weisse*, in keeping with his strict attempt to reduce his blood glucose.

"You should try one," he said. "It's delicious."

"Yes, but it won't make me tipsy, will it."

"No more than two or Judy will blame me and I won't get fed."

"I'll cook."

They ran on inconsequentially as a good conversation should. Bill was resolved to say nothing about his suspension. Why drag the mood into the grim arena of power's convoluted ways? There was a past to explore.

In their university days, Steve was a mathematician and rugby player. Maths and rugby involved fields Bill stayed away from and while he spent hours in the library or his room with thick novels, Steve worked rapidly at complex calculations and was always first to be ready for the evening bar. Once, he'd come looking for his mate and found him slouched in a chair, his feet on the wooden bar which traversed the tall window looking out over the greenery of the campus entrance a copy of *La Cousine Bette* opened mid-way in his hands.

"God," he said, grabbing the volume, "you'll be here till Christmas reading that."

"Forty pages an hour."

"How many are there? Four hundred and sixty-nine. Eleven hours forty-three minutes. How long have you been at it?"

"About that long," said Bill retrieving the book and displaying the annotated section.

"You should've done maths."

"My mathematical brain ran out with O Level."

"Rubbish. Addition, subtraction, division and multiplication. There's nothing else."

"And like they say, music is simply twelve notes and silence. But look what Bach did with it."

"The alphabet is twenty-six letters and look what this bugger's done with 'em."

In Steve's study room were a squeezed half dozen tomes occupying less than half the length of his shelf; in Bill's were novels, plays, collections of poetry, overspilling the single-stingy shelf, piled in the corner of the desk and by his bed. Picking up firsts for all his work, intending to become an actuary, Steve floated through the terms as if none of the tasks could challenge him. Rugby was as natural to him as calculus.

"I was born to be a fly-half," he would say, lifting his pint in the bar.

It was early in their second year he took up with Judy, the most attractive girl in the year and one of only two Physicists. Serious and intense, Bill found her daunting. When Steve began seeing her, Bill recalled the first time he'd set eyes on her. She was coming out of the library, her brown, fur-collared coat tied tight at the waist, a pair of thick books under her arm. He was heading towards her at a distance of thirty yards and she didn't spot him. There was something in her demeanour, in particular the set of her head, her chin slightly raised which made him feel she was to be avoided. Subsequently, he softened. She was sometimes part of their crowd and he tried to get along with her; but as she lit a cigarette with tense attention, as if the ritual had secret meaning, or delivered one of her decisive and final remarks about what was obviously controversial, his feeling sank and he wondered about her.

Bagging the most sought-after girl with no more effort than he needed to solve a simultaneous equation or flick a handy pass, brought Steve some kudos; but Bill noticed how his friend changed. Like a man who has always walked with a quick and easy stride but suffers some injury which makes him drag a foot, Steve's charming nonchalance was weighted with a permanent gloom. Towards the end of the year, Judy took an overdose of paracetamol and was zoomed off in an ambulance to have her stomach pumped.

"What's getting to her?"

The dark young man shook his head and stared into his pint.

"Beats me."

"Maybe you should get out of it, Steve."

"I can't do that. She'd probably try again."

"You aren't responsible for that?

"Aren't I?"

"Come on, Steve. You're as easy to be with as a carefree child."

It was easy to understand why any lad would want to stay with so beautiful a girl. Bill had often thought, in his teenage years, stunning looks could compensate for failings of character; but no extraordinarily pretty girl had ever suggested interest and the girlfriends he'd had convinced him of the opposite. The charm of a lovely pair of eyes was quickly evaporated by misery-inducing petulance. By the time he was eighteen he was starting to see the beauty in a facial expression rather than physiognomy: physical beauty was given, beauty of character achieved.

He didn't believe Steve was unable to pull away because of Judy eyes, lips, breasts, waist, hair. He was in thrall to something else. There was some odd, hypnotic attraction to her brittle loftiness. Bill could feel it in himself, as if she commanded attention, as if the very fact of her coagulated pride made loyalty necessary.

In the first term of the third year she became pregnant.

"She wants to have it."

"Do you?"

"I'm not carrying it."

"Are you ready to be a father?"

"Well, I was ready to deliver the necessary."

"Not deliberately."

"Kind of."

"Christ, Steve, you didn't want to drop her in it?"

"No. She dared me."

"You're joking."

" Too serious for jokes, Bill. She said, " I bet you daren't do it without a condom." What would you have done?"

"Worn two."

The register office was an unprepossessing, square, squat 1960s building, though the inner sanctum was improved by wood panelling; a nod to a previous era. On the steps the little crowd of a dozen covered the couple in confetti. There were sandwiches, pies and gateau in the *Black Bull* where Judy's father, a tall, grey-ing man with an emerging stoop was a taciturn, somewhat vigi-lant presence while his wife cracked jokes about the newly-weds soon "making ends meet" and Bill "getting on top" of things. By the end of the afternoon, Mrs Loxley was staggering and laughing ever more loudly at her own jokes.

"Best man around," she said to Bill, swaying.

"Thanks."

"Are you and Steve old friends?"

"No, we met in the first year."

"I see. Rugby I suppose."

"Not me," said Bill, " I think muddy fields are exclusive-ly for cows."

"What do you think of my dress? It's not too revealing is it?"

"Not at all. Very decorous."

"You'd say anything," she said, laying her hand on his lapel, "you're polite. But I bet you're as bad as your friend in the bedroom."

The first thing Bill noticed as he stepped into the hallway was the cleanliness: the wooden floor had obviously had recent attention and the stair carpet showed itself vacuumed. He won-dered if that was in his honour. Had Judy done it? No doubt they had a cleaner like the rest of the people in this buoyant nook. The house was on three storeys. The third had been converted into a flat to bring a bit of extra income. Downstairs was dominated by a huge dining kitchen heated by a log burner. There was a long sofa in lush material and colours, an Asian design, two armchairs to match and beyond this sitting area, a table extensive enough to seat twenty. The kitchen itself, dominated by the island lay at the back where patio doors led to a wide, enclosed garden where they grew their own vegetables.

Judy appeared as he set down his little bag. He was struck by her preserved beauty. She had the figure of a thirty-year-old and though there was a streak of grey where the lick of her hair rose from her forehead and the skin of her neck had lost its tightness, the odd combination of youth and maturity gave him a little shock.

"Hello, Bill. Lovely to see you."

She kissed him on the cheek and the odour of patchouli reminded him of university.

"Nice to see you, Judy. Thanks for inviting me."

"Have you no luggage?"

"Just that."

"You do travel light. You can stay as long as you like, you know. We've enough spare bedrooms to sleep a regiment."

The tone of her voice took him back nearly fifty years. He saw her in their shared first-year kitchen, a cigarette between her fingers. She smoked an expensive brand and he'd always been tempted to ask if they provoked a superior form of lung cancer. She was sitting in the square bay which looked out to the cars parked on the periphery. Her demeanour was tight and serious. Steve came in from his run, panting and sweating, his tight shorts above his sturdy, hairy legs.

"What kept you? she said, taking a drag.

"Ten miles."

"I've been sitting here for hours."

Steve went to the tap, filled a tall tumbler and swigged.

"Ten miles doesn't take me hours."

"What time did you set off?"

"Who cares? It didn't take me more than an hour ten."

"How d'you know?"

"It never does."

"Get a shower."

"I will. Give me a minute."

He sat down at the table, opposite Bill.

"You can buy me a pint, Bill, and I'll thrash you at table football."

"I'll buy you a pint."

"I'm not waiting much longer," said Judy.

"What's the hurry?"

"I'm sure Bill has some work to do. He has books to read. He can't get away with scribbling a few numbers like you."

"Scribbling a few numbers will get me a job as an actuary. Bill'll end up teaching kids from the rough end in some underfunded comp, won't you, Bill? It's called giving something back to society, and it gets you a poor salary, stress and a tin-plated pension."

"You should work in the City."

"Who?" said Steve.

"Both of you."

"You won't catch Bill in the City. That's like expecting a medieval Pope to frequent brothels. No, maybe a poor analogy."

"You'd be millionaires by thirty."

"Yes, but would we be happy?" said Steve.

The two friends looked at one another and smiled. Bill shook his head.

"You can't be happy if you're poor," she said.

"Oh, yes, you can," said Steve getting up. "Remember the days we were kids, Bill? Kicking a tin can down the cobbles, fifty nippers out in the street and thirty dogs from all over the neighbourhood. Bread and dripping for tea and tinned salmon as a Sunday treat. Freezin' our little bollocks off in the outside lav in February. Happy as pigs in shit, eh mate?"

"That wasn't your life," said Judy.

"No, but it was 'is. He's the genuine, northern, working-class oik."

"That doesn't stop him becoming a millionaire."

"She's givin' you career advice."

"Are you going for a shower?"

"Yes, ma'am," said Steve, bowing.

Bill was left alone with her. She smoked in silence.

"Fancy a coffee?" he said, for the sake of saying something.

"Okay."

"It's only instant."

She nodded. It was curious how hard it was to make contact with her. It wasn't simply the cultural gulf. He could make small talk with all kinds who didn't share his view. There was something else about Judy. Her remoteness was an absence of connection with the immediate, as if some part of her was held back, belonged to the past, to a set of relationships which no longer existed but dominated her feelings. As he spooned the cheap granules into the mugs he tried to think of some gambit to open conversation. It had always been easy with his mates, talking about nothing; somehow Judy demanded significance. Her mind seemed to be constantly reaching for something higher but out of reach, so she was permanently pulled tight and about to snap. He wanted to find some form of words which might make her ease and spill redundant language.

"We could have coffee and biscuits, if I had any biscuits," he said, putting the mugs down.

"Is it true?" she said.

"What?"

"Your background."

"He's just taking the piss."

"So you did have a bathroom."

"Eventually."

"How old were you?"

"When we got a bathroom? Oh, about fourteen."

"What did you do before that?"

"Stank."

"I couldn't live in a pigsty," she said, drawing on her filter.

He wanted to retaliate but oddly felt that her thoughtlessness made her vulnerable. He stirred his dark brown drink with the little chrome spoon wondering why he felt it unfair to treat her to a bit of sarcastic raillery. A pigsty. Maybe many people would have thought that of the house where he spent his first years, but for those who shared the conditions, they were ameliorated by mutual support. He had the curious feeling Judy was unaware of the pointedness of her remark. She was always jabbing people with her words, always going for their weak spots. Yet it was obvious she couldn't be jossed.

61

"The pigs would have to give permission," he said.

Judy showed him to his room. At the top of the stairs, the landing opened out into a space big enough for a double room and stretched in both directions to a far door in shadow. She turned left, followed the passageway to its end and showed him into a delightful little room painted sky blue to the dado rail and white beyond. There was a three-quarter bed covered in a pale blue counterpane decorated with a marine scene; a handsome chest of drawers beautifully polished; a little refurbished writing desk; painted green and embellished with chinoiserie;, and an armchair in dark blue velvet with two chirpy cushions decorated with breaking waves.

"No wardrobe I'm afraid."

"Don't worry."

"The bathroom's just on the left. Are you ready for a meal?"

"As Steve used to say, I could eat a scabby horse."

"See you in a minute."

The bathroom was a wet-room with a square-headed forceful shower, a floating hand-basin and toilet and an entire wall a mirror. He couldn't resist. The hot water pounding the small of his back relieved the tension and pain of his ancient pro-lapsed disc. The conversion was obviously recent. He thought of his own over-the-bath shower with its pathetic uneven dribble, as if the plumbing had a prostate. The spots in his bathroom ceiling two of which worked intermittently. The stretch of black damp-proofing plastic taped to the corner where the water which splashed over the bath side because the screen didn't fit properly accumulated and seeped through the ceiling to drip from the din-ing-room rose. A house like this, appointed to pernickety perfec-tion, was worth hundreds of thousands more. Property set a big gap between him and his old friend. Yet they still found easy common ground.

As he pulled on a clean shirt, quickly, he pondered how impossible life with a woman like Judy would have been. The best of everything. The most modern. Caroline had something of the same impulse. Perhaps all women who subscribed to the cul-ture did. Men married for love and found themselves taking second place to kitchen tiles. Was it something in the female brain the culture exploited, or was it altogether a cultural creation? Who could know? Who could see the join? Much about our own nature was shrouded in darkness.

They were four for dinner. The lodger from the third-floor flat was joining them.

"Daniel," said Steve, "this is Bill, my old mate from university. He comes from the north but he's house-trained."

"Nice to meet you, Daniel."

There was chicken soup to start, one of those home-made dishes, rich in real flavours and without the excessive after-taste of monosodium glucomate.

"That was lovely, Judy," said Bill. "Steve's a lucky man."

"She's a lucky woman. The food's from the organic kitchen round the corner. Cooked and delivered and at a price even retired teachers can afford."

"Are you going to give away all my secrets?"

"Certainly not, it'd put them off their food."

Daniel it turned out, when Bill could think of nothing to ask but how he earned a living, was a freelance, social affairs journalist.

"He earns more than me," said Steve, " and he lives in my house virtually cost free."

"Both atrocious lies," said Daniel.

"Now, where Bill comes from, you can buy a mansion for a hundred grand, isn't that right Bill? What do we do about that then, Daniel?"

"Oh, don't start on politics," said Judy, getting up to clear the dishes.

Bill got to his feet to help.

"Sit down, sit down, both of you," said Steve. "Leave it to me."

He was quick and secure, handling the plates as he'd once a rugby ball , balancing them as he went briskly into the kitchen.

"He does it to wind people up," said Judy.

"Mischief," said Daniel.

"I wanted to show you something," said Judy.

She went into the living area and came back with a small album, opening it at a photo from their undergraduate days.

"Ha," said Bill. "Where was that taken?"

"In my room, I think. Do you recognise him?"

"Yes, I do," said Bill, examining the picture closely. "Isn't it Ken Sturrock?"

"It is."

"Good journalist," said Daniel.

"Do you know him?" said Bill.

"Never met him. But his work is terrific."

"What you looking at?" said Steve returning in his stocking feet.

"Ken Sturrock," said Judy.

"And you tell me not to talk politics."

"It's not politics, it's nostalgia."

Ken Sturrock had been on the periphery of their circle. A diligent English scholar, his First had landed him a job with a right-wing national daily where he'd reported on cultural matters before being offered the job of Northern Ireland correspondent, which he accepted with like the sons of Eton accept directorships in the City. Bill hadn't been very friendly with him but he recalled sitting with him in the café by the library entrance, on one of those winter days when the wind howled through the campus as if it would lift the lecture theatres into the air. His resolve to spend his life in perilous journalism was already firm.

"Don't you want to live long?" Bill had said.

"I don't see much point in making the meaning of your life the length of time you managed to hold onto it."

"No," said Bill, trying to pretend he hadn't been facetious. " But you don't have to stop bullets to give your life meaning."

"What are you going to do?"

"Teach, I suppose."

"Sounds like you're set on it."

"I know. I don't want to join the corporate world. I believe in the public sector. I dunno. There isn't a fit, is there, between what we want to do with our lives and the jobs available?"

"That's right. What I want to do with my life is turn up a bit of the truth. I may have to work for a newspaper I disdain to do it."

"Will a newspaper you disdain turn up the truth?"

"I don't know, but I'll try to force it to."

Bill thought of journalism as a lower form of writing. What was there in journalism to compare to Tolstoy, Jane Austen or George Eliot? Ken made him aware of his superciliousness. He was going to risk his life for the sake of honest copy. That was a bit more courageous than challenging the conventions of the novel or submitting experimental pieces to *Poetry Review*. It hadn't occurred to him that people could be driven by a commitment to the truth which would take them to Vietnam or Northern Ireland. He'd always assumed those people you saw on the tv wearing a helmet with PRESS across the front, had simply been given the assignment and didn't want to turn down what might further their career. Ken was no careerist. He was a man with a fierce intent for honesty. Bill felt slightly ashamed. Was his instinct for safety merely cowardice?

"He's done well," said Steve. "Some say he's the best journalist in the Middle East."

"He's done what he wanted to do," said Bill. "Turned up the truth."

"He's a fine reporter," said Daniel, " and have you read his study of the Arab-Israeli conflict?"

"Ready for the next course?" said Judy.

Bill twigged only when Daniel was served shakshuka while they had smoked haddock curry . He hadn't noticed the yarmulke because it sat discretely among the young man's thick black hair and was visible only when he bowed his head. It hadn't struck him as unusual either that Daniel was dressed almost all in black. He was very dapper in a white shirt with three buttons on the collar, a merino v-neck sweater and tight trousers with sharp creases.

"Haven't they persuaded you to stand for Labour yet?" said Steve, still in the mood for a bit of raillery.

"They're pumping up a burst tyre," said Bill.

"I don't know. I'd say you've got plenty of life in you yet, eh, Judy?"

"Maybe that's why he doesn't want to stand for Labour."

Bill wondered if Judy's views had modified. Maybe she'd softened since the early seventies; perhaps Thatcherism had brought about a moderate drift towards the centre and she was now a Liberal Democrat, believing in capitalism but shaking her puzzled head at its injustices, celebrating the freedom of the individual while millions of them struggle through lives of poverty and neglect. In any case, the last thing he wanted was to sour the occasion's sweetness. Steve, he knew, treated it all as a joke. He would have liked to provoke Judy into some defence of opinions he didn't share and then laugh like Danton at Robespierre as she turned green in their defence.

"Do they want you to stand for parliament?" said Daniel.

"He has the makings of a leader, don't you think? He can shape a good speech. Eh, Bill, remember when you turned that meeting and swung the vote behind the rent strike? What was that line you repeated? 'We are three thousand. We are withholding our rent and we will not relent.'"

"Pretty corny," said Bill. "No, not parliament. Just voting fodder on the local council."

"He's modest," said Steve.

"Why don't you do it?" said Daniel.

To tell the truth might invite a little, domestic maelstrom of disagreement. Yet, why shouldn't he? After all, he'd been punished for nothing. He'd exercised his right to free speech. Maybe, in any case, Daniel would sympathise with him: if he sited himself in one of the orthodox categories, he might be at odds with the Zionists . Maybe he'd read Moses Mendelsohn or perhaps even sympathised with Noam Chomsky. All the same, this wasn't a public forum. Civic debate relied on a space beyond the personal. There, it was right to say what you thought freely. If people were offended, they could defend themselves. Danton would laugh, even on the way to the guillotine. This was someone's home and he was a guest.

"An old, white, middle-class male. Not exactly a challenging image."

"Middle-class," said Steve, setting his spread hands wide apart, "you were born in the gutter."

"England made me," said Bill.

"Now, Judy here, on the other hand," said Steve, "had the proverbial silver between her gums."

"No one can help the circumstances they arrive in," she said.

"'Course not, but Bill calling himself middle-class is like you claiming you're proletarian because you serve soup to the homeless at St Wilf's."

"If they want you to stand," said Daniel, "they must think you'd do well. No need to be ageist or hung up on class."

"Daniel's right," said Steve, "why shouldn't an ageing old fart with a teacher's pension and a white skin keep the local streets free of dog shit?"

"Steve," said Judy, "we're eating."

"Who do you write for?" said Bill to change the subject.

"Anyone who'll have me."

The dinner over , Daniel shook hands and excused himself: he had work to do. The three of them shifted into the comfortable living area. Judy turned out the dining-room lights and they were lulled by the soft glow of a tall lamp. Bill sank into the corner of the sofa. There was a hint of the old days when he and Steve would sit in one another's rooms and chat a few hours away in inconsequential banter. Even when they touched on serious matters, they were still, in a way, talking about nothing because keeping each other company was more important. If there was one thing missing from his life it was convivial evenings. The days were easy to get through. He could walk or cycle for a few hours, sit in a café with a book, come home and inevitably fall asleep, catch up with his e-mails, fettle a bit around the house. The hours from six in the morning till the evening evaporated; but between then and bedtime was the barren period, when a sense of loneliness crept up from the floor and he found himself thinking of newscasters as contacts. He listened to music, he read some more, but nothing could fight off the lack of easy togetherness, the soft evening feel of daytime consciousness and purpose melting. Everything seemed too directed, deliberate. He went to bed early or let himself doze on the sofa.

"Not a bad bloke our orthodox, is he?" said Steve, pouring a golden beer into a tall glass which fanned to its rim like a daffodil's bloom.

"Very pleasant," said Bill.

"Of course, it tries the patience, sharing a house with two fundamentalists."

"He's not a fundamentalist and neither am I."

"Doesn't he believe the Torah is the literal truth?"

"I'm sure he does."

"But he's adjusted to the modern world," said Bill.

"More than you, mate," said Steve. "He knows how to use his elbows in the capitalist scrum."

"Religion doesn't stop you getting on," said Judy.

"It didn't do much for Christ's career."

"That's just a clever-clever remark," she said.

"Thanks," said Steve.

He sipped his beer and relished its chilled delight.

"Judy," he said, "is learning Hebrew. Impressive, don't you think?"

"Where are you doing that, Judy?"

"Bible study class."

"Won't do to read the translation. Like you and Proust."

" Well, why not," said Bill. "Any kind of learning is valuable and Hebrew must be a bit harder than Spanish."

"But not so much fun," said Steve. "No sangria and salsa."

"Take no notice of him, Judy. If it's what you want to do…"

"It is, Bill. To get back to the root. I feel a need to do that."

"Maybe you should try Sanskrit. Isn't that even older and more venerable?" said Steve.

At length Judy took herself off to bed and the old friends descended into the pleasure of mutual company. Different though they were in many ways, they complemented rather than clashed

68

and the memory of youth, freedom and possibility wrapped them in an aura of timeless sharing.

"Bet you never had Judy down for an Old Testament prophetess, eh Bill?"

They batted back and forth till three. When Bill pulled the duvet over himself he reflected on how close he'd come to telling Steve; but what was the point? It raised such enormous questions it was bound to overturn the happy little boat of friendship and reminiscence. Judy wanted to go back to the root. His suspension did. It raised the most fundamental issue: power. Who had the right to do what to whom and why? It touched on the essential: were all human lives of equal worth? He believed so. He always had. Every definition but human was incomplete.

Tomorrow, he hoped, they'd go into the city. Steve would lead him to some good pubs. He'd keep the mood light.

*

A PROTEST

Fortunately, it was fine. They jumped on the underground and whizzed to Tottenham Court Rd where they mooched around bookshops for an hour and a half.

"My throat is dustier than a Yorkshire miner's," said Steve.

"There are no Yorkshire miners."

"Just as well. We've got to stop burning that stuff or we're all screwed."

"That's not why the mines were closed."

"We know why the mines were closed. To avenge Maggie's daddy."

"Amazing isn't it? I wonder if she clocked the environmental implications."

"She was a scientist. She applied her chemist's brain to the crucial matter of the elasticity of ice-cream. Look, they're selling the curly stuff over there. Fancy one?"

"Never touch it. On principle."

"What principle's that?"

"Beware of products invented by reactionaries."

"Apply that, you'll have to live in a cave."

The Jack Horner was busy but they found a table for two up against the wooden panels and Steve brough the brimming pints.

"What's yours?" said Bill.

"London Pride, what else? I've ordered fish chips and peas."

"Good. I'll maybe have a snack."

"Twice."

"You'll undo months of good work. I haven't had a chip since Christmas."

"Once in a while. Don't they tell you you're permitted an indulgence?"

"Sure, but that's for cissies."

"Cheers," said Steve laughing.

The battered fish lay from rim to rim, nestled by a little mountain of thick cut, pale chips with, here and there, a crisped darker edge and tucked into the gap between the thin end of the cod and the stacked potatoes, a round, little mound of Lincoln green peas blending into a generous dollop of tartar sauce.

"Can I get you anything else?" said the waiter.

"Many things," said Steve, "but I can't afford 'em. Oh, ketchup would be nice."

He squeezed his slice of lemon so the juice dripped onto the crisp batter, picked up the plastic bottle and gently spread an even line of red from head to tail before adding a swirl to his chips.

"Doesn't that look wonderful?" he said.

"Enter it for the Turner Prize."

"Tracey Emin's probably done it all ready. Leftovers or something."

Bill intended to eat the flesh, the peas and leave the rest, but a taste of chip impelled appetite and the delight of letting go to enjoy the familiar flavours and the glorious sense of filling his belly and devil take the consequences, made him eat heartily and clean his plate like a hungry school kid.

"Sticky toffee pudding?" said Steve.

"If you order two of those you're eating both."

"I'm having one. I might have a heart attack tomorrow."

"Very likely if you cover it in cream."

"Clotted. And ice cream, but not the whippy kind. Another pint?"

"Not yet."

While Steve was at the bar Bill noticed the headline on the paper the bloke at the next table was reading. The Supreme Court was about to deliver its verdict on the proroguing of parliament. Bill had no idea which way the judgement would go but the business sank his feeling. However you looked at it, there was cynicism in the manoeuvre. What did it presage? What it suggested, at least, was contempt for democracy and the people. It was obvious a long campaign was in progress to spread disdain for democracy, a supplement to the already highly successful promulgation of stupefaction. He noticed there was an article also about Trump defending religious freedom as a way of attacking the Chinese. Wasn't the goon in power because tens of millions

71

of Americans had lost faith in democracy and wasn't that because they elected apparent democrats like Obama only to have their noses rubbed in the fact of neoliberal elitism? He knew it himself, that resentment which stirred at the constant parade of the successful , the well-paid, the well-connected, the well-educated, the experts, the pundits, the self-regarding regiment of influencers, celebs, people who knew people, people who had been born into the right family, educated at the right school and university, the endless procession of time-servers, lick-spittles, grovellers, fawners, sycophants, the miserable daily circus of flunkeyism with its persistent suggestion that those who were not part of this dumb-show of benighted egotism and nerveless insensitivity were failures. A memory spring into his mind: Obama at some Democratic celebration declaring with airy stupidity: "Do I have the best-looking wife?" Enough to make you sick on the carpet. Were men with plain wives supposed to feel inferior?

The square slab of dark desert looked viscous, sweet and tempting. Steve drove the spoon through its resistance, dabbed the confection into the blob of clotted cream, lifted it to his mouth and withdrawing the cleaned cutlery, took up a tipfull of the frozen vanilla and added it to the scrumptious sugary, fatty mass.

"You know why your taste buds light up like Los Angeles when you eat that?" said Bill.

Steve raised his brows, opened his eyes wide and shook his head.

"Because you can't get that combination of fat and sugar in nature. Nothing like it. So natural selection wired in an extreme response. There are lots of calories after all. We didn't evolve in a world of supermarkets full of chocolate and cream cakes. If we had, your taste buds would go mad at Brussels sprouts."

"Want a bite?"

"When the quack tells me I've got six months to live, I'm gonna stuff myself with cheesecake, scones, fruit cake and marzipan, fruit and nut, chocolate covered toffee and rice pudding. For the moment, I'm watching my glucose levels."

Steve finished a third pint while Bill sipped a gentle cappuccino without chocolate.

"You know it isn't a cappuccino without the sprinkles?"

"Don't be pedantic."

"He says, who has just lectured me on the evolution of tastebuds."

They were on their way nowhere in particular, enjoying the sun and the crowds, the lovely swirl of humanity in all its beautiful variety, when they came upon a little protest. A woman of sixty or so, small and somewhat overweight, with grey hair cut short, dressed in a sweater made of hoops of blue, red, yellow and orange, had set up a tiny pavement dissent in defence of the Palestinians. A hand-drawn map showed Palestine in 1948 and today. There was a paper banner with a quote from Noam Chomsky and a series of figures about violent Palestinian deaths. A red biscuit tin sat behind a plea for donations. A small crowd had gathered and a few yards away a tall, gangly man, all arms and legs, with a bald head he was shoving into the face of one of the onlookers was ranting:

"They're anti-Semites. Get 'em off our streets. They're anti-Semites."

Bill reached into his back pocket, took out a two-pound coin and dropped it with a high-pitched clang into the tin. At once a second man was in front of his. Smaller and stocky, dressed in a dirty blue raincoat and wearing thick, black glasses, he had a head of untidy, dark hair which looked as though it had been frizzed by rain. He pushed his face close to Bill's and began shouting like his companion:

"You're an anti-Semite. Get off our streets, you anti-Semite."

Steve, who was mildly amused by the display, set his arm between the man and his friend.

"Hey, steady on, mate. He isn't deaf. Take a step back."

The big man lurched over and standing two centimetres from Steve, bent towards him and began to bawl in his face:

"You're an anti-Semite. Get off our streets. Don't touch my friend. You racist. Get off our streets."

Steve took a step back but the shouter followed, his face still almost touching Steve's.

"Anti-Semite, anti-Semite, anti-Semite," he chanted.

73

Riled, Steve dodged to the left and when the big man tried to stay with him, slipped to the right, skipped behind him and wrapped his arms round him so the bawler's arms were pinned to his sides. He struggled, kicked, pushed back on his heels, tried to throw himself forward but Steve gripped and rocked with him.

"You calm down, pal," he said. "Don't insult me or I'll get the police. Now, you gonna calm down or am I gonna hang onto you till the cops get here?"

But they already were. Two officers in peaked caps, appeared round the corner of a building and began to run to the scene.

"See," said Steve. "You want to explain to them what you called me?"

The shorter of the pair, seeing the police, backed away a few feet and stopped bellowing. The big chap calmed a bit and Steve let him go. The policemen approached the woman in the multi-coloured jumper, who pointed to the adherents of Zion as the officers surveyed her amateurish propaganda.

"Come on," said Steve. "let's get away while they're distracted."

"Why are they talking to her?" said Bill.

"Probably contravening some bye-law which prohibits material critical of Israel being displayed within five miles of the Commons. Come on."

"It's that pair they should be talking to."

"Yeah, but if we hang around they're going to be talking to us and I've just had Netanyahu's bodyguard in a bear hug, and the bastard stamped on me toe. Come on, Bill."

He took his friend by arm and they headed away. When they were twenty metres from the little huddle, the arms and legs appeared behind them.

"Don't let me see you on the streets again you fuckin' anti-Semites, or I'll have ya."

The ghost of Steve's rugby-playing days arose in him and he almost threw himself at the gangly accuser's legs, but some residual voice of sanity reminded him he was sixty-six and the pavement was solid. Bill put his arm round his shoulders and they hurried away.

"What's the matter with those people?" said Steve.

"They know the truth," said Bill.

"Crazy guy," said Steve. "What have I done and he calls me a fucking anti-Semite. Did you see the way they went at that woman?"

"They're no better than fascists," said Bill.

"What harm's she doing, the old girl? Makes her protest on a Saturday, probably keeps her happy. She gets harassed by a regressed hunk of muscle like him. Free speech, eh?"

"Free speech operates within very narrow limits, Steve."

"Well, it shouldn't. Speakers' Corner. Let everyone have their say. It's good fun and it lets off steam."

"Problem is the steam might scald the powerful."

"Wouldn't've believed it if I hadn't seen it. The guy belongs in a lunatic asylum."

"Or the IDF."

"Maybe the discipline would do him good."

"He'd enjoy shooting Arab children. He'd get quick promotion."

"I need a pint."

"You've had three."

"I hate odd numbers. I know a lovely little boozer…"

Bill admired the tiles, as Steve had told him he would.

"*Peroni* is the only non-alcoholic."

He set the green bottle and the decorated glass on the table, sat down and savoured the first sip of Nicholson's.

"That's a lovely beer."

"You were right about the tiles."

"Great, aren't they? George Orwell admired 'em."

"Yeah?"

"True. This was one of his favourite boozers. He probably came up with the idea for *Nineteen Eighty-Four* where you're sitting right now."

"I prefer *Homage to Catalonia*."

"Haven't read it."

"You should?"

"What's wrong with *Nineteen Eighty-Four*, then?"

"Not much. It's a love story, of course. Bit predictable. What's good about it is the way so much he saw around him is incorporated and he grasped the way the media would be used to undermine democracy."

"The Right say he was mocking communism, the Left he was castigating fascism. Bit like the Bible, find what you like in it."

"Sure, you always get those tendentious interpretations. People try to claim Shakespeare was a capitalist, but what Orwell was really getting at was the fear of freedom. That's why Winston ends up loving Big Brother. That's why you should read *Homage to Catalonia*. The opening pages give a taste of what freedom feels like."

"If it tastes like this beer, I'll have it."

"That's exactly what it tastes like, Steve."

"Freedom is beer. Now that's a political slogan that could get me shoving leaflets through letter-boxes."

"Freedom is your right to tell the Temperance Movement you like beer, and theirs to tell you it's bad for you."

"The first bit I like, the second I'm not so sure about."

"Orwell says liberty, if it means anything, is the right to tell people what they don't want to hear."

"And that ends up in a shouting match."

"What the anarchists told the capitalists and the communists and the liberals in Barcelona in 1936 was they didn't need either business or the State. People did things for themselves. Franco didn't like what he heard. Hence, thirty years of fascism."

"A shooting match."

"Well, what it boils down to Steve, is that if you show the capitalists there's an alternative to their system, they shut down democracy."

"If I show Judy there's an alternative to capitalism, she'll shut down my marriage."

Bill laughed.

"She seems more obsessed with the Old Testament than the stock market."

"Drives me nuts."

"The stock market?"

"Religious mumbo-jumbo."

"Maybe it meets a need."

"Yeah, what kind of need is that? I need a bit of evidence before I believe something."

"Sure, but people can get the evidence wrong. Look in the sky and the sun is going round the earth."

"I know. But 2019, Bill. Darwin, genetics, all that. Who can go on believing some intelligence assembled it all in a week?"

"She doesn't believe that?"

"She's a literalist. Like her old man."

"He still alive?"

"Ninety-one. Plays golf every day. Thinks Trump will save the world."

"Not running the business any more?"

"He pokes his nose in. I'm ready to pack it in, but he doesn't want to sell."

"Tell him what he doesn't want to hear."

"Yeah," said Steve, laughing, "but the money, Bill."

"Money is a good gag, Steve. It keeps many people silent. Especially to themselves."

When they arrived home Judy was beginning the evening meal. On the hob was a large pan into which she dropped a slab of mincemeat from its plastic packaging onto sizzling olive oil.

"Just in time," she said, " peel a large onion, chop two sticks of celery and grate two carrots."

Steve grabbed the chopping board and a Sabatier, searched out the veg in the fridge drawer and set to work while Bill took a smaller chopping knife from the drainer and began to peel the onion.

"Cut it as small as you can, Bill."

Judy's phone played the first notes of Cohen's *Suzanne*.

"Hello, Peter. Okay?"

She left the kitchen.

"Fellow Hebraist," said Steve. "Pain in the arse."

"I think this meat needs a bit of attention."

Steve took a wooden spoon and chopped at the compressed oblong breaking it up and turning it in the spitting oil so the red turned to brown and the little lengths, like raw worms, shrivelled a little and bundled.

"Where will I find the grater? said Bill.

"The greater grater or the lesser grater?" said Steve.

"Some are born graters, some achieve graters and some have graters thrust upon them. I'll settle for the latter."

"In the cupboard under the sink."

The onion, chopped into tiny white pieces filled the centre of the chopping board. Bill wiped his eyes and blinked. He rubbed the first long carrot against the rough peaks of the grater and watched the curling strips accumulate within. The second made a pile too big to fit on the board, spilling onto the marble surface. When the celery was chopped into thin, incomplete rings, he surveyed the colours. There was something marvellously attractive about fresh food prepared for cooking. He had no skill in the kitchen, hated following a recipe and would cut corners to shorten time; but he loved the sight of tomatoes sliced and waiting to be grilled, or courgettes cut lengthwise and chopped into cubes. More than the odour of the food, it was the visible appearance which charmed him. What could be more alluring than the open flesh of just ripe tomato or the white innards of a firm aubergine? It was when his children were young that he and Caroline had begun to cook from scratch. Avoidance of salt, sugar and fat seemed a parental responsibility, though both his offspring had grown into the takeaway gobblers the culture encouraged. He'd been appalled when Liam would call for delivery of pizza or chicken nuggets and chips when there was good, well-cooked food in the kitchen.

"But I don't want to eat that stuff," the lad would say, standing two inches taller than his father.

"You'd rather scoff heart attack in a box in your bedroom, eh?"

"I like take-aways."

"People like crack cocaine, Liam, but they don't live long."

"You can't compare McDonald's to drugs."

"The world is full of fat and sugar junkies. It's a corporate conspiracy for diabetes."

Steve turned from his coaxing of the meat to inspect the veg.

"You've got the job. I guess we'd better add the onion."

"Maybe you'd better wait for Judy. She was following a recipe."

"Where's she got to. That Pete could talk the balls off a giraffe. Come on, it can't do any harm. It all gets mixed together in the end."

He lifted the wooden board and swung it across to the still fizzling pan, sweeping the miniature bits onto the beef which he then attacked once more with the wooden spoon. Satisfied that the onions were softening in the hot oil when Judy returned he smiled:

"All under control chef. The onions are cooking nicely and the meat is beautifully browned."

She looked in the pan.

"Oh, no. We don't put the onion in with the meat. The meat has to be taken from the pan and the veg cooked in oil."

Steve was about to say there was no harm done when she took a plate from the drainer and began to pick out the specks of onion with her fingers, running them under the cold tap after each extraction. The two men exchanged a glance.

"Fancy a beer?" said Steve.

"You're not going out now."

"Bottles."

In anticipation of his friend's visit, Steve had bought a generous little stock of bottled, alcohol-free *Meisel's Weisse*. He opened one and handed it over before pouring a *Lancaster Bomber* for himself. The two of them sat in the living area and watched Judy who spent the next half hour fishing the offending particles from the meat. Bill wondered if it could really make much difference to the taste. Who would notice? Neither he nor Steve would care. Would she find it inedible? He couldn't believe the flavour would be so distinct. He almost wanted to suggest she should cook two portions and be put to a blind test; but what really gathered his attention was the feeling Judy had imposed this on herself for no purpose, as if she were obeying some odd, external impulse. As if the recipe were the word of god and to deviate in any particular was to risk perdition.

Was it true this was typical of Judy, or was he over-interpreting? He couldn't dispel the sense of her having some need to submit herself to such penances. Wouldn't it have been better to shrug her shoulders, dismiss the mistake with a laugh and carry on. The spiked little incident had made Steve slightly morose and it seemed like a glimpse into their intimacy where he had no right to intrude. His own feeling too was deadened a bit. As if he'd done something wrong. It all appeared ludicrous given Steve was trying to be helpful. Maybe she looked for these small opportunities to diminish him. His thoughts began to drift to the bedroom, but he stopped himself for fear it would disturb too radically.

"Remember our culinary watchword?" he said.

"If it's brown it's cooked, if it's black it's buggered."

"It served us well."

The table was laid with a white cloth, edged in lace which Bill thought somewhat old-fashioned for Judy who prided herself on being both up with the trends and top of the range.

"Nice tablecloth," he said.

"Heirloom," said Steve.

"Don't be ridiculous," said Judy as she turned back to the kitchen to fetch the salad.

"'It's her mother's," whispered Steve.

The bolognase sauce steamed in an earthenware bowl while the fresh spaghetti rested in a blue and white china dish. Bill was tempted to ask if it was Judy's mother's. The salad, tossed in home-made vinaigrette, filled a wooden vessel from which protruded the carved serving spoon and fork.

"No spaghetti for me," said Bill.

"No?" said Judy, holding aloft the gleaming server from which dangled the soft, yellow strands.

"He's on a diet. Trim, isn't he?"

"But you've been boozing all afternoon."

"Only me," said Steve, lifting his plate. "He's been on maiden's water."

"Seems a bit self-denying," she said, depositing the pasta.

"He's keeping himself in the market. Wouldn't you fancy him, if you didn't know him?"

"Blood sugar," said Bill, as if he should apologise. "Nothing serious, just have to lower it a notch or two."

"Is it working?"

"Slowly. Six months, down two measures."

"How far do you have to go?"

"Another one and I'm at the top end of normal."

"Oh, a bit of spaghetti won't hurt, then. It's fresh."

"And it'll replenish your resources after fighting off the Irgun."

"The what?" said Judy.

"Zionist terrorists," said Steve.

"Terrorists?" she said, spooning a heap of the luscious meat onto Steve's plate.

"In the middle of London, in broad daylight. But Bill was a hero, he fought them off. Nukes notwithstanding."

"Oh, will you stop it? What happened, Bill?"

"Chaos in a coalbox. There was a woman protesting the Israeli treatment of the Palestinians and a couple of blokes were haranguing her. When I tossed a bit of money in her collecting tin, they got a bit pink in the face."

"What does the woman have to protest for?" said Judy. "People don't want that shoved in their faces when they're shopping."

"It's called democracy, chuck," said Steve.

"I don't see the need for it," she said. "People always banging on about Israel or some such. Why can't they just get on with their lives?"

"Why can't they, Bill?" said Steve.

"People get on with their lives in different ways, I guess."

"They do. They do, Judy," said Steve, pointing his fork at her. "You see, Bill here, he can't live without radicalism. Shopping makes you happy, reforming capitalism out of existence cheers him up. The question is, how do we reconcile consumerism and anarchism?"

"What's wrong with consumerism?"

81

"Bill? This is your chance. No more than twenty words."

"You can only consume so much."

"There's a fine answer," said Steve. "He's right, isn't he, Judy? One planet. What do we do when we've used that up? Stephen Hawking says go and live on Mars but I've heard the boozers aren't up to much. Still, if half the world's population shoots off into space, think of the reduction in traffic. You'll be able to drive round the city at thirty miles an hour."

"My father says the Arabs are backward and Israel is a modern democracy, and he's been there."

"Yes, he's been there, Bill. That's conclusive. All you've done is sit in your northern slum and read Flapan."

"What?"

"It's a book," said Steve. "Seminal. I had to borrow his copy. Couldn't even find one on Abebooks and if there isn't one in Bezos's garage, where will you get one."

"I don't understand why people try to change the world. If we put our faith in god, he'll look after us."

"But will he look after the Palestinians?" said Steve.

"If they put their faith in him."

"They put their faith in Allah. Will that do?"

"God is god what ever you call him."

"Even if I call him Eric?"

"Help yourself to more salad, Bill."

Bill nodded and shifted the bowl beside him, lifting out the soaked leaves which gave off the enticing smell of balsamic and black pepper.

"Anyway," said Steve, "Bill was saved by the Old Bill. Even the righteousness of Zion cedes before a couple of graduates of Hendon."

Judy ate a small portion of spaghetti and sauce and an ample supply of salad, but Bill noticed that before her plate was clean, she'd filled her wine glass three times. He recalled her spliff smoking. She'd been one of those who would sit in the corner of the union bar, roll and light up, filling the place with the sweet odour of slowly burning hemp. Neither Bill nor Steve had dabbled, Steve's quip being that he preferred the expanded consciousness of *Newcastle Brown*. There was something reminiscent of her dope days in her drinking, some driven need to change her mood. Serious and intense in a way which seemed somehow troubled, there was a joyless tenor to her imbibing. Steve drank beer happily and without any sense that he couldn't relinquish. He seemed intent on enjoying his mood rather than ridding himself of it; but Judy seemed to drink as if it was work, as if she had to, as if it was ordained.

Before long she began to speak more loudly and authoritatively and lurched to the fridge for a new bottle, which she banged down on the table.

"Steady on," said Steve.

"Open it," she said, holding it out to him.

"Of course, the Rabbinic texts are god's word. That's why I'm studying Hebrew. You have to go back to the root."

"Isn't that the Urtext?" said Steve.

"Yes, but that hasn't been discovered yet."

"There we are then," said Steve, twisting the cork from the neck, "we're all waiting for the truth to be revealed. Bit like a whodunnit, isn't it?"

"Don't be facetious."

"I like being facetious."

"Well, don't, it doesn't suit you."

"I think it suits me very well. What about you, Bill?"

"I'm biased."

"She's hardly objective. She's had to share a bed with me for decades."

"You can say that for the Jews," said Judy, "they stick to the truth of the Torah."

"You have an enlightenment empiricist eating your bolognaise, my love. He might not quite agree about the origin of truth."

"The enlightenment is a failure. Everyone knows that."

"Yes, rockets to Mars, the internet, satnavs, antihypertensives, paracetamol all thanks to the Old Testament."

"It was you who used to quote U Thant: "We have reached the moon but we haven't reached one another.""

83

"Very good. I'd forgotten that. Who did you used to cite, Bill? One of your Frenchies who said the Christians have had two thousand years and have managed little but warfare and strife."

"Diderot."

"Diderot. He's an enlightenment wallah."

"And how has he helped the world?"

"What would you say, Bill?"

"He wrote some interesting books."

"As interesting as the Bible?"

"She's got you there, Bill. It's a best seller."

"So is David Walliams."

"Is he the new messiah?"

"You can't argue with the word of god," said Judy.

"Unless you're willing to take the consequences," said Steve.

She finished another glass and poured once more. Bill watched her drink. She was killing herself. It was slow and pleasurable but inexorable. It made him think of Walt Davidson who he'd worked with in his first teaching post. A clever linguist who'd studied Latin and French at university he drank and smoked as if his life depended on tobacco and alcohol. A neophyte, Bill had agreed to help him out at fund raising barbecues and discos. Invited to his house to end the evenings, he was astonished to watch him drink till he collapsed, sometimes on the sofa or in an armchair, but once in the garden, his torso on the lawn, his face in the soil of the flower bed, his glasses skew-whiff. Three or four blokes hauled him into the house, dragged him upstairs, yanked off his shoes, socks, trousers and shirt and shoved him under the duvet.

Lucre fascinated him as much as stimulants. Thick wads of used tens and fives in his hands as the left-over hot-dogs were scoffed by the helpers or tossed into the overflowing bins, or stacks of silver counted into neat piles and set in symmetrical rows on a trestle table, induced the same I've-left-myself-behind obsessive attention.

Judy exhibited the same failed reaching beyond herself, as if the drink contained the secret of self-transcendence. She was killing herself and Steve was watching her and knew there was nothing he could do.

"Peter was praying, just before the London Bridge attack. He was praying for peace and god told him to stay away from the Bridge. He was going to walk to visit a friend and would have been there when the white van mounted the pavement. God saved his life. What has the enlightenment got to compare with that?"

"The theory of evolution?" said Steve.

"That came after," said Judy.

"Exactly. Newton, Hume, Darwin. Wouldn't work the other way round."

"Life is empty without god," she said, grabbing the bottle and tipping the last thimbleful into her glass, "empty, empty."

She thrust back her chair which scraped hard against the tiles and brought another Cava from the fridge.

"Is that the last?" said Steve.

"No, I bought a case. Open it, please," and she sat down heavily, her head falling forward.

At ten, when they were sprawled in comfort, she announced, in a tone which suggested reproach, she was going to bed.

"Okay," said Steve, smiling.

"Night," said Bill.

"Goodnight," she said petulantly, banging the door behind her.

Steve turned to his friend, gave a little puffy grunt, shrugged and shook his head.

"She's very drunk, Steve."

"She's an alcoholic, mate."

"You think so."

"She held back for your sake."

"Shouldn't she get help?"

"I will lift up mine eyes to the hills. From whence cometh my help, my help cometh from the lord."

"Maybe AA would be better."

"You can take a horse to water but you can't take a drunk to self-awareness."

"She'll kill herself."

"She will. I don't know which will get her first, the religion or the booze."

"Religion won't kill her."

"Don't you believe it. It's killed millions."

In bed, Bill reflected on Steve's fate. He was well set-up materially. His mathematical brain had landed him the actuarial job he'd always wanted and being willing to work for whoever would pay, he'd moved around shrewdly. No longer working full-time, he earned more for a couple of days a week than the average employee for forty hours. He was jaunty. He took life as it came and he pursued his pleasures with relish. Yet there was clearly deadness at the heart of his relationship to Judy. Why did he stay with her? Because he didn't want to see her decline. She was the mother of his children. He was holding things together.

"Listen," said Bill as they were parting at the tube station , "why don't you come north for a weekend?"

"Judy's allergic to it. She thinks Birmingham is on the Scottish border."

"Come on your own."

"Yeah."

"She'll be okay for a weekend."

"She'll be flat-out pissed, but yeah, why not?"

Coming out of the train station, Bill didn't feel like going home. What was at home, after all? He strolled to the library where in the entrance above which rose a great empty column, three floors high, ending in the galleries where visitors could read hieroglyphics and see Egyptian relics, there was a little, makeshift café: a dozen tables of various styles, accompanied by vagrant chairs and in the corner a counter behind which was the tiny kitchen where the woman who ran the place and her assistants toasted teacakes, buttered scones, or stirred hearty soups.

He'd got to know Alison, the busy supervisor by dint of being a regular. Cafes provided social contact. Once, it had been pubs, but propping the bar when you didn't drink was awkward. In any case, he liked coffee and to sit and read was pleasant.

"Hello, luv," she said. "Decaf large cappuccino?"

"Please."

"Going somewhere?" she said, nodding to his bag.

"No, coming home. A couple of days in London. What sandwiches have you got."

She rhymed off the selection. He looked around for a table and spotted, in the middle, in a smart suit, alone, biting into a thick BLT, his MP, Sir Jack Swift, who he knew in passing from meetings and rallies. A more or less invisible presence, except at election time, he was obviously here for something special. He was one of those backbenchers with a safe seat, an office and an efficient secretary who, for a quarter of his salary, kept the constituents at bay, banged off the letters he dictated from home, and ensured he could live the quiet life of a half-competent hack and enjoy the conviviality of the Westminster bars. Bill had once shared a platform with him in his days as a union activist and, making a rousing speech which had got the three hundred folk assembled in the square cheering, had left the dullard parliamentarian with a reluctant tongue. He wondered if he should permit the poor bloke to get on with his lunch but craving a bit of company and moved by a chance of mischief he approached.

"All right, Jack? Mind if I join you?"

The politician looked up through his heavy glasses and shook his head as he chewed.

"Don't often see you around," said Bill, settling in and trying in vain to tear open the cardboard and plastic packet in which his chicken salad on brown was imprisoned.

"Meeting," said Swift.

"Ah, one meeting after another, I suppose?"

The other nodded and chewed on.

"I've just got back from London myself."

Swift nodded and chewed some more.

"How are things in the great chamber where our fate is decided?"

"Fine," said the people's choice, nodding.

"Chaos, I would've thought," said Bill. "Is there going to be an election?"

"Who can tell?"

"Well, I thought you might," said Bill, jabbing a knife into the impenetrable packet.

"Hard to say what's in the PM's mind."

"Nothing, surely?"

Swift pretended to laugh.

"What do you think the outcome would be?"

"We can't win with Corbyn."

"No, but he could form a minority administration."

The tribune shook his head.

"The Party has to come back to the centre."

"The centre will not hold," said Bill, at which the lobby-fodder looked blank. "After all, look at 2017."

"Things have moved on."

"Isn't it odd how they will? What will lose it for Labour is the second referendum nonsense."

"We can't turn our back on the remain vote. Most Labour voters chose to stay."

"Yes, but the ones who didn't are raving mad at Starmer."

"I don't think so," said the legislator. "The message has to be made simpler but Starmer is right."

"Well, he's on the right."

Swift poured his tea from the little, rotund white pot which reminded Bill of the gentle days of his childhood, when aunts and uncles or his parents' friends would come to call and his mother would prepare a polite tray of home-baked cakes, biscuits and freshly brewed tea. By lingering on the periphery of the incomprehensible or tedious conversation he could feast on fruit cake, flapjack, scones, Victoria sponge, Chorley cake and swill them down with tea into which he'd dump four heaped spoons of *Tate and Lyle* granulated. Adults liked to meet and talk for a few hours which provided an atmosphere of protection. Although he saw his uncle George and auntie Beryl no more than twice a year, they were part of his inner landscape, like distant hills seen in a mist when out for a country walk, never known but reassuringly enduring.

The MP, who was a little younger, must have known that different time too, before the violent incursion of the doctrine that we are solitary competitors without natural sympathy whose well-being inheres in measuring our property against another's and in priding ourselves on any advantage.

"People don't want left-wing intellectuals or endless talk about what's wrong with capitalism. They want sensible, moderate policies."

"Like visiting hell on Iraqi children."

"The Americans would have gone in anyway. The right thing was to stand by our best ally."

"I suppose you could have said that about Vietnam."

"There's no point falling out with America. They lead the world."

"Towards disaster, it seems to me," said Bill. "If Trump gets a second term we're doomed."

"He won't."

"I hope you're right. Pity Bernie Sanders won't be President."

The deputy shook his head in further despair.

"He's far too left."

"What does he propose that Harold MacMillan would have objected to?"

Lifting his cup, Swift stared through his heavy glasses, as if at a dangerous lunatic.

"The Americans will vote for an Obama but they'll never elect a socialist."

"Obama was as bad as Bush in his foreign policy. Drone strikes. Unalloyed support for Israel."

"You have to support Israel," said the representative, setting down his empty cup, "it's the only democracy in the Middle East."

"You're right, it's in the Middle East."

"Corbyn has got us in a mess by criticising Israel."

"Isn't that democracy?"

"I've been to Israel," said Swift, as if having flown to Tel Aviv and spent a weekend as guest of HaAvoda his perspective was superior to anyone who hadn't breathed Israeli air.

"Have you read Flapan?"

The backbencher looked blank again.

"The influx of anti-Semites under Corbyn has done us terrible damage. We have to apologise to the Jewish community."

"You think all the people accused are anti-Semites?"

"Of course."

"But how do we know? Accusation isn't guilt. There's no due process. It's the perfect context for whipping up false allegations."

"Oh, there's plenty of evidence. Abuse of Jewish MPs. Vile language."

"Which Jewish MPs?"

"All of them."

"Do you recall a *Dispatches* programme some years ago when Peter Oborne explored the Israeli lobby in the UK?"

Swift shook his head.

"You can catch up with it on YouTube. Worth it. One of his points is that anyone who criticises Israel is quickly dubbed anti-Semitic."

"It's well known, people use criticism of Israel as a cover for their anti-Semitism."

"Some may, but look what the Tories say: criticism of capitalism is a cover for people's jealousy. Is that true? Are you simply jealous of Boris Johnson's millions?"

"That's not the same."

"It's exactly the same, Jack. It's a way of deflecting all criticism, of claiming that what you represent is so virtuous only the malicious can be opposed."

"You can't deny there's anti-Semitism in the Party."

"You can't deny there are paedophiles in the Party, or alcoholics, or shoplifters. Among half a million people there are bound to be, given paedophilia, alcoholism and shoplifting are phenomena of our culture. But no one claims the Party is institutionally alcoholic."

The head-shaking became more vigorous, as if there were flies buzzing around his brain.

"Alcoholics in the Party aren't insulting a particular community."

"I should think tee-totalers might be a bit narked."

"It's just not the same. We have to be especially sensitive about the Jews."

"Why?"

"The Holocaust."

90

"Have you been reading the Perlmutters?"

Furrowing his brow, Swift continued to shake his head in tiny movements.

"If we don't get rid of these people, it'll destroy us. You can't have racists at the heart of the Party and expect to be elected."

"I agree. Kick out the Zionists."

"Oh, that's ridiculous," said the MP.

"What's ridiculous about it? They imprison nearly two million people in the Gaza Strip, because they're Arabs. That's racism. They minutely control the lives of Arabs in the West Bank, because they're Arabs. That's racism. They deny citizenship of Israel to non-Jews. That's discrimination. Chaim Weizmann said "There's a qualitative difference between a Jew and an Arab". Pure racism."

"Israel has a right to exist."

Bill was stunned by the non-sequitur. How could Swift's mind leap from a statement which was clearly an expression of racial superiority to the assertion of an abstract right which no State on earth enjoyed. It was such a miserable collapse into non-thinking, into the acceptance of a reiterated formula without meaning whose purpose was to conceal the truth, that for a moment he perceived Swift as an idiot, in the literal sense. Was he thoroughly bereft of the basic capacity to think on the basis of evidence, or even to think at all? How could it be that a mind could give up thinking so spectacularly?

Of course, people for centuries had trotted out pat explanations of what they couldn't comprehend; but it was understandable that without telescopes people looked into the sky and assumed the sun was orbiting the earth which was at the centre of everything. When evidence is lacking what can the mind do but invent?; and there is such a vast range of potential explanations, that thinking without evidence is bound to produce bizarre theories. What was pole-axing about Swift was that he lived in an era of easy, fulsome evidence. Anyone who could read was able to find out the facts about Israel, and one of them wasn't that it had a right to exist.

"Does the UK have a right to exist?" he said.

"Of course," said Swift.

"So what happens if the Scots vote for independence? The UK isn't the UK any more, is it? So where is it's right to exist?"

"It will exist, but in a different form."

"Does Czechoslovakia exist in a different form?"

Swift looked serious and forbidding and didn't answer.

"No State has an abstract right to exist. That's not how the international order works. Functioning States are recognised as such, but they come and go. Israel is recognised as a functioning State, that doesn't mean it has an eternal right to exist. The USA doesn't have a right to exist, it has wealth and power and international recognition, but things change."

"Israel is insecure. It's surrounded by countries which want to eliminate it."

"For example?"

"Egypt."

"Does Egypt have nukes?"

"No, but it attacked Israel in 1967."

"That's not what Ben Gurion says."

" Nasser was massing his tanks in the Sinai."

"And did he attack?"

"Of course."

This time it was Bill's turn to shake his head.

"Not at all. Ben Gurion admitted it. We attacked him, he said. It was a war of Israeli aggression, but as always, Herzl's children have to claim they are victims. They appropriate the privileged status of victim and use it to traduce anyone criticises them as an anti-Semite or a holocaust denier. That's why The Holocaust was invented in 1967."

Swift sat back in his chair, his chin tucking towards his tie, as if he'd just been told his tea was spiked with anthrax.

"I don't agree with that," he said, as if his status as lawmaker gave him the right to disagree that natural selection was responsible for the variety of species.

"Well, take a look at the evidence, Jack. Go to Hansard, to the press archives, try to find references to The Holocaust, capital T, capital H, in the post-war period before the Six-Day War.

They barely exist. Simple. During the Cold War, Germany was America's ally. Not a good idea to remind them too much about the Nazi genocide. The Soviet Union, on the other hand, loved to talk about it. For obvious reasons. It all changed in 1967 because the war convinced the US Israel could prevail against the Arab armies of the Middle East. Israel became the guarantor of US power in the region. Hence, The Holocaust. The Jews were victims and must be protected and never criticised."

"That's all theoretical," said Swift. "We have to deal with the realities. The Jewish Community perceives Labour is anti-Semitic and that's enough."

"What's the Jewish Community, Jack?"

Immediately angry with himself for losing his temper, Bill toyed with the remnants of froth in his cup.

"The Party has had representations from the BoD, the Jewish Labour Movement, the Campaign Against Anti-Semitism, the CST..."

"I'm surprised Netanyahu himself hasn't knocked on your door."

"These groups represent the Jewish Community."

"No, they don't. They represent a strand of political opinion. Not all Jews are Israeli Statists, Jack."

"Anyway," said the tribune, looking at his mobile, "I'll have to be going. I've a meeting in quarter of an hour."

Bill was tempted to ask if it was with Rabbi Mirvis and to suggest Swift ask him about same-sex marriage, but shied from intruding on Swift's well-known private life.

The MP gone, alone in the inner circle of the library's ground floor, he was surprised to discover he found even Swift's uncongenial company comforting. Who was it who wrote that inviting your worst enemy into your house was better than living alone? Maybe Carson McCullers. He remembered that when he first heard the name he thought it was a man. A second young woman from behind the counter came to clear the table.

"Have you finished?"

"I think so," he said. "I have, anyway. And the politician's gone, no doubt to bring a bit more misery into the world. Did you know that was your MP?"

"Was it?" she said, blinking at him.

"If you live in the city."

"No, I don't"

He handed her the little plate with the remnants of the legislator's petty feast.

"Where do you live?"

"Out in the sticks."

"Ah, and you come to the wicked metropolis in pursuit of lucre?"

"Sorry?"

She was a pretty girl whose age he would have guessed at nineteen, but she might well have been thirty given how wayward his estimates had become. Slender and shapely with hooded blue eyes and fine, light brown hair brushed behind her ears and touching her shoulders, her little pink mouth and soft white cheeks were those of a child. He became sharply aware she might think he was trying his luck and felt thoroughly *de trop*. Why hadn't he simply let her take the things and thanked her politely? Well, he wanted human contact, but there it was, the indefeasible fact that if an old man alone makes conversation with a young lass, all that's on his mind is seduction. The idea was too ludicrous. Had she responded flirtatiously, and what girl in her right mind would to a grey-haired, lonely old fool, he'd have skedaddled like a rat from a terrier. How odd it was to live in a society of strangers where friendliness and approach were signals of danger. Had there been a time, thousands of years ago, when people lived in tiny communities and everyone spoke to everyone, the famed hunter-gatherers, our fortunate ancestors?

"Thank you," he said, lifting his cup and saucer.

As he made ready to leave, it struck him how few people there were in the world who meant anything to him personally. Every one of the billons meant something. They were people. There was a connection between all of them. It was impossible to sever yourself from the lives of those you shared the planet with. They were part of you by being human. You had to take the wider view and see humanity in the round. Yet, personally he knew hardly anyone. Oh, he could count up dozens of acquaintances, as people would, asserting them all as friends, but people he really knew, and more importantly, who knew him in any sense that mattered. There were hardly any.

"Yes," he said to himself, as he crossed the square outside the library, "there are tens of thousands of people in this city and I know hardly any and they know nothing of me. What might he be?" he thought as he looked at the man he passed, a bloke of forty or so, chubby, balding, apparently hurrying. "Now, if he happened to be my neighbour or if I'd worked in the same place or if he'd married my sister, I might know him well, we might spend hours together, there might be common ground between us. But there we are. Strangers. He'll live out his little portion and so will I, and mine will probably end well before his. Inhabitants not of the same planet, continent, country and time, but city. His feet have trodden the same pavements as mine. Maybe we've been in the same pub at the same time and never noticed one another. Maybe he knows people I know. But if I spoke to him, he'd think I was mad or on the make."

All the same, Bill liked cities teeming with people. He liked quiet country paths too, where if you passed someone you'd never seen and would never see again, you did say hello and not to would be thought uncivil. How odd it was. Intimates. Acquaintances. Friends. Strangers. Were our minds made for it?

There was a chance he might bump into someone he knew. Chance encounters, after all, had shaped his life. Part of him was still the eighteen-year-old Bill who couldn't come into town without meeting ten people he knew, whether he liked them or not. How quickly the decades had passed which had brought him to this. There was just a chance. He walked slowly, as if that might improve the odds. But he knew it wouldn't . The ground for it had retreated. School, work, the pubs, parties, just being young and *disponible*. In between had come the long task of child rearing. He emitted a little puff of laughter at the thought of his paternal idealism. Yes, it was good. He'd done the right thing. Yet, how things had turned out. How impossible life would be if we knew how things were going to turn out.

The click of his front door behind him was the sound of an evening alone. He had no difficulty filling the hours, in fact they were too brief. Every day was too brief, just as, when he was a teenager in school every hour seemed eternal and infinitely heavy. He could fill the time before bed with cooking, the Radio 3 concert, a bit of reading, answering e-mails. It would fly by; but what was missing was contact, those idle hours he and Steve had spent in one another's rooms, chatting and laughing before a few pints in the bar and back to one or other room for more idle talk to midnight or one o'clock. He was perfectly all right alone, but he was alone. Another person, even someone you didn't get on with particularly well or whose opinions you thought wayward made all the difference.

In his little kitchen which hadn't caught up, where there was no island or stainless steel fridge which told you the cricket score or the state of the stock market, where the hinge of the corner cupboard was constantly flicking loose so the door hung to the right like a drunk against a lamp-post, where the laminate flooring displayed patches of exposed brown shaped like countries no one cared about, he switched on the small radio which sat between the microwave and the kettle. It was tuned to Radio 3 and the first bars of Chopin almost made him leave it; but he liked to keep up with the news and important things were happening. Important things were always happening but he was caught in these important things. He'd been suspended from the Labour Party. His democratic rights had been curtailed because he'd sent a short e-mail to a Zionist who treated all criticism as "trolling"; and the Party, which ought to have responded by saying: "It's nothing to do with us. This is a private e-mail. We aren't permitted to reveal if Mr George is a Party member. That would be to breach data protection laws. This is none of our business..." had meted out swift punishment.

What the Party had done was to treat him as guilty because accused. He'd responded to their inane questions, a few months had passed. Nothing. Such was the contempt in which the Party held its members.

He wasn't surprised as the voice emerged to hear discussion of Corbyn and anti-Semitism. He found Evan Davis irritating. There were those of a sentimental, nostalgic turn who regretted Eddie Mair. *Les morts*, thought Bill, *sont tous des braves types*. It was a foolish idea that a change of broadcasting personnel could make much difference, like the ridiculous focus on the psychology of individual politicians: Thatcher supposedly possessed of an inner sternness that would make a whale tremble; Foot of a bumbling, confusion which made him intellectually incapable of leadership; Kinnock of an indefatigable sunniness, Major of the accountant's steady attention to detail and probity. It was all looking for the cause of rheumatism in the movements of the planets. What mattered were institutions and what kind of institution was the BBC?

All for public service broadcasting, Bill couldn't but be sceptical of an institution born more or less by accident, headed up by an engineer and given assent by royalty. Why not the people's assent? Educate, inform and entertain; but what mattered was who benefitted and who was pulling the strings. Oh, for a people's media, but it was a fantasy in a world ruled by property. The collective mind had to be shaped to conformity and among the many nexuses implicated, the media were crucial. The BBC's famed impartiality inevitably tipped to conservatism because to question the status quo was by definition partial while to confirm it merely looked like common sense. What was it Montaigne said about custom? He'd have to look it up.

Some woman whose name he didn't catch was claiming Corbyn had brought hordes of anti-Semites into the Party, Jews were under constant assault, prejudice festered in every corner and *these people* needed to be expelled unceremoniously. Being one of *these people* he wondered what gave her the right to judge him. What did she know of him? What did she know of his case? What she knew was that he, along with a couple of thousand others had been accused. Nothing more. Yet the BBC, like the rest of the media, without exception, assumed the accused were guilty. Impartiality? This was a propaganda machine any dictator would have been pleased with.

His mind flicked back to a tv debate from years earlier: Roy Jenkins in the studio and Noam Chomsky from the US. At a certain point, Jenkins had descended to insult. He tried to recall the form of words: "I have great respect for Professor Chomsky as a linguistic philosopher, but this is really a farrago of nonsense..." Chomsky raised an eyebrow in objection. What struck

Bill was that it was Jenkins who was damaged by the exchange. He sank while Chomsky rose. By sticking to argument, based of course on his precious empiricism, Chomksy had remained dignified and respectful. It was the politician who had revealed his true nature. Failing in argument he'd resorted to nastiness, and there was revealed the low creature behind the urbane front. Jenkins, of course, was hailed as the great liberal, the man who wanted to get the State out of people's private lives, to extend the arena in which people were free to choose how to conduct themselves. Bill had never liked him but it was only now the thought occurred to him that Jenkins was motivated more by opportunism than principle. Of course, letting people make their own choices was a fine notion, but Jenkins wasn't in favour of workplace democracy; he wasn't for people having real choice over their lives but was rather focussed on the personal, the intimate, the sexual. It was a good thing to lift guilt and opprobrium from people's intimate lives but there was a sleight-of-hand by which Jenkins claimed to be socially liberal when in fact his essential position was conservative.

He was, of course, an infamous womaniser. Nothing wrong with that. A man wants to have affairs with many women, why shouldn't he, if they're willing and happy? Yet what Bill despised about Jenkins was the slick hypocrisy. His emulation of the loose ways of the aristocracy sat ill with his claim to represent working folk. No one, after all, was suggesting that Jenkins' kind of behaviour would be acceptable for a bus driver, a joiner and most definitely not for a hairdresser, a nurse, a shop assistant. The morality of "family values" was held aloft by Tory, Liberal and Labour luminaries alike. The idea that ordinary women should have multiple lovers would have turned most politicians purple. And, of course, the response would have been utterly different if Jennifer Jenkins had been the Home Secretary, Chancellor of the Exchequer, leader of a new party, while he played the supporting role, taking on responsibilities on one committee or another and remaining faithful and dutiful while she went to bed with the husbands of her best friends.

The truth about Jenkins was that his narcissism made him adulate the aristocrats, he loved wealth and power, he was a sexist

98

who took for granted that women would take on subsidiary responsibilities, he was bisexual (Crosland having been his young
lover) and promiscuous, but he carefully styled the demeanour of
the faithful, dutiful *pater familias* to protect his political career.
Had he admitted openly how he behaved, he would have lost
credibility, because the politics of the day rested on the notion
that politicians were steady, conformist people, whose rectitude
could be taken for granted. And if Jack Jones, Hugh Scanlon, Joe
Gormley or Nye Bevan had been womanisers, they would have
been torn limb from limb by the media.

Jenkins was spared by the media because he represented
the interests of the rich and powerful and was never going to challenge them. His spoilt behaviour was indulged. He wrote highly-
praised biographies of Gladstone and Churchill rather than Keir
Hardie and Sylvia Pankhurst. He was a perfect example of the
Labour man, claiming to support working people, while enjoying
the high life, liberalising those elements of legislation which
made his way of life easier, but brooking no criticism of capitalism. They wouldn't have criticised him if he'd been having sex
with dogs. He deflected the malcontentedness of working people,
gave them the false idea he and those in his party were on their
side, while always ensuring the interests of the rich and powerful
were protected.

There was the source of the insult to Chomsky, who really was on the side of the common folk, who saw an alternative to
capitalism and could articulate it. Jenkins's dissembling collided
with Chomsky's honesty and the only resource the statesman
could grab was the vicious insult based on no evidence; but it was
he who declined; it was his dignity which was stripped; it was his
integrity which lay in shreds on the studio floor.

THE GREAT DUCK POND DISASTER

The same was happening every day. Bill was listening to the radio again while he grilled tomatoes and mushrooms for breakfast. There was yet another accuser peddling Perlmutterism, the demented notion that whatever didn't serve the interests of Israel was by definition anti-Semitic. The BBC could have done a simple thing: invite Ilan Pappe into the studio, just once, and ask him what he thought of events in the Labour Party. Why would that have been outrageous? Wouldn't it have been fully in the defence of impartiality and balance to have an internationally renowned, expert voice from the opposing side? Of course, the reason he was never heard was obvious: he might have convinced the public the hullabaloo was factitious. There was voice after voice accusing Corbyn and all his supporters of racism but never a serious argument from those who exposed the accusations. There was a statue of Churchill outside parliament though his racism was clearly expressed more than once, yet Corbyn, whose anti-racism was inveterate, was castigated as an anti-Semite. Madness.

The landline rang. Bill liked the phone in the hallway. It was what and where a phone should be, except he received a dozen calls a day from people in distant centres offering him insurance or recorded messages telling him the Amazon Prime account he didn't have was about to be shut down. The mobile phone performed something of the same function as the cigarette of old. He recalled how people used to get on the bus, sit down and immediately light up: I'm doing something; I've got something to think about; I'm not alone, I'm with my fag; I'm occupied. These days he would be on a train when a fellow passenger would start up: "Hello, yes, I'm on the train. I'll be there in half an hour.." or "I've just been to the doctor, it's my verrucas..". Loneliness. People were heartbreakingly alone and needful of connection. The obsession with devices was neurotic and narcissistic. He'd developed a bad habit: on the bus he could see, over the shoulder of the woman in front, what she was scrolling through. He'd rubberneck for a few seconds: images of dresses or shoes or blouses. Trivia. How much energy was being used? What resources had been

100

gobbled up so a woman could browse through clothing on a bus on her way home at five? It was indulgent and silly and it was bound to lead to mountains of discarded devices in poor countries and kids getting cancer from rummaging through the heavy metals in search of what might put a plate of rice on the table. But of course, much profit was made from this nonsense.

It struck him too how adherents of the mobile were ruled by heteronomy: as if by being connected for twenty hours a day, they were in touch with something which might deliver satisfaction. It was a form of mysticism, a deflection of life's inadequacy in a society organised around the colossal boredom of buying and selling. Perhaps, he said to himself, the new opium of the people.

"Hello, dad. Okay?"

"Hello, Liam. Fine. You?"

"Yeah. No probs. Heard from Jess?"

"Not for a week or two. Haven't you been messaging?"

"Yeah, she sent me a text last night. She's going to Morocco."

"Permanently?"

"Ha, no. About a month, I think."

"What's she going to do?"

"Study the cooking, apparently. I think they've got the idea of setting up a Moroccan restaurant."

"Why Moroccan?"

"No idea. Maybe there are a lot of Moroccans in Fulham."

"When you say, they."

"Yeah, Candida and those people."

"Have they won the lottery?"

"I don't know. I think one of them has well-off parents. You know, the one whose dad set up a business making fertilizers."

"Oh, yeah. Well, Morocco sounds interesting."

"Sure. Anyway, I was thinking of coming up for the weekend."

"Fine. This weekend?"

"Yeah."

"Okay. I'll stock up on crisps and *Red Bull*."

"I don't drink that stuff anymore."

"I'm glad to hear it. Just crisps, then."

"I wanted to ask. Is it okay if I bring a friend?"

"Of course. A bloke?"

"No, Rachel. She's my new girl-friend."

Occasionally, Liam visited with one of his mates. Joe had been three or four times and was easy to accommodate. He slept on the floor on an old inflatable with a slow puncture so that by four in the morning he was unsupported and had to grab the foot-pump. Nor was catering a problem: they took themselves to McDonalds or ordered a pizza, habits which struck Bill as gas-tronimically base and culturally distressing. But a girl. Bill's thoughts switched to the bedroom? How much of a mess was it? Used infrequently, he went for days or perhaps weeks without poking his head around the door. He would have to change the sheets. Did he have any clean? And the bathroom: the lock had finally fallen from the door and the pull-cord for the spotlights had snapped. He couldn't expect the girl to shower in the dark and without being able to lock the door. Then there was the win-dow. He'd unscrewed the opening light when there'd been a few warm, dry days, chipped out the rotten timber in the corners, slapped on some wood-hardener, filled the gaps with putty (a tip a glazier had given him: "It keeps out water, dries hard, you can paint it and it's cheap"), painted the frame with ten-year gloss and screwed it back in place; but the repairs were feeble against cli-mate change. The heavy rains came and the insistent winds, the water was blown, crept, slid, sneaked into the gaps, the frame ex-panded at both bottom corners and the window wouldn't open.

He couldn't expect the poor girl to make use of a dark, unsecured, tiny bathroom that would fill with steam which couldn't find an escape.

"That's fine. Anything I should buy in for her?"

"She's vegetarian and she doesn't drink caffeine."

"Okay."

"And she likes to sleep on cotton sheets."

"Cotton?"

"Yes, Egyptian cotton if you've got any."

"Is Egyptian cotton different from any other?"

"Apparently it's particularly comfortable. But if you don't have any.."

"Maybe I have. I don't know. Anyway, cotton sheets. I can manage that."

When he put down the phone he went straight to the bedroom. He'd forgotten about Stan's boats. His ex-wife's brother was a model boat builder and had asked if he could store some of his yachts and launches. Bill had let him pile them in the bedroom. There was a great, blue-keeled effort white two huge white sails in the middle of the floor, a red speedboat with a little outboard motor on the bed and numerous vessels difficult to categorize, in the corners on the bookshelves, on top of the wardrobe, on the window-ledge.

Someone knocked at the door. He went down the stairs wondering if Brian would be able to collect his fleet before the weekend.

"Look at my new ball, Bill? Want to play?"

Rakesh held out a pristine, white football.

"I'm a bit busy just now, Rakesh."

"What you doin'?"

"Sorting out some boats."

"Can I see?"

His dad poked his head out of the door.

"Rakesh, don't pester Bill."

"It's okay, Nathan. He can come and have a look."

"Kick him out if he gets on your nerves, Bill. He can talk the legs off a camel."

Rakesh was six, a very clever little boy who, since he'd moved in next door had befriended Bill. He appeared frequently with his football in his tiny hands, or under his arm like the head of a ghost:

"Fancy a kick around?"

Behind the houses was an unmade alley, six or seven feet wide. Impromptu goalposts- a sweater, a track suit top, a discarded drink can, a handleless bucket – were set up against the concrete sides of the garage which blocked one end of the track.

"You're in nets, Bill."

Rakesh flicked the white orb into the air with his dainty but skilled foot. He bounced it on his instep, his knee, his forehead, ran wide with it at his feet and turning with a neat body-swerve as if outwitting and outpacing the entire Manhester City defence launched it towards Bill who stretched impotently as it pinged against the stone.

"Top bins," called the lad, executing a celebratory lap before the bemused audience of the neighbour's sleepy, black and white cat.

These extempore games might last two hours.

"I'm getting a bit cold now," Bill would say.

"I'll go in nets."

Or:

"I think I'd better make my tea now, Rakesh."

"Just five more minutes," and five would expand to fifty.

Or Nathan would appear at the far end:

"Rakesh! Rakesh! Come in, your mother wants you."

"Coming, dad," and the dusk would turn to full darkness before he shook hands with Bill, saying, "well played."

"Where are they?" he said standing at the foot of the stairs.

"In the spare bedroom."

The quick, slender legs scurried up the steep stairs and the boy was among the boats before Bill was halfway up.

"What's this?" the boy called, holding a speedboat and pointing to its outboard.

"It's the engine."

"The engine?"

"Yes."

"Does it work?"

"If you put fuel in it."

"What's fuel?"

"Petrol."

"Have you got any?"

"No."

"Let's go to the service station."

"That's not the right kind of petrol."

"Where can we get some?"

104

"I don't know. But we can't get any just now."

Bill was in the room.

"How fast does it go?"

"Oh, I don't know, twenty knots."

"What's twenty knots?"

"The speed. On land we say miles per hour, on water we say knots."

"How fast is twenty knots in miles per hour?"

"I don't know."

"Look on your phone."

"I don't have a mobile phone."

"Why not?"

"I like a quiet life."

"Why does this have two sails?" said the child leaving aside the disappointing speedboat and picking up a yacht.

"I'm not sure. I'm not nautical."

"What's nautical?"

"To do with the sea and boats."

"Will it sail?"

"I guess so."

"Let's go to the park."

"The park?"

"We can sail it on the duck pond."

"Maybe one day."

"Why not today?"

"I'm a bit busy."

"Can I go on my own?"

"No, don't do that. Your mum would go hairless."

"It won't take long, Bill. It's only round the corner."

"Another day."

"What are you busy with?"

"My son is coming to visit at the weekend. I've to tidy this room for him."

"It looks tidy to me."

"You're a lad after my own heart, Rakesh, but his girl-friend won't want to share the bed with a model ocean-going vessel."

"I'll help you, Bill. Come on," and the boy began to shift the boats, pick up the odd sock from the floor, pull open drawers.

"It's all right, Rakesh. I'll do the tidying. You should play."

"Let's go to the park, then."

Judging a quick visit to the park the swiftest way to satisfy the lad, Bill searched for the retrieving pole for the yacht.

"Look, dad," Rakesh said to Nathan, "a cool boat. We're going to the duck pond."

"Are you sure, Bill?"

"Yes, Nathan. Just a quick half hour or so."

"You listen to Bill, Rakesh, and do as you're told."

"Okay, dad."

There were a dozen people walking their dogs and feeding the ducks which glided in noisy delight to the bank where the bread was being broken and tossed. An unleashed Staffordshire terrier was running wildly among the legs trying to get to the birds as its owner, a man of thirty-five or so with a thick brown beard, dressed in baggy leggings, pristine, white trainers and a black t-shirt emblazoned with BORN TO BE WILD, called ineffectually:

"Killer! Come here, killer!", grabbed the collar, stood in its way, diverted it by snatching it and sending it in the opposite direction, anything but putting on its lead.

Two little girls approached Rakesh.

"Cool boat, innit?"

"What you going to do?" said the youngest, taking the keel between her thumb and forefinger.

"Don't touch it," said the boy, "it cost a lot of money."

Bill suggested they try the opposite side to the duck feeders. He held the yacht by its mainsail and lowered it the sixty centimetres into the water, hooking the pole onto the eye at the rear.

"There," he said, "hold the pole and let it sail a bit."

Rakesh took the shaft and squatting by the edge moved the hull backwards and forwards in the water.

"Do you think it'll sail to the other side?"

"No."

"Why not?"

106

"The breeze is in the wrong direction and isn't strong enough."

"Which way will it sail if I let it go?"

"Don't let it go, Rakesh."

"I won't," said the boy looking up at the man, "but it isn't sailing much here is it?"

He raised his hand to shield his eyes from the sun and at the same time, his attention no longer on the boat, pulled sharply when he felt a tug. The eye sprang out of the timber. The pole became light. Rakesh turned quickly to see what had happened.

"Look, Bill, it's sailing. Cool !"

It was true the yacht was cutting an elegant stripe across the rippling surface, the gentle wind billowing its white sails, tilting to port but continuing to glide. The children on the remote bank pointed and their parents clapped.

"Wow," said Rakesh.

Even Bill enjoyed the sight of the little craft bobbing in stately progress, dignified and balanced, but he was conscious of its direction and was looking at the mass of floating weeds it was heading towards, hoping, like a man who has punted his life savings on a horse trailing in the Grand National, that some *deux ex machina* would intervene and send it to safety. It veered starboard and for a second he thought some kindly eddy would let it avoid the matted green peril, but in an instant it was back on its inevitable path.

"Come on," said Rakesh, "let's run round there and wait for it."

"No, stay here and see where it ends up."

"Is it going to get stuck in the weeds?"

"What do you think?"

"Shall I go and get it?"

"No, Rakesh," said Bill putting his hands on the boy's shoulders. "Just wait."

They waited, as people wait for a hurricane to strike, for dictators to stage coups, for governments to become unpopular, as the boat cut silkily through the grey water and hit the vegetation, full prow, coming to an ignominious halt, and lilting further to port.

"What do we do now?" said Rakesh.

"We need a very long pole."

"My dad has a fishing rod."

"I know. It cost him a lot of money."

"Let's go and ask him."

"Let's see if we can find something."

Between the pond and the canal was a wood through which cut a path well worn by dog walkers. They searched at either side for fallen branches. Rakesh took hold of the thick end of a limb two rugby players couldn't lift.

"What about this, Bill?"

"Yeah, hang on, I'll go and hire a crane."

There was a miscellany of scrappy twigs, odd little branches snapped by the wind, but nothing Bill could use to reach from the bank to the boundary of the weed-bed.

"Come on, let's go back and see what's happening."

They walked to the edge where the greenery began its fulsome growth. The family with the unleashed dog, still running between people's legs and haring after the ducks, like greyhounds after the hare, came to join them.

"You'll not get that back, mate," said Born To Be Wild.

"No, it's looking a bit tricky, isn't it?"

"Bit tricky. You're fucked."

Bill smiled, nodded and led his charge away.

"That man said a bad word, didn't he Bill?"

"He did."

"Why?"

"Because he's an idiot."

"Why is he?"

"Who can say. Maybe nobody ever taught him to think before he speaks."

They stood at their original spot and surveyed the disaster. The weeds were entangled round the boom. Even with a pole long enough to give the hull a shove, it would be unlikely to come free. There was only one solution. Bill pondered taking off his trousers but a sixty-eight year-old man stripping to his underpants in the park would no doubt send some paedophile hunter into a panic and in minutes the police would have him in handcuffs and he'd have to explain that it was all for the good of his erstwhile brother-in-law's maritime collection.

"Listen, Rakesh. I'm going into the water. I'll be okay. It isn't deep. But you must stay here. Understand? Don't move from here. Don't talk to anyone. Just stand there and watch me. And put these keys in your pocket and leave them there."

Rakesh nodded.

Bill kept his shoes on. You couldn't know what might be on the bottom. They were five years old and he'd had them soled and heeled three times. Just as well, he reflected, he hadn't decided to show off his Loakes. The water wasn't deep but it was stunningly cold. His knees were just above the water. All the same the chill went through his entire body. He decided he should move as quickly as possible to generate a bit of animal heat. His first few steps were successful but suddenly the bottom of the pond sloped severely as he set down his right foot. It slid as if being pulled by some mysterious subterranean force. His arms spread to balance him, he rocked backwards, Rakesh put his hands to his mouth, he lurched forward and sank up to his shoulders as he fell to his knees.

Upright, he went gingerly, with tiny steps. He began to shiver.

"Get a fuckin' move on mate," shouted the helpful Born To Be Wild.

The dog came running to the edge beyond the weeds, barking as at some intruder in the night. Bill dragged his numb legs, held out his arms like an ice-skater, focussed on the trapped yacht and tried to convince himself he would be out of the water in five minutes. He was two metres from the boat when the ground simply disappeared and the dirty water covered his head. He kicked his legs in a futile effort to swim, effected a miserable doggy paddle and after a minute of struggle, managed to right himself. He could taste the muddy water. He tried to spit the unpleasantness away. Soaked, cold, there was no point any longer trying to carry out a reasonably seemly rescue. He threw himself forward, lunged, splashed, fought with the element which leapt into his face and made him wince. When, finally, he got his right hand on the stern, a cheer went up from the little crowd and the dog began to yap frantically.

He tugged. He twisted the hull. He grabbed at the weeds and pulled a handful free, but the integuments were twisted round the rigging. Part of him wanted simply to yank it free and to hell with the damage, but another part was thinking of his brother-in-law. He would weep if his precious vessel were injured. So he began delicately pulling stands of weeds away from the boom, the mast, the wheel, all the time pulling gently and finding it fast.

"Just pull the fucking thing," shouted his landlubber supporter.

It was half an hour before enough of the tough stems had been dislodged for him to extract the yacht. Next, he had to make his way round the thick, green patch to the bank. He tried to go quickly, to tread confidently, but the slime tricked him again and he fell backwards, his head ducking briefly under. In frustration and desperation he regained his feet, pushed hard against the unstable bed, and thrashing, lurching, tumbling to left and right, slipping so his face hit the water, he struggled like a man fighting for his life to the concrete edge, lay the yacht safely as Rakesh appeared.

"You got it, Bill."

"Took your fucking time," said Born To be Wild.

The bedraggled pensioner tried to lift his right leg onto the hard surface but his fatigue forced him to pause. Born To Be Wild came forward, grabbed him under the armpits and hauled him, sack-of-potato-like to his soggy feet.

"It's okay, Bill. Look. Shall we sail it again?"

He was shivering, his wet clothes clung to him like octopus tentacles, his mouth was full of the acrid taste,.

"Come on."

They made their sorry way off the park, Bill dragging the heavy, saturated shoes which made his quaking legs feel weak. Dog walkers, young mothers with prams, a group of hearty walkers brandishing their Nordic poles like trophies of super-fitness, teenagers pulling wheelies on heavy-framed, thick-tyred bikes, a shuffling old man whose daily exercise was a hundred yards from his front door to the porter's lodge and back, a few solitaries moving at impossible pace seemingly to conceal their self-consciousness about walking alone and with no ulterior purpose, eyed him with dismay, incredulity, horror and amusement. Rakesh dawdled beside him, carrying the proud craft which had negotiated the water so majestically, delighted it was undamaged and hoping he might persuade his neighbour to let him keep it.

The final stretch, once they'd crossed the railway bridge was two hundred yards, more or less in a straight line. Bill stopped and looked at the distance. His courage and his heart failed.

"Run and get your dad, Rakesh. Give me the yacht."

Looking at the boat and fearing it might never return to his hand, the boy looked up at the drowned man.

"I'll keep it safe, "he said. "I'll give it my dad."

"No Rakesh. Give it me and run as fast as you can."

The boy's face filled with grief, his lower lip began to quiver. Bill ruffled his black hair.

"Don't worry, you can come round and hold it whenever you like."

He set off like a whippet, his skinny legs swift and nimble.

"My god! My god!" said Nathan when he arrived at a trot. "What happened to you? Rakesh, what've you been up to?"

The young neighbour supported the old man as they painfully fulfilled the final stretch, like marathon runners coming in exhaustion and blisters to the tape.

"Come in, come in. You can have a shower and some curry."

"No, I'll be okay. I'll get under the shower at home, but I'll accept the curry."

The little pile of wet clothes on the landing was a symbol of near defeat. Under the poor shower which, though the water it delivered was hot, dribbled as ever, Bill relaxed, worked up a full lather in his hair, let the heat penetrate his chilled flesh and wondered why he hadn't left the damn thing to its fate. What was it after all but a child's model? That a grown man could get worked up about it was perhaps indicative of the culture; but he knew he couldn't have faced its owner who loved his toys like a baby its rattle. He couldn't have said:

"Sorry, but we lost it on the park. Shipwreck in the duck pond. I'll buy you another."

Another was never any good in such circumstances. It was like stealing a man's wife and offering him a replacement.

He stayed under the inadequate spurt for a good long while, positioned himself so its splash hit him full in the lumbar region where he ached most frequently, turned to let it gurgle on-to his hairless, unimpressive chest and dribble down to his feet and the plug hole. At length, all that was left of the cold which had made him shiver like a malaria victim was the memory. He could summon up the idea but no longer the experience. He couldn't provoke the cold in his thighs, his calves, his hands, his biceps. It reminded him of something he'd read in Hume thirty or forty years earlier. When did he read the *Enquiry*? He was usually quite good at identifying the time he read a book: *Sons and Lovers*, 1967; *Combray*, 1972; *The Divided Self*, 1977; *La Vie Est Ailleurs*, 1980; *Die Blechtrommel*, 1982; *The Unbearable Lightness of Being*, 1984; but he couldn't pin it down. Sometime in the 70s, he was pretty sure. Yet what was more annoying was being unable to recall what Hume had written. He must dig it out.

Dressed, warm, the odour of the pond dispelled (though at moments a noxious soupçon seemed to steal into his nostrils) he pushed his foot into his *Rockport*, a good, comfortable shoe, suitable for the town, for a café, for a restaurant, for a pub, but no good for long walks by the river, over the hills, along the shore, like those he'd ruined in the Great Duckpond Disaster. In the cupboard with the hanging door, he searched for a packet of coffee. Nathan and Jasmine didn't drink, nor did he. An offering when invited by imbibers was easy. Somewhere he was sure there was an unopened packet. He took out the jar of peanut butter, the yellow tin of mustard powder, the little bottle of tabasco, the bigger bottle of Worcestershire Sauce, the packet of basmati, the packet of spaghetti, the beef stock cubes, the tea bags, the suet, the tomato ketchup (bought because Rakesh liked it), the Puy lentils, the baking powder, the desiccated coconut, the bouillon powder, the cornflour and his eye caught the pale blue he recognised.

He reached into the back corner. An unopened packet; but decaf. Could he present that? Would they be offended? Did he have some biscuits (bought for Rakesh). No, the shortbreads were half eaten.

"Coffee, Nathan. I'm sorry, it's decaf."

"Come in, Bill. That's perfect. I don't drink caffeinated, it gives me palpitations."

"Oh, him and his palpitations," said Jasmine appearing in the hallway her hands full with a big pan, "he bothers the doctor about them and he's as fit as a flea."

"You'll be sorry if I drop down dead."

"Don't be so sure," she said, disappearing into the kitchen.

Handy in a way Bill admired and was amazed by, Nathan had extended and improved the rear room. Where Bill's rear wall was, began a pleasant addition with a sloping roof adorned by two big Veluxes. At the far end, hardwood patio doors:

"UPVC," Nathan had said to him, "I won't have it. Bad for the environment and ugly. Don't you think it's ugly? All these plastic doors and windows. Doesn't a good, old-fashioned wooden front door cheer you up?

The extra room allowed them to accommodate a long table where they invited family and friends for cheerful meals and uplifting conversation.

"Sit where you like," said Jasmine.

"Next to me, Bill," called Rakesh.

The guest settled himself next to the boy, put his arm around his shoulder.

"Well, did we have a good time this afternoon?"

"Cool. Where's the yacht?"

"Back in its pride of place among the other boats."

"Tomorrow I'll help you tidy up."

"Good lad."

"Maybe Bill would like to tidy up on his own," said Jasmine.

"No," said the boy shaking his head, "he's too old."

On the table was an array of dishes which were a delight to the eyes alone.

"Will you have some samosas, Bill?" said Jasmine who was seated opposite him.

"I will."

"Help yourself. Don't stand on ceremony."

"She makes them herself," said Nathan, putting two on his side plate.

"It's not difficult. You should make your own, Bill."

"Yeah, it'd be a change from cheese on toast."

"Not difficult," she says. "The time she takes."

"What d'you mean."

"I tell you, Bill, hours she spends in the kitchen. Once she starts, you can't disturb her. Concentration."

"I like cooking. I like to do things properly."

"She's an expert, Bill. Those samosas. There's a technique, you know. It's in the fingers. Sensitive fingers she has. You have to mix the flour and oil, you see. Don't work it too much. She gets it just right. I can't do it. If I make them, they aren't flaky and crispy. I haven't got the fingers, Bill."

"You haven't got the patience."

"Look at that. Aloo Keema. No one makes it like, Jasmine. When the family gets together, she has to make it. And the naan. She doesn't buy them. Help yourself, Bill. Tuck in, as you say. Tuck in."

"Anyway, have you recovered, Bill? Nathan said you were in a state."

"He was all right, " said Rakesh. "I was looking after him."

"The hot shower revived me."

"You should've used ours," said Nathan. "Power shower, hot as you like."

"Is yours a power shower, Bill?" said Jasmine.

"It's getting on a bit. Like me. But it's hot."

"Was it Rakesh's fault the boat got stuck?" said Jasmine.

"It wasn't, was it, Bill? There were weeds. I didn't do anything."

"No," said the neighbour. "It was my fault. I should've known better. Still, no harm done."

"Be careful," said Nathan, "you might have caught a chill."

Hot nourishing food attracted him as if he hadn't eaten for days. The aromatic air nursed him to relaxation. Two samosas were enough. He would ruin his appetite for the rest if he indulged his desire to scoff another pair. The blue oval dish of Aloo Keema sat before him, steaming, the potatoes visible just below the sauce's surface like scuba divers in clear water.

"May I?" he said, taking hold of the long-handled, silver spoon.

"Of course," said Jasmine.

"Tuck in, tuck in," said Nathan. "Fill your plate. Whatever you like."

It was some time since he'd eaten lamb. It was one of those things he tended to avoid, almost semi-consciously, in response to the confusing and contradictory alimentary advice about cholesterol, diabetes, obesity, strokes. He had no more fat on him than an Ethiopian marathon runner, but he half-attended to the broadcast strictures and found himself in the supermarket wondering why he shouldn't buy the pack of four appetising pork pies.

The first forkful brought the taste of tomatoes. He'd always had a predilection for them. As a boy he would take one from the kitchen and bite into it, sprinkle a bit of salt and devour it with sensual relish. His tongue picked up a hint of garlic, cumin, paprika. The meat was tender, tasty and left that slightly fatty feeling in his mouth which he'd sought after when he was young and loved to eat the fat off a lamb chop along with a heap of hot, brown chips. The potatoes, soft, full of the flavours of the sauce, bringing that anticipation of fullness which had made them in any form- roast, mashed, sauted, chipped, sliced – the easy way to satisfy teenage hunger, provided instant satisfaction. He could eat the lot. To hold himself back he took a naan bread, tore it and dipped it into his sauce. The soggy consistency, the doughy promise of a replete belly, the lovely hints in the sauce, fleeting flavours of its expertly combined ingredients saw it quickly swallowed and he tore again.

Jasmine got up and disappeared, returning with a jug of sweet lassi.

"Shall I fill your glass, Bill?"

He vaguely recalled being told it was fattening, but just now he would have eaten a jam doughnut with cream and felt no twinge of guilt. The liquid slid smoothly down his gullet, sweet and cold and soothing. The curry was relatively mild but all the same the emollient effect was delightful and inspired the desire to eat more of the spices.

"Would you like to try the Haleem? Bill. It's beef."

"I would."

Jasmine spooned a hungry-man's portion of the porridge-like stew and he dipped his naan. When he forked it into his mouth he could taste the star anise, the nutmeg and his tongue recognised the texture of rolled oats, his favourite breakfast.

"She puts everything in it," said Nathan. "Any spice in the kitchen. Eh, Jasmine? Nigella seed, mace, cumin, pepper-corns, coriander, caraway.."

"I could get carried away," said Bill, cringing at his limp humour.

A few hours earlier, he felt close to death. His teeth chat-tered, his hands shook, he sensed in what seemed to be his stom-ach, right at the centre of that visceral part of him which was usu-ally warm and health-giving, an absence of energy which made him feel he couldn't carry on. Yet here he was glowing, replete, with that seemingly inexhaustible supply of force emanating from his organs as if his life would never end.

When the time for the green tea arrived, Rakesh was sent to bed.

"It was very good of you to take him to the park but you shouldn't let him pester. He gets his own way too much," said Jasmine

"Oh, listen to her who spoils him like a prince."

"Me? Who takes him to the corner shop for sweets three times a week?"

"Three times. Once."

"I don't mind," said Bill. "He's a lovely lad. I like having him around."

116

"Yes, he's a lovely lad but he knows how to press your buttons," said Nathan.

"He knows how to press yours," said Jasmine.

"Anyway," said Nathan, "how are things going in the ward? I hear Bobby Bridge is standing down."

Jasmine and Nathan were members. They signed up for Miliband's supporters' scheme in order to vote for Corbyn and when he won, converted to full membership. Though Nathan liked to think himself the informed politico, it was Jasmine who'd prodded him to join, and his opinions were mostly harvested from her comments about what she heard on the news, read in the paper or ferreted out on the Web. She was one of those women whose thinking cuts through verbiage and obfuscation, who assume that a politician, any politician, is out to bamboozle but who resist absolute scepticism as just as much a fool's position as absolute idealism. Her scepticism went far enough to make her question the slick speeches of a hack on the make, but behind it lay firm belief at whose core was a simple perception that fairness is written into our minds. Everyone has a concept of fairness, even those people, like her father, who would say "life isn't fair".

"Well," she would say to him when she was a girl, "you couldn't say that if you didn't know what fairness is, and as you know what it is, you would be up in arms if you were treated unfairly."

Nathan had done an Open University degree but she'd missed out, being a girl with three brothers. She didn't sulk, she read. In their living room were two ceiling-tall bookshelves of her volumes, some horizontal on the top of the vertical, others in little piles on the already crammed boards. What struck her was that through all her reading of the philosophers, political thinkers, historians, novelists, poets, dramatists, critics, her essential orientation remained the same. Her ideas had changed, but not that. She'd always believed, even as a little girl, that the natural thing to do was to treat others as you would like to be treated. It seemed to her that if you stripped away what culture superimposed, that's what you came to: the human core. And just as it was indefeasibly true that we had two feet and one nose, two lungs and one heart, because nature had done its work well over millions of years, so it was true we had an in-built sense of fairness and justice which impelled us to behave well.

The religionists evoked original sin and pointed to the evil in the world, but she wasn't convinced. All the evil, she felt, came from our defiance of nature, in the way smoking provokes lung cancer, bronchitis or heart disease; it was when people did what they knew to be wrong but found some self-justifying excuse that evil appeared.

Tories, she believed, knew what they were doing was wrong, which is why they said stupid things like "life isn't fair". Everybody knew it was wrong for excessive wealth to co-exist with food banks, children going hungry, old folk unable to heat their houses. Tories had to find an excuse: it's the operation of the market; let the market do it's work and wealth will trickle down; it's free enterprise; people must stand on their own two feet; management has the right to manage; and worst of all the invocation of that creature as mythical as the unicorn, the *entrepreneur*, the *self-made* man or woman.

An *entrepreneur* was supposed to be the source of our well-being, without whom none of us would work and we'd all be living in caves when the contrary was obvious to any five-year-old. How did the billions in Donald's Trump bank contribute to the common good? Even Bill Gates with his generous foundation was defying the principle that made him rich. Accumulation out of greed to permit a modest philanthropy which left you rich, was a stage magician's cheap trick. *Entrepreneurs* got rich through other people's work. Richard Branson didn't do the work which made his fortune, his employees did. It was a banality so vapid she could barely tolerate reminding herself of it. Yet the tyranny of custom kept injustice in place and children went hungry so the self-regarding rich could preen at the notion of their election.

She'd usually voted Labour, but had baulked at the despicable, mendacious Blair after the Iraq war and put her cross next to the no-hope Green; but Corbyn had ignited her hope. She quite warmed to him not dressing like a tailor's dummy and his hit-and-miss oratory gave him more of a human feel. There was nothing quite so unnerving as a trimmed-hedge speech delivered with the passion of a bored jobbing actor or the worked-up enthusiasm of a pay-me-for-salvation evangelist. They partook of the debased motivations of mass entertainment. What she heard from Corbyn was what she knew: the gross inequalities and injustices were imposed by those they served; change was necessary.

The 2017 election made her believe victory was possible. All the same, she wasn't a meeting rat, one of those peculiar individuals who love standing orders, agendas, tedious speeches, petty local council aspirants parading their egos. Rather, she spread the word subtly in her community. Nathan was devout and she accompanied him to the mosque. She felt it was probably good for Rakesh, in small doses. She never talked politics. It was too intrusive. Nevertheless, there were ways: what a shame it was Mrs Uddin had to rely on the foodbank; a country as rich as this; Mr Nawaz had bought another house to let to students and the reputation he had; perhaps landlords should be more carefully regulated. She never let an argument develop. It was always possible to smile and change the subject.

"Yes, he is," said Bill. "Some family problems."

"Shame," said Jasmine.

"Why don't you stand, Bill?"

"Bit long in the tooth."

"You stood in Eastway, didn't you?"

"Yes, because they'd vote for Bolsonaro if he promised to protect their property."

"It'd keep you busy, and you'd be good," said Nathan.

Bill nodded, wondering if the best was to tell them. What held him back? It was such a nasty, convoluted business and he'd already been blanked several times by people he used to sit in branch with and enjoy a chat before and after the business. People were easily convinced that smoke meant fire and long commitment to the party militated against sympathy. He couldn't believe they would turn against him, but pushing his case might sound like special pleading and it was easy to become strident. What chance Nathan and Jasmine understood the background? Maybe, like most people they felt the Jews must be treated with special care because of the Nazi genocide and fell into the propaganda web which equated any criticism of Israel with anti-Jewish prejudice? What did they know about Herzl? If he mentioned the Perlmutters would their eyes glaze?

"I'm busy enough, for a codger. It's all I can do to keep the house reasonably tidy."

"I'll give it a clean once a week, if you like," said Jasmine.

"Oh," said Nathan, throwing back his head and showing his white teeth in a great laugh, "you'd never find anything, Bill. She tidies the kitchen, all the spoons disappear."

"They go in their rightful place, you're just too lazy to look there."

"Twenty pounds an hour," said Bill.

"I'm not taking any payment. The hours you look after Rakesh."

"He looks after me."

"Anyway, you should stand, Bill, They've pestered you to, haven't they? I'd help your campaign."

"Me too," said Jasmine, "and Rakesh could shove leaflets through letter-boxes."

There was no doubt the Israeli lobby had done its work well. The party was in a blind funk. Corbyn himself didn't fight back vigorously because, Bill felt, he was deterred by the fear of being deemed blind to what was happening. By trying to placate the accusers, he was implicitly admitting guilt. His reiterated repudiation of racism in all its forms did no good against the morally abject dishonesty of the Israeli statists. These were people defending the indefensible, willing to fabricate whatever would secure their malicious end. They weren't exercised by anti-Semitism – some of them sided with far-right groups- they were troubled merely by criticism of the Israeli state. The claim of institutional anti-Semitism took flight after Corbyn defeated the feeble challenge of the smart-suited salesman Owen Smith. To anyone with their eyes open, the coincidence was too neat. Unable to remove Corbyn by constitutional means, the Israeli lobby had sunk to the lowest skulduggery. That Labour was institutionally racist was too out of proportion to be worthy of a flicker of attention. In most branches there wasn't a whiff. In most CLPs the issue was as dormant as the Black Death. What was in the wind, of course, were Palestinian rights. That was the real issue. Israel's indefensible and crumbling position was the issue, but to defend that was difficult. To cry *Holocaust, Denial, Anti-Semite* at the first hint of dissent from Israel's orthodoxy was the conscienceless, gutter-level, cheap, dissembling, amoral route to quick sympathy from the uninformed and unthinking, and slow suicide as the truth emerged like water seeping from a cracked sewer.

It was vile, malicious, underhand, an insult to the memory of those slaughtered by the Nazis, but it worked, as unprincipled means often do, for a while. His democratic rights in the party had been curtailed. They took his money every month, but they made no response. He had fulfilled what they requested. Their questions were answered. They had indicated a desire to settle things in a timely manner, but months had elapsed and it was obvious the party was intent on leaving him in limbo. What could be expected from an organisation which treated its own members so badly? How could Labour offer social justice when it celebrated injustice at its core, when injustice was in fact its *modus operandi*?

All this and more he had thought through so often it was installed in his consciousness like the alphabet. Yet what would Nathan and Jasmine think? Would they assume the party couldn't be so corrupt as to suspend people on feeble evidence and leave them dangling in a crass denial of even the most elementary due process? They wouldn't be captious adversaries; he knew they'd be sympathetic; but beneath their neighbourly sympathy would they harbour the suspicion that he was guilty of some oblique anti-semitism? The guilt which attached to accusation was recognised of old. The Israeli lobby knew how to make use of it. They were as negligent of evidence as the most far-gone metaphysician; but worse: they were fully conscious of their evil; they accused the innocent in order to defend their felonious regime. If he told them, perhaps forever there would be a morsel of grit in their relationship. Yet if he didn't, wasn't he certain to appear evasive? How would he explain no longer going to meetings or dishing out leaflets? In any case, by hiding the truth, wasn't he giving in to

the evil? Why should he behave as if he belonged in a Kafka novel?

"Well, what would you say if I told you I'm suspended?"

"For what?" said Jasmine, straightening.

"Bringing the party into disrepute, it seems. Though just
what I'm accused of I haven't been told."

"I can't believe it," said Nathan.

"That I'm guilty or the party could do it?"

"Either," said Jasmine.

"There we are. I won't be standing."

"Oh, they'll have to change their minds," said Jasmine.

"I don't think they will."

"It's outrageous. What do they say you've done?"

"I sent an e-mail to an Israeli lobbyist."

"And that's a crime now, is it?" said Jasmine.

"It is if you tell him he should look for anti-Semites in his
own backyard."

Nathan bridled slightly and looked bemused.

"Quite right," said Jasmine, "Zionism has long embraced
hatred of Jews who refuse it."

"Has it?" said Nathan.

"I told you to read those books. You left them by the side
of the bed."

"I read one."

"You feel asleep on page four."

"Anyway, when do I have the time to read?"

"Oh, when do you have time to watch the cricket?"

"Are you going to deny me my simple pleasures, now?"

"But how did the Labour Party find out you'd sent it? "
said Jasmine, turning her face from her husband.

"The gentleman complained."

"Did you send it on behalf of the party?"

"Of course not."

"Did you identify yourself as a member?"

"No."

"Then how could he complain to the party?"

"Speculatively."

"That's despicable. The party had no right to disclose you were a member."

"They may not have."

"I don't get it, Bill. How could he complain to the party if he didn't know you were a member? Did the party reply to his complaint?"

" No idea. Maybe."

"Maybe. I think the chances are more than maybe," said Jasmine. "If they did, they broke the law. You should take up your cause, Bill."

"Hard to take up a cause against a sponge . They refuse to respond. People try FOI requests. Zilch. They appeal to the information commissioner. Nothing. Too many complaints. You may think I'm getting paranoid, but its systematic. Everything pulls together to prevent the truth being exposed. Just look how the matter is dealt with in the media. It's taken for granted people like me are guilty. I'm a racist because I've been called a racist. The Israeli lobby is vicious but efficient and everyone with power is on their side."

"It makes me so mad," said Jasmine getting to her feet. "Make some more tea, Nathan."

"She's right, Bill," he said, obeying, "you should fight your corner."

"Is the branch defending you?"

Bill shook his head.

"Doesn't work like that. They're sympathetic but they won't take up the cudgels."

"And where's the fuss about Islamophobia?" she said

"I know."

"Jews are mistreated in the UK? I don't see it."

"They're thriving, by and large"

"No, we're pretty lucky too, here. We don't get much trouble in this town. Nathan had some teenagers shouting "Paki bastard" at him when he was walking home a couple of weeks ago. I get the odd offensive e-mail. But things are good here. My sister in London got one of those letters in 2018, you know, Punish a Muslim Day."

"Shame."

"And the police say the definition agreed by parliament is too broad and might get in the way of free speech. I haven't heard them say that about the IHRA definition."

"Ah, well defending Israel comes first."

"I know the far-right is anti-Semitic, but people like you..."

"People like me think the Palestinians are ill-treated."

"Of course they are. It's a disgrace. It makes me so mad, Bill."

Nathan returned with the teapot.

"I'm shocked, Bill," he said. "I'm shocked."

"What can we do to help you?" said Jasmine.

"There's little can be done against something so co-ordinated and extensive."

"I'll write to the paper," said Jasmine.

"I doubt they'd publish it," said Bill, "in any case, I'm not allowed to tell you about my case under threat of expulsion."

"How are you supposed to defend yourself?"

"You can't, that's how it always works."

"This is a country of the rule of law. The law can't allow things like this."

"Institutions can get away with a lot, Nathan."

"But the Labour Party is supposed to stand for justice," said Nathan.

"Supposed to," said Bill.

"Write to Jeremy Corbyn. I can't believe he supports this."

"No doubt," said Bill, "but he's the political leader, he doesn't control the bureaucracy."

"The bureaucracy? Who elects them?" said Nathan.

"That's what makes them powerful," said Bill.

"Oh, that's not right," said Jasmine. "That makes me so mad. The members are supposed to run the party."

"Yes," said Bill, "if all the *supposed tos* were realities, the world would be a different place."

"Well, complain to the head of the bureaucrats. Who is it?" said Nathan

"Jenny Formby, but she's trapped. The idea is now entrenched that people like me are racists. She can't dismiss it. And there are members of the party staff doing the dirty work of the accusers. Faceless people, fairly low level people, but at the heart of the machine and that gives them power."

"No one should have power in a democracy unless the people give it them."

"All big organisations need bureaucracies and they are opaque and reactionary. Always."

"Well, they should have power taken from them," said Jasmine.

"Yes, but that would need a very different kind of organisation."

"Well, then," said Nathan pouring the tea, "let's have it."

"Let's have it indeed," said Jasmine. "Away with the bureaucracy. Leave power at the grassroots."

"The party system," said Bill, "it's essentially corrupt. Why should power be concentrated in two big parties? Why should we elect people who stand for parties? Parties are a way of keeping power in few hands. They always were. Once it was the landed interest against the commercial. When the people got the vote, they decided to join in. But parties simply suck power into themselves. It's supposed to lie with the people but it lies with the party machines, the State bureaucrats, the media billionaires, the opinion manipulators. That's what we call democracy."

"I'm not giving money to the Labour Party for it to suspend people like you," said Jasmine.

"Nor me," said Nathan. "I'll give it to Amnesty International."

"Or the Palestine Solidarity Campaign," said Jasmine.

"Watch it," said Bill, "that'll get you expelled."

"Do we live in a democracy? Do we have freedom of expression and association? Am I being told I can't support Palestinian freedom and be a member of the Labour Party? And you, Bill, where are your democratic rights. The parties are the conduits of the people's will and you're stripped of your rights in the party. Oh, it makes me livid."

"The rich have been organising against democracy ever since the franchise became universal. The world order rests on the antipathy of property towards poverty. That's the simple principle which explains why the world is as it is. The natural sympathy between people has been replaced by the antipathy of those with money to those without it, because equal distribution threatens their advantage. And out of that simple fact the tragedies go on day in day out."

"Yes, natural sympathy, I like that," said Nathan.

"What a mess we're in," said Jasmine.

"Have some more tea," said Nathan.

"No thanks, I'd better be going. I need to go to bed with the hens, as the Italians say. The great duck pond disaster has worn me out."

As he climbed the stairs and his legs muscles hurt he remembered what he'd intended to do before Rakesh interrupted. He poked his head in the spare bedroom and switched on the light. Much to do tomorrow. In bed he found himself wondering how authentic Nathan's and Jasmine's responses had been. They were nice people. Sympathetic people. It was true, there was a given sympathy between people for no other reason than their shared humanity. It was the work of biology. The antipathy was the work of culture. How odd we should have created a culture which denies what's best in us. Anyone could get annoyed or fed up with anyone else, but a systematic antipathy took hard work. When we made the choice to pursue lucre we erected the barrier between one another. Yet could it be true they harboured a suspicion of his guilt? Maybe they were talking it over now:

"He must have done something bad," Nathan might say.

"He's a nice man, but maybe he went a bit too far."

"They wouldn't suspend him for nothing."

"No, I can't believe it. He must have made a mistake."

He stopped himself. What was he doing, attributing negative feelings to the neighbours who had fed and supported him? It was the germ of paranoia, planted by accusation. Someone must have been telling lies....He was reminded of Kundera's *The Joke*. Would it have made any difference if he'd cast his e-mail in the form of a quip? Of course not. The Israeli State could no more take a joke at its expense than the Stalinist. Yet his situation wasn't quite so bad: his fellow members' hands hadn't been raised against him. It was merely the dark bureaucracy. Nor was he about to be sent to a gulag. No need to exaggerate. All the same, the germ was there and things could rapidly descend. Once it was accepted that the accused were guilty, there was no justice. Not even cold justice, let alone the warmth of sympathy.

It took effort to convince himself Jasmine and Nathan were entirely sincere, which made him feel an alien force was operating in his mind. They were his lovely neighbours who turned up at five o'clock on a Saturday with a tray full of samosa, rice, Balti, naan. They trusted him with their little boy. When the pull cord in the bathroom broke, Nathan fitted another and he climbed on the roof on a cat ladder and replaced two cracked slates when rain dripped onto his duvet. There was no question about the authenticity of their reaction. Yet the little demon wouldn't be quelled: he dreamed he was before a court. Netanyahu was the judge. The members of the jury were pointing at him, laughing mockingly. Nathan took the witness stand and said he was guilty. Jasmine followed him and asserted he was a well-known racist. He was seized by the court officers and marched outside were a firing squad made up of members of his branch waited. He woke to feel his heart pounding. His t-shirt was damp. He got up, went to the bathroom, found a clean one. When he slid back beneath the sheet he felt it too, damp and clammy. He had to tear it off, find another in the packed chest of drawers and tuck it in the mattress. He looked at the alarm's digital display. Four twelve. At six fifteen he was still awake. With so much to do he might as well get up rather than waste time reluctantly awake.

A mundane, necessary task, before it's begun threatens boredom, but once he was under way tidying the room and one task led to another, he found himself enjoying the limited nature of what he had to do and the approaching sense of accomplishment. It was odd, and out of kilter with prevailing ideas: simple, ordinary tasks weren't supposed to provide a sense of fulfilment. He was unpleasantly reminded of the many lessons he'd taught towards the end of what he refused to call his career when the pupils had been unruly, reluctant and even downright nasty and the hour had ended in a feeling of inordinate frustration and waste. Nigel Reed, who sometimes gave him a lift half-way home, would be tense and quaking when he'd spent the final hour with a bad Year 10 who refused to do a stroke of maths and drove his anger and humiliation beyond toleration; and John Newman complained over and over when they went for a pint together of the hopelessness he experienced when his classes subverted his every effort.

The irony was that this circus was the result of the work of OFSTED and the league table culture. Having experienced the before and after, Bill had seen how quickly a culture can be transformed. Prior to Major's laughable "citizens' charter" schools had operated on the assumption that the State was on their side; they were doing an essential and hard job; teachers were professionals but not richly paid; public money funded the system; the understanding was, those who rejected the provision were at fault; unruly kids were unruly kids, not a proof of teacher incompetence. Once OFSTED was in place and the charter established, it was open season on teachers and everyone went for them: politicians, the media, parents and, of course, the youngsters themselves, given the excuse for bad behaviour by the PM himself because the orthodoxy became: there is no such thing as an unruly, difficult, recalcitrant or malicious pupil, just uninteresting lessons.

In his last few years, fulfilling hours were few. Yet here he was, on his hands and knees using a floor wipe to remove the dust from skirting boards and finding it satisfying to see the result. It was intrinsically replenishing to see what needed to be done and to do it, even if it was nothing more than pushing the vacuum over the polished floorboards, polishing the windows and making the bed with clean, ironed, cotton sheets. Little was worse than being undermined in seeing through a task, and of course, teenagers looking to rib a teacher knew it. They couldn't be blamed. They were just kids kicking against the pricks. It was the pricks in government who were responsible for the appalling decline.

Cleaning and tidying occupied the central hours of the day. Finished, he sat on the sofa with a cup of tea. No doubt Liam and Rachel would want something to eat when they arrived. He wasn't going to subject them to his who-needs-a-recipe cooking. Where could he take them? If they favoured Italian, they could walk into town to *Marco's* and he could have the lovely red pepper soup and the pan-fried cod and a cappuccino. Nothing to stoke up calories or send his blood sugar soaring.

The phone rang.

"We'll be there in twenty minutes, dad."

"Okay."

"Can you pick us up?"

"What in, a wheelbarrow?"

"I scrapped the car, Liam. It was diesel. I'm an eco-warrior. Get a taxi, I'll pay."

They arrived in a diesel people carrier, big enough for seven.

His son's hair was cropped short, which gave him an odd twitch of disappointment. On his shoulder was a neat, little grey overnight bag. His white trainers were out-of-the-box clean but his jeans and fleece were lived-in, worn and friendly. His girlfriend was small and dark. Her pale complexion clashed with the black curtains of her perfectly centrally-parted hair. She was strong-looking, her arms and legs short and sturdy and she carried her big, pink suitcase with ease.

"Welcome to George Towers," said Bill. "Put your bags down. I'll brew up. How was the journey?"

"Fine," said Rachel showing her big white teeth.

"Yeah, no probs. I'll take the stuff up, eh dad?"

"Aye, back room."

Liam lifted the plastic case, wriggled through to the kitchen and they heard his clump as he climbed.

"Tea okay, Rachel?"

"I'd love a coffee, if that's possible."

"Everything's possible chez Bill. Decaf or the stay-awake stuff?"

"Ordinary coffee, thanks."

"Take a seat. I'll get the coffee maker gurgling."

As he spooned the coffee into the little, holed device which sat between the lower chamber of water and the upper into which the black liquid rose and spluttered, Liam bounced down the stairs and came to stand beside him.

"Good to see you, son. Everything okay?"

"Yeah, dad. Cool, cool. Just one thing. Do you think you could pay for my train ticket?"

Bill experienced that little jab of discomfort in his stomach such requests always brought. Part of him wanted to turn to his lad and say:

"Liam, you're a fully grown adult. I'm nearly seventy and on a pension. You're not a teenager anymore. I'm not subbing you to go to the *Moon* with your mates any longer. It's time to be independent."

He turned and smiled. Liam had a curious expression, half assertive, half reticent.

"Sure," said Bill. "I'll get the cash tomorrow."

GUESS WHO'S COMING TO DINNER?

There were tables on the pavement of the little square. Marco had extended his arena without permission but for the time being the councillors hadn't bothered him. One was a regular; a bustling, committee-addicted Tory who in spite of what she thought was her free-market ideology, got up a petition and worked vigorously to save the little heritage centre, funded by the council-tax payers, which risked being slaughtered by the austerity. Marco knocked ten percent off her bill, and considered himself a wily operator.

They were early enough to avoid the descent of the evening chill.

"If it gets cold, they'll bring blankets," said Bill.

"That's nice," said Rachel, perusing the menu.

As ever when meeting someone new he wanted or needed to get to know, Bill was impelled to fire questions: where did you grow up?; what do your parents do?; where did you to university?; what are doing now? It was the way to understand someone; to have all the details which combined into the full picture. He always thought it odd there were people he'd been friendly with for years who knew nothing about his origins and had shown no curiosity. Jimmy Villiers was like that. What he knew of Bill was what he experienced, but what Bill had experienced to make him what he was, he had no inkling of. There was something fundamentally reassuring about someone who would say: "Were you born here?" or "Are your folks still alive?" It testified to an interest beyond the superficial.

"What do you fancy?"

"Don't know," said Liam.

"There are plenty of vegetarian options, and Marco is obliging."

"What are you having?"

"Soup and fish."

"You always have soup and fish."

"I like soup and fish."

"The soup sounds nice," said Rachel

"And you'll get some lovely warm bread with it, and heated olive oil."

"Yes, I think I'll have that."

With a little dish of assorted olives , Marco, dark, sturdy, mustachioed, aproned, brisk and proud arrived.

"Buona sera, Bill. Come stai?"

"Bene, grazie. Mio figlio, Liam, e la sua ragazza, Rachel."

"Piacere."

The Italian shook their hands as he surveyed his customers.

"Treating your dad, eh? I bring Champagne?"

"Pago, Marco."

"Allora, due bottiglie."

"What's he say?" said Liam.

"You're paying and he's bringing two bottles of Champagne."

"Your dad paying, you have what you like, eh? Bistecca di girello. You like?"

"What's that?"

"Rump steak. È vegetariano, Marco."

"Peccato. I give you few more minutes, eh?"

"Please," said Bill.

Liam found the olives too salty and the garlic bread he ordered, just to have something to chew while they ate their soup, not firm enough.

"Let me try a bit," said Bill, and tearing off a little ill-shaped corner he slipped it into his mouth between spoonfuls and chewed. "Mmm" he said nodding, "lovely flavour though. Plenty of garlic."

"I don't like too much," said Liam.

Unpleasantly reminded of Caroline, Bill recalled, not any specific instance, but the negative feeling which accompanied it. What was the name for that feeling? Disappointment? Frustration? Exasperation? A combination of the three or more which had no name? Nothing was ever right for Caroline, except what she did for herself and then it was supreme. If he cleaned the bathroom, she'd see only the bits he'd missed and would com-

132

plain there were still stains in the toilet bowl. When he checked , he couldn't see anything but bleached it again for good measure. On the rare occasion she might attend to the bath (she hated housework and did virtually none) she would claim it gleamed with pristine cleanliness like no bath ever had. Had Liam learned from her or was it something in-born? There was no way to know? The puzzle ran up against the limits of his understanding. Probably the safest was to assume it was an amalgam of both, but that was nothing more than an assumption.

"Well, you can have something else if you like. Enjoy yourself, son."

Bill cast a glance at him as he put his slice of garlic on his plate with a look of disgust.

"What is it you do, anyway?" he said to Rachel, while they waited for the main course, his curiosity forcing him.

"I'm in tech," she said.

He wasn't rude enough to say that was the end of the conversation.

"Oh, who for?"

"Myself."

"The Zuckerberg of Ealing, eh?"

"She doesn't live in Ealing, dad."

"No, sorry to conflate your addresses."

"Stoke Newington," she said. "Do you know it?"

Bill shook his head.

"The only bits of London I know are the theatres, some of the galleries and a few cafes and pubs."

"You know Steve's neck of the woods," said Liam.

"Yeah, that too. I went for a weekend a bit back."

"You could have told me."

"Sorry. I wouldn't have had time to meet up. It was one of those come-and-go, weekends."

"I could have come to Steve's."

"Yeah, sorry Liam. Thoughtless of me."

It hadn't failed to pass through Bill's head that he could hook up with his son while he was in the city, but the truth was he had no desire to. The idea bothered him at first, but he quickly overcame his discomfort: Liam was a grown man with his own life to live and this was joining up with an old friend he hadn't seen for a long time. It was simply easier to keep the two separate; but it wasn't only simpler. He didn't want Liam' negativity to invade what he hoped would be a thoroughly pleasant time.

"Next time you come, we'll show you round some interesting places," said Rachel.

"Yes, good idea. So, you work for yourself."

"I do."

"Keep busy?"

"Very."

"She's a tech expert, dad. She gets commissions from all over the place."

"Right. Did you do a tech degree?"

"No, Physics."

"Clever stuff. I failed O Level."

"What's taking them so long?" said Liam, twisting in his seat to try to see what was going on inside.

"Patience. Want another beer?"

"Yeah."

They walked home in the gathering dark and the thickening chill. Bill knew a short cut. They had to pass through a little copse which blocked out what was left of the light and made Rachel shudder and Liam put his arm around her. It led them past the new Mosque built in the suburb much to the outrage of a swathe of its residents. Bill thought it a relatively aesthetically pleasing building. They'd chosen a stately, grey-greenish stone and the design was restrained and high-minded. He thought it an architectural addition. As for the religion, people had a right to it. He'd long since rejected the idea that humanity could be cured of its need for faith. Evolution and natural selection had made nothing perfect. The human mind had contrary tendencies. His was towards what tallied with the evidence, but if people needed gods, they should have them, as long as they didn't impose them on everyone.

"How long has that been there?" said Rachel.

"They finished it about eighteen months ago. Not bad, is it."

"There must be a lot of Muslims here."

"No, not as a percentage."

"They're taking over London," she said.

Bill walked on, the two of them a pace behind. There was silence for thirty seconds during which the gross conception of Rachel as an anti-Muslim racist formed itself. He had to restrain himself from mocking disdain of her remark. It brought to mind the unpleasantness of Enoch Powell, the dismal spectacle of trade unionists marching under banners reading KEEP BRITAIN WHITE, the miserable National Front and the puffed up John Tyndall, the humourless, pathetic, anti-Semitic, follower of Hitler, the BNP, the EDL, the neo-Nazi football thugs, and above all the deadly, hapless, confused nexus of misconceptions which attributed biological superiority to a particular section of humanity. Taking over London? The idea was so remote from reality it might be on a par with the claim crabs were taking over Brighton, or seagulls in St Ives part of a Jewish conspiracy for world domination, or beetles secretly planning to subvert democracy. It was of the same tenor as Hitchcock's *The Birds*: a fantasy of a horror which simply couldn't happen.

He wished he had the figures at his fingertips. How many Muslims were there in London. He would have liked calmly to put the evidence as he walked beside her. Of course, evidence meant little to a mind determined to submit to its own irrational fears. In a way, it was akin to his claustrophobia: he knew there was little risk in taking a lift, but unless he had to, he would climb the stairs. There was, at least, an element of rationality to his fear: a lift could jam. He wasn't afraid of what wasn't possible, just susceptible to too ready an anxiety. Nor did his peculiarity threaten anyone. It might be inconvenient if he was in company and the others took the quicker way, but no one was in any way injured.

The idea brought what seemed like an insight: racism wasn't simply an irrationality, it was a maliciousness. At its core was a desire to inflict pain. Perhaps that came first. Maybe the will to hurt was primary and it sought an outlet and excuse. Was that true of this apparently charming, innocuous young women he'd just spent a couple of hours in the restaurant with?

"This is where Liam imbibed his first learning," he said as they passed St Stephen's, "in the care of the highly skilled Mrs Wells."

"I hated her," said Liam.

Bill laughed.

"You were five," he said, "you just didn't like learning the two times table."

The levity delivered them home.

"I hope the room's okay for you," said Bill.

"Yes, it seems fine," said Rachel.

They were eager to be alone while he would have enjoyed a bit more conversation, but with Liam being gainsaying and morose he was glad enough to wish them goodnight.

Starting up the laptop, except for some lengthy session, always got on his nerves. It told him he hadn't entered his password before it gave him the chance, took five minutes to warm up and he had to run the virus killer before shutting down to avoid one of those horrible incidents he'd known when the screen went black or turned upside down. He found what he wanted: there were about 1.2 million Muslims in London out of a total population of nearly 9 million. Some takeover. The alarming figures were incidences of Islamophobic violence. What was much more likely to take over was racial and religious hatred.

What was Rachel's animus? He hadn't managed to discern her background but he wondered if she was Jewish. Was that an anti-Semitic thought? Ridiculous. She might well be and it might explain, in part, her wayward remark. There were no more than about 300,000 Jews in the UK. They were vastly outnumbered by the Muslims, but that was thanks to Enoch Powell, to colonialism, to the chickens of conquest coming home to roost and pecking in the dust of working-class areas where the established population felt they were imposed on. They weren't wrong, essentially. The rich could always choose their neighbours and often they chose what they saw in the mirror. The people at the bottom end had to put up with the results of the policies which served the rich and powerful, and when they felt aggrieved, they read the tabloids, listened to the demagogues, because it was easier than finding out and thinking hard, and turned their ire on the wrong target.

In the sixties and seventies Bill had many conversations with bigots who began: "Send 'em back", or "I hate Pakis", or "They eat cat food and they stink". He never convinced them, or at least he didn't think he had; but maybe hearing the arguments did make a difference to them. Perhaps he should have a discussion with Rachel. He ran the virus check and got up to look out at the quiet street. He wouldn't have racism under his roof. Yet she was here for only two nights. All the same, he was disappointed in Liam. He wanted to say to him: "I'm surprised at you, Liam. Muslims are taking over?"

The next day the young couple didn't appear till noon, quickly devoured a breakfast of toast and coffee and disappeared with their railcards in their pockets to spend the day in Manchester. Bill was glad they were off to enjoy themselves but he hoped Liam had slept off his disagreeable humour and the ethnic mix of the city wouldn't disturb Rachel too much. He was at that age where hours went so quickly and a day could accommodate so little, he'd done nothing more than shave and shower, breakfast, read a few pages of Kafka, walk three miles by the river, have a snooze and Jasmine was knocking at the door and calling:

"Bill, I've got some food for you. Are you there?"

He roused himself as she came in.

"Oh, I've disturbed your nap, I'm sorry."

"No, I needed waking up. I'd've dozed till midnight. Must have been the nip in the air that made me tired."

"I'll believe you. There's curry, naan, basmati rice, tomato and onion with lemon and a ginger relish. Does that sound okay?" she said, setting the tray on the little three-legged table by the corner of the sofa where he liked to sit and read.

"No cucumber raita, Jasmine? You're backsliding. I don't know if I can accept this."

"Oh, you're right," she said, bringing her hand to her mouth, her brows rising, "You like it so much and I forgot it. I'll go and make some right away."

She turned for the door. He pushed himself effortfully to his feet.

"No, no, no. I've got cucumber and yoghurt in the fridge. I'll make myself some."

He put his hand on her shoulder to restrain her from going.

"Have you? Well, perfect, let me make a dish. You sit down and eat while your food is hot."

He followed her into the kitchen, took the tub of fat free natural from the top shelf and dragged the week-old, still firm, chilled length from the jumble of veg in the lower drawer.

"Give it me, give it me," she said. "I'll be much quicker, I've made it a thousand times."

"A thousand and one now," he said, pulling the foil lid from the plastic tub.

She was quick and handy, very neat and capable. As she was chopping the peeled cucumber the sound of a key in the front door, the voices of the couple and the click of the lock reached them. She looked him in the face.

"My son," he said, *sotto voce*, " and his girlfriend."

They came through looking fresh air bright, contented and slightly city-weary.

"Good day?" said Bill.

"Yes, cool," said Rachel.

Liam nodded.

"This is my neighbour, Jasmine. She's looking after me as usual. Jasmine, Rachel."

"Lovely to meet you," said Jasmine, "sorry, my hands are wet from the cucumber."

"Oh, that's all right," said Rachel, turning away.

"Have you eaten?" said Bill.

"We had lunch at Mr Thomas's," said Liam.

"Nice. Bet it cost you a pretty penny."

"Have something to eat with us," said Jasmine. "Bill, I'll take your food back and we can all have dinner together."

"No, thanks," said Rachel. "I'm not really hungry now. I had a good lunch. I'm a bit tired actually. I think I might have a bath."

"You don't have to eat much," said Jasmine. "A few samosas, a poppadom, some dips. I'll make you some lovely green tea, very refreshing."

"No, I really don't feel like it," said Rachel. "Can you run the bath for me, Liam."

"Sure."

"Don't leave the taps on and let the water come through the ceiling, again," said Bill.

Jasmine watched them climb the stairs.

"Did he do that?" she said.

"Twice."

"Oh, kids."

"Who'd have 'em?"

The garnish filled the low white bowl. Jasmine took the coriander from the window ledge and chopped a little heap which she let fall from between her thumb and forefinger onto the white surface through which poked the pale green peaks.

"There," she said. "Now you can eat," and she carried the dish to the tray.

Having grown used to eating alone, Bill had no dining table. It was comfortable and convenient to eat on the sofa with the tv tune to Radio 3.What could be better than curry and Chick Corea?

"I'll be back for the dishes," said Jasmine.

"No, you won't. I'll pop them back."

As ever, the food was full of delicate flavours. His reward for spending time with Rakesh, Bill felt it was more than he deserved. Jasmine would have fed him every day, if he'd let her. Her generosity spilled from her four walls. She would have fed the entire avenue. She was one of those people whose sympathy didn't defend itself from abuse or insult. Not that she was naïve. She was perfectly aware of widespread ill-feeling which served nothing but itself, but her delight in kindness carried her through.

He was at the end of his meal, mopping the last of the sauce with a wad of naan, when Liam and Rachel came down and settled in the armchairs.

"You don't have a hair dryer do you, dad?"

"No, I gave it away with my curlers."

139

"Rachel forgot hers."

"I'll ask Jasmine," said Bill.

"No," said Rachel, shaking her head and running her fingers through her hair. "It'll be okay."

For a second, Bill was inclined to insist: it was no trouble; Jasmine wouldn't mind. He thought better of it.

"What did you get up to in Manchester?" he said.

"Had a look in some music shops," said Liam. "Mooched around a bit."

"It's a nice city to mooch in. Plenty of folk around I guess?"

"Yeah."

"And the Hoochie-Coochie Mancunian?"

"Who?"

"Busker. He's not at all bad. I think the council should pay buskers. It should be compulsory for every town in the country to have at least one regular."

"I went to the Synagogue," said Rachel.

"Which one?"

"Manchester Reform."

"Ah, handy?"

"Jackson's Row," said Liam.

"There used to be a restaurant there I went to a couple of times," said Bill, "what was the name of it?"

"There are about fifteen synagogues in Manchester," said Rachel.

"Yeah? I think the Jewish population is about thirty thousand," said Bill.

"Pity there isn't one here."

"Hardly any Jews."

"Not enough for one synagogue?"

"They bulldozed the last one a year or so ago, but it'd been a Hindu temple for a few years. I believe there was a Jewish community in the late nineteenth century but it dwindled.."

"Too many Muslims, I suppose."

"How many is too many?" said Bill, unable to restrain himself.

"I'm getting peckish," said Liam. "Fancy a take-away."

Bill was about to remonstrate there was lovely, cooked-from-scratch food next door, but the weight of the junk food culture's hold and Rachel's resistance held him back.

"Yeah, I could eat a pizza,"she said.

"I fancy a Maccy."

"You have that, I'll have a *Dominos.*"

"They won't deliver free under ten quid."

"Get me a Ben and Jerry's and coke and you can have a McFlurry and a milk shake."

"Okay."

Liam began keying the number.

"No need to buy drink," said Bill. "There's juice in the fridge, tea, coffee…"

"I like Coke," said Rachel, especially after a pizza.

Bill had to hold back the sarcasm which urged him to ask if she liked diabetes. He got up and went to the kitchen to calm himself. Two deliveries. Over twenty quid for the pair and he was expected to pay Liam's train fare. To be asked suggested there was need, but where was the need if money could be thrown away on fat and sugar when there was healthy, delicious fare on hand? It was one of those moments when the transformation of the culture he'd grown up came into clear focus. For Liam, ordering take-aways and paying for delivery was almost a daily matter. At his age, the only over-the-counter grub he ate was fish and chips, and the notion of paying for them to be brought to your door would have been thought insane. Asking his mother or father for money was he was the other side of twenty was unthinkable. As a student, if he was down to his last few bob, he'd walk or cycle rather than take the bus. Where did it come from, this overwhelming sense of entitlement characteristic of Liam's generation? Was that truth or was he maligning? No, it was true, the old culture had collapsed under the weight of failing opportunities, the impossibility of buying a house, extortionate rents, aggressive marketing, the death of the notion that minimal material means was a good trade off to be able to spend your time learning.

It was taken for granted, once, that when you started earning, you no longer relied financially on your parents. Now, how many people did he know who had offspring of thirty or older at home, paying nothing? Vic, whose stepson worked in Morrison's, spent virtually all his free time in his room playing computer games, never wiped a surface or took the vacuum for a walk, dumped his breakfast pots in the kitchen as if the fairies would wash them; Sally whose eldest son was now past forty and still occupying his bedroom, leaving his clothes on the floor for her to wash and iron, paying several hundred pounds a month for the new Toyota on the drive and asking her for money for petrol when he'd *maxed-out* his credit card.

It was alarming to have lived through the collapse of a culture and its displacement by an inferior. Was he right, or was that merely nostalgia? Would anyone looking at the changes objectively see the later as worse? Maybe he was falling for what Montaigne identified: custom makes us blind to our failings. Yet he couldn't agree with his scepticism. Parents had a responsibility to bring up their children but once they were adults the responsibility switched: freeloading on your ageing parents was no way to behave. He ran a little thought experiment: supposing he was rich. If he had ten million would he think differently? Only slightly. He'd buy Liam a house, give him half a million and tell him now he had to look after himself. In any case, the fact he was living on a pension wasn't nugatory. It was true he had sixty thousand in the bank thanks to his retirement lump sum, his little inheritance from his mother and frugality, but there were costly possibilities ahead: care homes and other unthinkable outcomes. In any case, the fact that Liam knew he had a bit put away didn't give him any right to claim it.

When the food arrived, Liam came through in search of ketchup.

"Never use it, Liam. Disgusting stuff."

They ate in the living room, Rachel with her feet tucked under her.

"Let's find something on *Netflix*," she said.

"Dad doesn't have it."

Bill had resumed his place in the corner of the sofa.

"Really?" she said, her mouth bulging with vegetarian pizza.

"The films I like to watch aren't available," he said.

142

"You can get anything on *Netflix*," she said.

"Closely Observed Trains?"

"What's that?"

"A film. Very funny, and tragic. I've got the DVD some-where."

"We don't want to watch that," said Liam.

"Why not?"

"It's old-fashioned. We like to keep up with the new stuff."

"That's how they've got you hooked."

"I couldn't live without *Netflix*," said Rachel.

"I think if we examined that statement fully we'd find your survival is perfectly possible without it," said Bill.

"Without what?" said Jasmine, popping her head round the door. "I've just come for the dishes. How was the food?"

Bill got to his feet and picked up the tray.

"Delicious as ever."

"I'll bring your dessert," she said, taking the tray from him.

He sensed her unease.

"As you can see," he said with a smile, "these two can't get through the evening without their fix of saturates, salt and sucrose. Fortunately, there are plenty of dealers. I bet sugar has killed more folk than heroin, eh Jasmine."

"Don't ask me, Bill. Anyway, your pudding is low sugar, no fat."

"I wish my mother had known how to make a healthy spotted dick."

She laughed, which relieved him.

"Raspberries, strawberries and blackberries with fat free yogurt. I looked it up. The fruits are very good for you."

"Tell you what," said Bill, "I'll come and eat it at yours, if that's okay. Have a chat to Nathan."

"Of course, but don't get Rakesh too excited. It's his bed-time soon."

Liam zapped the tv and scrolled through the channels.

"Does that woman walk in when ever she feels like it?" said Rachel.

143

"Neighbours are like that round here."

"There are a lot of Muslims. I'd move away."

"My dad doesn't care about that."

"Well, he should."

Nathan was watching cricket. Bill had little interest. He'd played recreation ground, impromptu stuff with his mates but never the organised game. Batting and bowling were okay, but long periods in the outfield during school games lessons put him off for life.

"Whose winning?" said Bill.

"He knows the result," said Jasmine. "It's a recording."

"Bill is going to eat his dessert with us," said Jasmine. "Perhaps you could pause that for a few minutes."

"Sit down, Bill," said Nathan, turning off the set. "What about the youngsters, don't they want to come round?"

Bill cast a glance at Jasmine who looked inscrutable.

"No, they've tired themselves out in Manchester. They're slobbing in front of the box."

"She seems a nice girl," said Jasmine.

There was an opportunity to say something. It was appalling, in Bill's view, to have refused her food and bought junk. He might have criticised the fire-up-the-tastebuds culture and confined himself to the regrettable proclivity of the young for whatever was easily consumed; yet he knew Jasmine suspected. It might just have been possible that Rachel claimed not to be hungry but was tempted by melted cheese and a thick bread base once she'd been in the bath; but Jasmine was a sensitive and astute woman. If he opened a discussion, she would have known he was staying the right side of the issue.

"Yeah, I think she is," he said, "but it's early days."

He wasn't insincere. She was a nice girl. To all common appearances, she was a calm, pleasant, friendly lass. Many racists weren't unpleasant people in most situations. They were good spouses, friends, neighbours. The fault in their sentiments and ideas wasn't pervasive. There were the far-right thugs who were inherently nasty, but they were a small minority. It was the pervasive, low-level racism of the nice folk that was the problem.

"She's Jewish," he added.

144

"Oh, that's nice," said Jasmine, setting his bowl in front of him.

"Well, everyone to their own. I don't mind so long as no one disturbs me in my paganism."

"You were brought up a Christian, Bill?" said Nathan.

"I was," he said, taking up his first spoonful, "I was washed behind the ears and dragged to church on Sunday mornings, and I stood in the school hall mumbling the Lord's Prayer every morning along with six hundred other kids who knew it by heart but never reflected on what it meant. There were sown the seeds of my atheism."

Jasmine laughed.

"Yes, but you took it in when you were young, Bill. It had an influence," and he tapped his forehead with his index.

"It did, Nathan. Who knows if for the better?"

The conversation drifted away from religion and Rachel, but throughout, at the back of his mind, Bill was conscious of his disturbance. When he went home, the couple had gone to bed. He sat and let his mind run on for a few minutes. Should he mention his suspension to Liam? He could broach it in the morning, cheerfully, over breakfast, and explore the ideas as far as they wished; but his instinct was to restraint. Rachel's anti-Muslim sentiment needed challenging, but obliquely. To take her head-on would produce that fierce resistance creed-believers exhibit when their shibboleths are breathed on, however, lightly. Once the defences were up, all sensible discussion was over. There was nothing like evidence for defeating a fallacy; but the dinosaur bones failed to convince millions of Americans the world must be more than six thousand years old. It was odd how emotion could attach itself to an *idée fixe* with such intensity people felt their very existence was under threat if it was at risk. It wasn't even a matter of ideology: Caroline would respond with vicious wildness if some purchase she'd set her heart on was cancelled. He recalled a scene in the bedroom when she'd raised her fists at him over something he'd said they couldn't afford. What was it? A wardrobe? Yes, she'd spotted it in *Powell's* the high-class furniture shop and come home insisting she must have it. How much was it? He couldn't remember. All the fights over money. Three thousand or

145

something, but when he'd argued an antique wardrobe wasn't necessary and they could get a perfectly serviceable one for a thousand, she'd responded as if he was about to kill her.

It was queer. She was perfectly capable of acting rationally when she had to. She didn't go to work and throw tantrums or raise her fists at the boss: she knew the consequences; but her mind could turn from rationality to this mad torment over some consumer good in an instant.

Was it his business to make Rachel think? Maybe he should let it drop. She would be gone in a day or so. Liam, if true to form, would be with some other lass in six months. Yet, it would be just his luck if they stuck together. She might become his daughter-in-law. Wouldn't that be pretty, a Jewish woman with an anti-Semite for a father-in-law? He gave a little snort of laughter and resolved to go to bed. What had happened to his life? He was as loveless as a lone, shipwrecked sailor. Caroline contacted him only when she wanted money. Liam was as affectionate as a brick and he heard from Jessica twice a year. He sat in his curiously contented gloom. His life rolled along pleasantly enough from day to day. He was never at a loose end. There was always a new walk to be tried, books to read, music to listen to and the thousand little tasks required even in a small house on your own. Quiet desperation. He snorted again. Too self-pitying.

His mood blended with his intention. There must be something he could do. He switched off the lights and went up. From the bathroom he could hear Liam and Rachel talking and in the background the sound of whatever they were watching on his i-pad. Brushing his teeth an idea came to him: the girl who worked in the *Hand and Dagger*. What was her name? Layla? She served him his glass of non-alcoholic many times and then he'd bumped into her on a Free Palestine demo. Hadn't he said she must come round and meet Jasmine and Nathan, and, of course, Rakesh? He'd invite his neighbours first thing, before they could make other plans, nip to the pub at lunchtime and see if she was working. How to prevent Liam and Rachel sneaking off? He'd think of something. He went to bed content and mildly excited at the scheme, but as he turned off the beside lamp no-

ticed the lumps in the wallpaper on the chimney breast and reminded himself he must find a decent roofer.

Nathan was in the yard by seven, tending to his tubs. Bill
looked over the wall.

"Been at that all night?"

"Never went to bed," said Nathan, without looking at
him.

"You want to be careful, while you're nursing your plants
someone might take your place in the bedroom."

"I padlock the door."

"You're an enlightened husband, Nathan."

"What's for breakfast, I'm starving."

"Get your hands washed, I'm frying up."

These masculine breakfasts had become a habit. Bill
would go next door for scrambled eggs or omelette with parathas,
chole, mangoes, melons, bananas, honey, sheermal and tea when
Jasmine was having a lie in or had gone for a jog, and Nathan
would reciprocate by feasting on the traditional English with a
veggie burger in place of black pudding because Bill felt guilty
about having fed him so much of the cholesterol boosting delica-
cy.

"Sit down and get your gnashers round that. Keep you
going for a week."

"Ketchup?" said Nathan seating himself at the little table
and sniffing the aroma.

Bill opened a cupboard and handed him the HP brown.

"No ketchup."

"You promised to get some."

"I'm a liar."

"This stuff is probably just as bad," said Nathan, shaking
loose a large dollop onto his bacon.

"I know, but they don't serve it in McDonalds and it re-
minds me of my childhood, a time when children got a free bottle
of unchilled milk at playtime and secretaries of State for education didn't think it a Bolshevist conspiracy."

"Where did you get this bacon, it's lovely?"

"From a pig."

"Slaughter it yourself?"

"Don't report me to the council. My cellar is an abattoir."

"Where's the teapot? Your organisation has gone to pot."

"But not to the teapot," said Bill getting up from his chair opposite his friend. "Anyway," he said, raising his voice a little, "tonight you're eating chez George. I'm going to spend the afternoon in the kitchen and cook the best egg, chips and beans you've ever tasted."

"Can't wait."

"You've not got anything planned?"

"Jasmine might."

"Well, get her to unplan it and be here for seven."

"With a big enough lever a man could move the earth, but no man on it could change Jasmine's mind once it's made up."

"Tell her she can help me finesse. She can't resist taking over in the kitchen."

"Good thinking, appeal to her desire for power.

There was volley of rapid steps on the stairs and Liam appeared, followed by a sleepy Rachel, running her hands through her hair. Nathan was laying a rasher on a slice and dousing it with sauce.

"Gorgeous breakfast your dad's made," said Nathan.

Rachel looked down at the plates before the two men.

"I don't know how you eat that stuff," she said.

"Want some Coco Pops?" said Liam who'd found the packet.

"Check the sell-by date," said Bill, "I think I bought them in 1982."

"Is there some coffee?" she said, moving away from the table.

"I need you to help me later," said Bill.

"With what?"

"Bringing some stuff up from the cellar. Can you be here at six?"

"Six? Why not do it this morning?"

"I've got to go out. Assignation."

"In your dreams."

"You wouldn't want to know what goes on in my dreams."

"No, I wouldn't," said Liam.

"If MI5 knew, I'd be shot at dawn."

"They aren't interested in superannuated ex-hippies these days, dad. There are Jihadists trying to blow us to kingdom come."

"Didn't we do the same to them?"

"Evil people," said Rachel.

"True," said Nathan, pouring a cup.

"Anyway," said Bill, "make sure you're here at six. Warm your muscles up."

He was lucky: Layla was working.

"I've come to chat you up," he said.

"How original. Usual?"

He poured the golden beer into the tilted glass slowly so it formed a centimetre head. He missed the alcoholic stuff, not because he liked intoxication, but for the flavours. All the same, this was a lovely drink and it allowed him to pop into a pub and prop the bar, usually finding someone to chat to.

"What are you doing tonight?"

"Washing my hair," she said with a smile and a tug on the pump.

"How original."

"Touché."

"Remember I told you about my neighbours?"

"Your neighbours?"

"Jasmine and Nathan and their boy Rakesh. They're keen to meet you. Jasmine is a radical."

"Oh, yes. I'd like to."

"Well, tonight, chez moi, c'est la grande bouffe."

"Je suis au regime."

"Don't worry. Nothing to add calories. Vegetables of all kinds, a spray of olive oil here and there. I've told them you're coming."

"What?" she said, standing with a customer's tenner between her fingers.

"They're lovely people."

She turned to the cash till, registered the purchase and handed over the change.

"That was very cheeky of you."

"They pestered me. I told them about you after we had a chat on the demo. Jasmine is very much a supporter of Palestine. You're not working I hope."

"No."

"Perfect."

"I might have something arranged."

"You might. Think of it as in support of the cause."

"Are they PSC members?"

"Good question. If not, you can sign them up. This is lovely beer."

He smiled and she pushed her lips together and looked at him askance as she might a child up to innocent mischief.

"Seven. 29 St Wilfrid St."

"I'll think about it."

"Don't think too long. As Mark Twain said, he must have a considerable amount of mind because it takes him a week to make it up."

On his way home, he bumped into Jimmy.

"Taking the air, Mr Payne?"

" Yeah. Fancy a pint."

Bill shook his head.

"Just had one. You okay?"

"No," said Jimmy.

His face assumed a pleading, anxious look.

"What's up?"

"Prostate cancer."

"Christ, that's bad luck. Are they treating it?"

"They have been." They can't operate. Too far gone."

Bill put his hand on his friend's shoulder. He would have liked to hug him but he wasn't sure he would accept it. Words, which serve so well for easy banter, lose all their force when faced with the gulf between a healthy and a dying man. The commonplace expressions of sympathy and support were almost an insult. To say you were sorry was to acknowledge you would still be walking, sleeping, having a pint, watching the telly, when he would have gone through the pain of death and was a pile of ashes.

150

"Tomatoes," he said.

"What?"

"Eat tomatoes."

"Are you taking the piss?"

"They contain a chemical they think may combat prostate cancer."

"Too late."

"No. No, it isn't Jimmy. It's never too late. You're on your feet and walking. Give it a try."

"I'm on my feet and walking but I'm ready to drop."

"Don't give up. Eat well, rest well and get a bit of exercise. You never know, Jimmy. Don't give up."

What he'd told him might be cod science. It was one of those things you read in the press and it sticks because it relates to your own health. He always had liked tomatoes and he ate them every day, for pleasure; but he didn't know if there was any weight to the theory. The journalists picked up on bits of research and reported something provisional and exploratory as more or less confirmed. All the same he felt glad he'd been able to say something positive. Maybe Jimmy would go home and look it up on the internet, as everyone did. Perhaps he'd find something encouraging. In all likelihood, eating a kilo of tomatoes a day wouldn't make much difference, but if it gave him a bit of hope, if it made him feel during the last months of his life that he didn't simply have to give in to the illness.....

Bill felt more at one with himself than if he'd looked Jimmy in the eyes and said, "I'm sorry, mate." What did that mean except: "You'll be dead in a few months and I'll still be knocking around, and you're five years younger."

Jimmy left school at sixteen and started work in the truck factory. He was a time-served turner at twenty-one, married with his own little terrace at twenty-two. Because he was willing to speak out and could put a decent sentence together, he was elected shop-steward, which got him into trouble, which he enjoyed. When the company tried to get rid of him, as they always do effective advocates of the employee cause, the entire workforce walked out and he was reinstated in three days. He was very touched. Hundreds of men and women had risked their own jobs for him. There was an element of self-interest in it, but the quiet solidarity, the genuine belief that an injury to one is an injury to all and the swift action, pushed him towards politics. He joined his Labour Branch, was spotted as energetic and honest and by the time he was thirty was on the council.

Chivvied to try for a parliamentary seat, he felt it was a reach too far. When they tried to persuade him he could be a solid backbencher, he felt he was being recommended as voting fodder. Wasn't that what most MPs were, of any party? Weren't they the dutiful troops, rounded up like sheepdogs and directed into the appropriate lobby? On the council, he could work with unions and get things done. In parliament he would be eclipsed by the slick, privately-schooled boys and girls who thought of a place in Cabinet as their birth-right.

In his early fifties, he was made redundant. The package wasn't bad and his wife was a primary school teacher so they didn't sink too much financially; but it was still a hurt to his pride. Thirty-six years. He was a skilled man. Yet he could be thrown away like swarf.

To Bill, he represented that intelligence and generosity of the common folk which, given its chance, could change the world. Jimmy would have been no good in an Oxbridge philosophy supervision, but he was bloody good if you were in trouble. And what had his culture made of him? It was a scandal and a tragedy and now he was going to die before he got to enjoy his grandkids and some quiet years with Joyce.

He had to find something for Liam to help him with in the cellar. There was an old trunk, unopened for years, shoved in the corner. In it he discovered yellowing piles of *The Guardian* and *The New Statesman* from the eighties. Fascinating to read about what he'd lived through; the ludicrous Falklands War, the vicious miners' strike, the despicable Gang of Four doing all they could to destroy democratic equality while lining their pockets and polishing their egos. He beguiled he didn't know how long leafing and recalling. It was odd and illuminating to see the photos: Kinnock, who he'd hoped would be a leader in the spirit of Nye Bevan, but who had turned out to be all speechifying and little substance; Hattersley, who he'd thought had a real commitment to equality but was one of the first to distance himself from social ownership and who he now recognised as an old-fashioned liberal paternalist whose belief in capitalism was unshakeable because he was committed to the State it created which allowed men like himself to have fancy careers and write bad novels; Thatcher summoning the support of millions in the lower half, seduced by her cutting-the-pound-in-half domestic economics, until the Poll Tax taught them what was really in her head was an idiot's view of the world in which taxation was a punishment for being alive; Major, the cardboard cut-out accountant bamboozled into bed by the glib recycler of *free enterprise's* vacuous platitudes, Edwina Currie, drinking his warm *Double Diamond* as he watched cricket, sinking into the fantasy that England (yes, England not the UK) was a country of fair play where every chap and chapess had the chance of a decent innings. From today's perspective, the whole circus crew looked shallow, age-serving and incapable of an original insight. Yet at the time, he'd put his faith in Labour. He still did, or at least the current surge of membership and enthusiasm for policies which could eradicate poverty and start to give people some real control over their lives.

He thought himself an anarchist-socialist: the aim was a self-governing society, the means were socialistic, because that was the only way to transition. And where were we now? It wasn't looking good for Corbyn because the entire Labour machine was against him. He was the vertical invader. The careerists in parliament and the bureaucracy loathed him and the democracy which brought him to the leadership. Truth was, they would prefer the hack snob who blamed the Liverpool supporters for ninety-six deaths and called people of colour piccaninnies. Truth was, they made use of the radical sentiment among the common folk as a means to power, money and status, without a glimmer of belief in serious change.

"What's to be done, then, dad?"

Liam ducked his head under the low ceiling at the stair foot.

"Just what I was thinking. We need to get this in the recycling."

"Is that it?" said his son, looking at the heaps.

153

"There's more than you think, and they're heavy."

"God, dad, we could have done that in half an hour this morning."

"Don't worry, I'll feed you."

"We'll get a take away."

"No, you won't. The food is cooking. Take-aways are banned in this house for one night."

"Oh, for fuck's sake, dad."

"Did you hear me swear when you were a child?"

"No."

"Then watch your language in front of me, I'm old and fragile."

The task was fulfilled quickly. Bill was regretful at dumping the past, but there was a limit, the papers had no monetary value and what they contained was no doubt accessible digitally. He got Liam to sweep and tidy which kept him busy for a further ten minutes.

"Bring Rachel to the table."

"What's for dinner?"

"Wait and see. Go and get her."

"She might not like it."

"She'll be okay."

To get the two youngsters seated before the others arrived would, he hoped, prevent their absconding. Maybe they'd be hard-faced enough to get up and leave, but he doubted it.

Rachel appeared looking demure in black. Liam joined his dad in the kitchen, trying to work out what was to eat.

"Sit down, I'll get you a drink."

"I'll do it."

Bill, wondering how they would react to the guests, heard them chatting in the background. It was important to get the timing right: guests and food arriving at the table simultaneously was requisite. He assembled the carrot and celery batons around the big dish of hummus, bought from the Palestinian market which served the huddle of streets on the eastern side of town populated almost entirely by people whose origins or ancestors weren't British. It was an area the middle classes merely drove through on the way to the motorway. Its reputation ramped up fear to the point that parents in the suburbs would have had seizures at the idea of their youngsters visiting. Bill liked to walk there. He could finish one of his rambles through woods and by the river by climbing to its rear edge where houses and bungalows with big gardens, garages and newish cars on the drive provided the barrier between the little cluster of expensive places, assembled around the now defunct Lower Bank Farm, and the huge expanse of the estate, built post-war, into which the poorest families with the most severe problems were herded, as if they should be grateful for a roof the middle classes would have seen as a humiliation.

Having wandered the streets many times and exchanged greetings with the folk he passed and never having encountered any trouble, he felt comfortable there and had discovered its wonderful shops: the Turkish supermarket, the Polish store, the remarkable little Asian, corner place where he could buy every spice and vegetables the conventional shops didn't sell; the grocers run by a little, old Asian man with poor English who always greeted him with a wide smile and shook his hand and where the enticing, fresh produce was piled on pavement stalls, bringing a bright flash of distant places to the drab town; and the delightful Palestinian market, housed in a former lock-up garage where he could buy ready-made dishes.

One of its treats was hummus made as you waited, unlike the tubbed, wrapped-in-cardboard stuff he used to buy from the supermarkets.

There was a knock.

"I'll get it," he said, putting his hand on Liam's shoulder to keep him in his seat as he passed behind him.

Layla had brought taboon and a bottle of orange blossom and honey lemonade.

"Come through and meet my son and his girlfriend."

On time, as they entered the little dining-room, Jasmine and Nathan appeared.

"Good," said Bill, "all assembled like players in the last act. Layla, Liam and Rachel, and my neighbours Jasmine and Nathan."

As they seated themselves he gathered the *crudités*.

"Bon appétit à tous."

155

He heard Jasmine expressing her love of hummus in that sweet, keep-everything-friendly tone of hers as he attended to the food. He'd bought freekeh, musakhan and kebabs which were always on offer but securing Jewish dishes was more difficult.

"Can you make shakshuka?" he asked Latif.

"That's not one of ours."

"I know, but I'm having guests. If I make it it'll be a catastrophe. For you, it's as easy as cheese on toast."

Latif shook his head.

"I don't know. I'm very busy."

"Because you sell fine stuff."

"Good try."

"I'll pay, whatever you ask."

"You may regret that."

"Is it hard for you? Am I a good customer?"

"How many guests?"

"Five."

"Okay. But keep it to yourself."

"I need kugel and latkes too."

The stallholder threw his hands in the air.

"You want me to serve it?"

"Good idea. Are you free on the twelfth?"

"Enough for five?"

"Yeah, can I collect it on the day?"

"Day before."

"Will it keep?"

"Of course."

Confined to reheating, he was still nervous of getting something wrong. All the same, there was an array he'd intended. He went through with the steaming musakhan.

"All my own work. Nathan, you serve it up."

"That looks delicious," said Jasmine.

"What is it?" said Liam.

"Musakhan," said Layla.

"What's in it?" said Liam.

"Chicken, sumac, saffron, pine nuts," said Layla.

"What's sumac?" said Liam.

"A spice," said Jasmine. "It's said to lower blood pressure. Nathan should eat it."

"There's nothing wrong with my blood pressure."

"Until Pakistan lose at cricket."

"Let me serve some for you, Rachel."

"No thanks, not for me."

"Liam, give me your plate," said Nathan.

He was about to hand it over when Rachel effected a little dig which Jasmine noticed. Meanwhile, Bill had returned with the shakshuka.

"That's for you, Rachel," he said, setting the hot dish in front of her.

"Hey," said Nathan, "I'm having some of that."

"You'll have to fight over it," said Bill.

"Oh, gorgeous," said Jasmine.

"What is it?" said Liam.

"Shakshuka," said Rachel.

"Is it Jewish?" said Liam.

"Yes, it's a typical dish for us."

"Shakshuka means mixture in Arabic," said Layla.

"That's interesting," said Jasmine.

"Do you speak Arabic?" said Nathan.

"Yes."

"We're in the tower of Babel," said Jasmine. "Urdu, Arabic, Bill with his French, Spanish, Italian and who knows what."

"And Hebrew," said Rachel.

"Of course," said Jasmine.

Bill put a challah and the taboon in the middle of the table, spooned a portion of hummus onto a side plate and sat next to his son.

"I'll just have a mouthful," he said, "then I'll get the rest."

"Stay where you are," said Jasmine. "I'll get it."

"You're a guest, you're not allowed to work."

"I'm going to have a bit of everything," said Nathan. "Variety is the spice and all that."

"You don't mind as long as you can fill your gut," said Jasmine.

"Listen to her. I'm as slim as the day I married."

"The day you married you weighed seventy kilograms."

"So I do today."

"You'd have to lose a leg to weigh so little."

His mouth full of the oily hummus and celery, Bill nipped to the kitchen and came back with the potato kugel and latkes.

"There you are, Rachel. I hope you're hungry."

"I hope she isn't," said Nathan.

"That looks lovely too," said Jasmine. "Is it traditional?"

"We eat it at celebrations and on the Shabbath."

"Kugel," said Bill, "it's German for ball as in Kugelschrieber."

"It's a German dish then?" said Nathan.

"It originated in Germany," said Rachel. "But it's Ashkenazi now."

"Good things will travel," said Nathan. "What do you call this bread?"

"A challah," said Rachel.

"Can I have some?"

"Of course."

Nathan tore off a chunk.

"I'll have some too, please," said Layla.

"Here," said Nathan, handing her his clump, "if you don't mind my fingers."

The lemonade was on the table, a bottle of sparkling water, and another of Sauvignon blanc. Bill added the kebabs and roasted cauliflower freekeh.

"Everyone got what they need?" he said.

"That would be too much to ask, Bill," said Nathan.

"Oh, what needs do you have which aren't met?" said Jasmine.

"That's not for public discussion," said Nathan.

He talked about his hydrangeas, which weren't flourishing. Jasmine accused him floricide. Things rolled along gently and Bill was glad of the success. At a certain point, Nathan, who was one of those people always curious to know as much as he could about people he met, asked Rachel where she came from.

"Tel Aviv."

"Nice place?" he said.

"Yeah, a modern city. Very go-ahead."

"Modern?" said Nathan. "I suppose it's origins are ancient though?"

"Jaffa is, Tel Aviv grew out of it in the early twentieth century, as the Jews started to bring civilisation."

"Pass me the lemonade," said Jasmine. "And where do you come from, Layla?"

"Ramallah."

"Nice place?" said Nathan.

"It's twinned with Hounslow," she said.

"Where's that?" said Nathan.

"West London," said Bill. "Lovely place if you like passenger aircraft. On their way to Heathrow they brush your television aerial."

"That's progress," said Nathan.

"Is that what you call it?" said Jasmine.

"Funny you two should end up here," said Nathan, "of all the places in the world."

"Yes, you too," said Bill.

"I was born here," said Nathan. "I'm British."

"But you're a Muslim," said Rachel.

"So he claims," said Bill, "his true religion is cricket."

"I was born to a Jewish mother in Israel," said Rachel, "so my nationality is Jewish."

"Your nationality," said Nathan, stopping chewing.

Rachel nodded.

"More challah, Bill?" said Jasmine.

"Well, that's a funny thing," said Nathan. "I didn't know that. Isn't that a funny thing, Bill?"

"Hilarious."

"I was born to a Muslim mother in Birmingham, does that make my nationality Muslim?"

"You weren't born in a Muslim country," said Rachel.

"I was," said Layla.

"Then your nationality is Muslim too," said Nathan. "We belong to the same country."

"Her nationality is Palestinian," said Jasmine.

159

"There's no such thing," said Rachel.

"What about you, Bill? You were born to a Christian mother in a Christian country so your nationality must be Christian."

"What makes you think I was born in a Christian country?"

"The Archbishop of Canterbury told me."

"The Pope will tell you priests are sexually abstemious, choirboys will disabuse you."

"Bill," said Jasmine.

"What if I'd been born to an atheist?" said Bill.

"Ha," said Nathan, waving his fork in Bill's direction, "then you'd be an atheist."

"I am an atheist."

"By belief," said Nathan, "but if your mother had been an atheist, you'd be Atheist with a capital A."

"My mother's an atheist," said Liam.

"But you were born in a Christian country," said Rachel.

"So says the Archbishop," said Bill.

"Most people think of themselves as Christian, I'm sure," said Jasmine.

"Most people think they speak English because they have English brains," said Bill.

"Well, me and Jasmine are Muslim, Bill is Christian, Rachel is Jewish, Layla is Muslim and Liam is Atheist. What a mix of nationalities," said Nathan.

"Christianity is nothing to do with me," said Bill.

"You say so," said Nathan, waving his fork some more, "but if what Rachel says is true, you're Christian whether you like it or not."

"I'm British whether I like it or not."

"Why wouldn't you like it?" said Jasmine.

"Henry Morton Stanley, the Battle of Plassey, the Opium Wars, the East India Company, the creation of Ulster…"

"Israel is unique," said Rachel.

"What happens to someone born to a Jewish mother in Finland," said Nathan, "are they Jewish or Finnish?"

"Finnish, of course," said Rachel.

"What a silly question, Nathan," said Jasmine.

"That's a bit unfair, don't you think," said Nathan.

"Why?" said Rachel

"Why shouldn't a Catholic born in France enjoy Catholic nationality or a Presbyterian born in Moscow, Presbyterian nationality?"

"Israel is unique," said Rachel.

"All the same,…" said Nathan.

"So why did you come to the UK, Layla?" said Jasmine, offering her the lemonade.

"Study."

"Oh, that's interesting. What's your subject?"

"Fine art."

"Art?" said Nathan. "Jasmine is a good artist."

"Don't listen to him," said Jasmine, "he thinks Vettriano is a good painter."

"He is. I like him. What do you think, Layla?"

"I prefer Banksy," she said.

"He's a criminal," said Rachel.

"Yes, but he can paint my gable end whenever he likes, eh Jasmine?"

"He doesn't do it for the money," said Jasmine.

"No, but people buy it. Millions they pay. He can have my gable end for a canvas, I tell you."

"I think he's right about the art world," said Layla.

"He should be in prison," said Rachel.

"He'd certainly improve the décor," said Bill.

"I like graffiti," said Liam.

"What does he say about it?" said Jasmine.

"It's a disgrace," said Layla.

"It is," said Bill.

"Why?" said Nathan.

"Because it's organised around money. It's a playground for the rich."

"Why shouldn't people make money out of it?" said Rachel.

"All art should be free," said Bill.

161

"That's why painting on walls is operating at a higher level, as Banksy says," said Layla.

"Couldn't you find the course you wanted in Ramallah?" said Jasmine.

"There aren't the same opportunities in the West Bank," said Layla.

"Except for terrorism," said Rachel.

"You did the right thing, coming here. Good for you. I hope you do well."

"Yes," said Nathan, "If you're going to be the next Banksy, you can start on my gable end."

"Oh, put your gable end away," said Jasmine.

"Anyway, you're almost neighbours," said Nathan. "Tel Aviv, Ramallah, how far are they from one another?"

"Depends on the route," said Layla.

"About ninety kilometres," said Rachel.

"Ninety? What's that in miles? About fifty? You'll be able to visit one another if you go home," said Nathan.

"I never go to Ramallah," said Rachel.

"I like to travel," said Nathan. "Don't we, Jasmine? We could drop in on you."

"Will you go back to Tel Aviv, Rachel?" said Jasmine.

"I might."

"I'm not living in Tel Aviv," said Liam.

"Why not?" said Rachel.

"Have they got a McDonald's?" said Bill.

"I like London."

"Plenty of McDonald's," said Bill.

"London, we love it, don't we Jasmine?" said Nathan.

"I like Islamabad," she said.

"City of Islam. You should visit," he said, waving his fork at Rachel and Layla.

"It's not a place I want to go," said Rachel.

"I might," said Layla.

"Take a walk down Constitution Avenue," said Nathan. "Unforgettable, eh Jasmine?"

"The world has many beautiful cities," she said.

162

"Paris," said Bill. "Not only beautiful but liberal. Josephine Baker, James Baldwin, in the US they were abused, in Paris they were hailed."

"We should go, Jasmine," said Nathan. "We've never been," he said to Bill, raising his eyebrows.

"We have," said Liam.

"What did you think?" said Jasmine.

"I liked the Marais," said Rachel.

ASYLUM

The visitors left very early. Bill heard them moving and registered the time as five. When he got up at six thirty, he was alone in the house. Liam had left a note, scribbled on the back of one of the used envelopes Bill kept for jotting (he took the climate crisis seriously): Thanks, dad. See ya. Probably the last communication for months.

Bill thought the previous evening a success. Convivial and pleasant, but he'd fulfilled his intention. He liked Rachel, but if she was going to visit his home, she needed to leave prejudice against Muslims at the door. Not that he wasn't willing to discuss the shortcomings of Islam. The shortcoming of religion, as far as he was concerned, was the belief in a deity; but he'd never thought that was what kept religion alive: it was its social power which people responded to. When he saw people coming out of the Mosque, it was just like the days when he was sent to church as a boy: getting together with other people was the pleasure, god was the excuse.

He hadn't read the Koran, any more than he'd read much of the bible. He'd had it read to him, by teachers' pet pupils in school, by vicars in church, but to sit and absorb it was boring beyond measure and the chapters he'd scanned had scandalised him. Only the song of songs was worth attending to, and that because of its poetry and its frankness about sensual life. No doubt if he did read the Koran or the Torah, he'd throw them across the room in frustration. Yet that didn't for an instant impinge on his recognition that people had a right to freedom of belief. If the flat-earthers gathered in a building round the corner and praised the lord of flatness, they should be left alone to do so. Freedom of belief was absolute, but so was the right not to have other people's beliefs forced on you.

Jasmine had promised to come round and help with the clearing: he must get it done before she arrived. She was such a lovely, generous woman and worked so briskly, if he didn't have everything in order, she'd elbow him aside, gather, scrape, wash, dry and store leaving him standing idle like a great, useless bumpkin. The mindless tasks gave him room to think.

164

Did he resent that Christianity had been forced on him? He did when he pondered the hypocrisy: preaching love and peace while employing maximum violence in pursuit of lucre. Then there was the subtraction from everyday life which faith in an after-life entailed. Much better to recognise that life has a beginning and an end and to make the best of what's in between. His thoughts settled on his teenage years and the religious prohibition of sex outside marriage. It was almost ludicrous now, but the message had been conveyed by teachers, parents, vicars, priests, politicians, journalists. At fourteen, he and his mates had expected to be virgins till they married at twenty-one or two; yet at the same time the air was thick with prurience and stories abounded of lads who'd done it with Gloria Kenyon or Marilyn Ashton. Only diligent masturbation kept them sane. All his close pals, finally, broke the prohibition. Nor were the girls reluctant: they were fed up of being hungry and seeing food all around but being forbidden to eat.

There were one or two lads though: the memory of Pete Weaver drifted into his mind. He'd always liked him. He was one of those people who radiate harmlessness, always ready with a smile and laugh. He came from the town, though not the mean streets or one of the troubled estates; rather a little road of modest semis on the periphery where the urban reached

out to the suburban, separated by a busy road and the fields not yet snapped up by developers. The year's outstanding athlete he played rugby for the county, was the cross-country champion three years on the trot, won the local schools' long-jump trophy every year and outpaced all his contemporaries over the mile, the eight-eighty, the four-forty, the two-twenty and the hundred, as they were measured in the sixties. His intellect didn't excel, but he was dogged and diligent. The teachers loved him, while Bill they were ambivalent about because he could produce brilliant results in English or language exams, but was nonchalant as a gorged flea. When lads began to grow their hair and got pulled in by the deputy head, Pete remained requisitely short-back-and-sides. The questioning atmosphere of the time didn't penetrate to where his ideas were formed. He was one of those lads who assume obedience is moral. Yet he wasn't at all pompous or arrogant. When they inevitably made him Head Boy, he was still unassuming and friendly and Bill could recall pleasant chats and banter in the form room.

At fourteen or so he'd taken up with a girl who also excelled at sport. What was her name? Pam or Diane? He couldn't retrieve it. They'd stuck like magnets and married in their early twenties. Maybe they'd consummated the relation long before, but Bill suspected they might have adhered to convention. A few years earlier he'd run into Pete at the railway station and had one of those brief, not-seen-one-another-for-fifty-years conversations in which decades of life are condensed to a few trite sentences:

"Any kids?"

"Yeah, boy and a girl."

"Grandkids?"

"Three. You?"

They'd been together for more than five decades. It was heartening: people could make a good choice and find pleasure in sticking with it. Yet he couldn't help wondering now if Pete had known only one woman, as if the bible was right. There was nothing wrong with that. There was nothing wrong with anything which made people happy and did no harm. That should be everyone's motto: be happy and do no harm. Yet if they'd waited six or seven years to discover one another naked, what a waste. If an external injunction had kept them from what made them happy, that was a sin.

The youngsters of his generation were let down by the official culture. Mostly, they rebelled and found their way, and the rebellion was uplifting; but there were dismal periods when the conflict between what was imposed and what was obvious caused anguish and much pain and confusion could have been avoided. Religion, why did it go for people's genitals if not because that was the most effective means of control? Control he despised. Encounter in equality he celebrated.

By the time Jasmine arrived the place was as spotless as a nun's reputation.

"Bill," she said, "you've been up all night."

"Don't the neo-liberals say sleep is for wimps?"

"Who cares what they say, they're liars."

"You're just in time for a brew anyway. Sit down."

"I didn't come here to idle my time away."

"You should. Idling your time away is a good thing to do with your life. All the great people do it. Shakespeare idled his time away writing plays, Einstein trying to work out what gravity is."

"That's hard work."

"No, standing on a production line is hard work, or sitting in a call centre or changing beds in the middle of the night, or saying "Do you want fries with that?" for the five hundredth time in a shift."

"You have a curious idea of idling."

"I have curious ideas about everything."

"Everybody enjoyed themselves last night anyway."

"Rip-roaringly."

"Oh, stop it."

"You think Rachel enjoyed it?"

"She ate plenty."

"Yes, her stomach took part unreservedly, but didn't you detect a tiny frisson of discomfort?"

"Perhaps she isn't used to being in mixed company."

"Mixed company is human company."

"It was mischievous of you to invite Layla."

"Nice lass, don't you think?"

"Very."

"Not even the reduced circumstances of Ramallah could eliminate her charm."

"I thought everyone remained very civil."

"They did, Jasmine. Under considerable pressure."

"It's the food. People are much more civilised when they sit and eat together."

"Than when they do what?"

"Almost anything else."

"It's a nice idea, Jasmine. The solution to the world's conflicts lies in cookery."

"Well, where does it lie Mr Clever Clogs?"

"In recognising our nature."

"If we all have the same nature, what's Rachel got against Layla?"

"That we all have the same nature."

"You don't make any sense," she said, wiping the work-surface for the fifth time.

"Rachel's problem is she wants to believe her nature is distinct from Layla's. She's Jewish. She's superior. Her people have a right to Eretz Israel. It's because that isn't true, because we have the same nature, the problem arises. If it were true there would be no problem."

"Why? Wouldn't Layla still be aggrieved?"

"Not if her nature really was inferior. You can see the same thing throughout history: slaves in revolt, peasants in revolt, employees in revolt, women rising up, blacks rising up. Why? Because they've been asked to accept they're inferior and it isn't true."

"Does being an employee make you inferior?"

"Employment is a moral outrage, Jasmine."

"How do we run the economy without it?"

"Much more efficiently. People work best when they're in control of what they do. Suppose I suggested we go back to slavery. It's a neat system. You can work people to death. You own them. You can whip them, kick them, have sex with them. You can give them just enough to keep them fit for their work. We could shut down the schools and the hospitals, no more pensions or social care. There's a lot of money to be made from slavery. Why not go back to it?"

"You can't treat people like that. It's an insult to their dignity."

"And employing them to serve your enrichment isn't ? In a way, it's worse. Slave owners owned the people who worked for them so they had an interest in looking after them. Employers just rent them. They have a lesser incentive to care for them. In fact, most of the ways people are cared for in our society fly in the face of what employers want. A production-line operative has a heart attack and gets NHS treatment, is off work for three months, gets free medication which prevents further problems. The employer has to keep the post open. Do you think most of them wouldn't rather say: "Your health isn't my problem. Your employment is over."

"Some of them do."

"It isn't the employer-employee system which has given us the decencies we enjoy, but the effort to overcome it."

"Isn't that the half-way house, Bill? Let the employers do what they do and the State intervene to look after people?"

"The State does some good things, but never as well as people can do them for themselves."

"We can't take out our own tonsils."

"No, but we can co-operate to ensure it's done without needing the State."

"Doesn't the NHS do it well?"

"Of course, the doctors, the nurses, the porters, the cleaners, the cooks, all of them. Their work makes it work."

"Well then, why get a bee in your bonnet about them working for the NHS?"

"Because the State isn't essentially benign. Its benign functions are an exception. What it's best at is war."

"We aren't at war all the time."

"No, but we're on the verge of it all the time. State squaring up to State as they fight one another for lucre. The world lives on its nerves because of the pursuit of money."

"I know, but people like to live well and whoever offers them new cars, gadgets and holidays is going to get the votes."

"Not my vote."

"You're an exception."

"No, Jasmine, I'm just a bloke."

"A bloke who knows four languages."

"That's nothing unusual. Everybody's creative, everybody's intelligent in their own way. The narrow definition of intelligence the education system uses, serves the needs of employers. I'm no exception, I've just been lucky enough to have thought things through, But everyone agrees with me. Who do you know who doesn't complain about their boss?"

She laughed.

"Yes, everybody knows the boss is incompetent."

"If the newspapers ran stories for a week, just a week, saying that everything would run more efficiently if the hierarchies were levelled and people controlled their own work, the entire country would agree, because people know it already."

"But would it be more efficient?"

"It would be more human."

"I know, but factories are efficient because they break tasks down into small functions. Your laptop is put together by people who perform one small task over and over and have no idea how what they make works. Same is true of your car, your tv, your washing machine. People like those things. They're not going to give them up."

"Not while they're told having them gives their life significance."

"Who's going to tell them anything else?"

"I think they know it already, and anyway, most of the world's population doesn't enjoy those things."

"But they want to. They call it aspiration."

"For the wrong things. Give people a real choice and I think they'd change their minds. Three days work a week instead of five and public transport rather than the car on the drive, I think a lot of people would go for it. People are on the merry-go-round and it's moving too fast for them to jump off."

"I'd live in your world, Bill, but I'm not sure many people would. Anyway, I know you."

"You know, if you read the testimonies of people who saw the few, brief occasions when self-government was given a chance, like Orwell in Barcelona, they all say how it felt like a new world; how people gave up their petty competitiveness and became relaxed and generous; how pleasant relationships became more important than money or status or power. They're tiny glimpses but they're telling. Once the spell is broken, people change."

"But what's going to break the spell?"

"There are flashpoints everywhere and constant tension. That's how the rich run the world. Paranoia is normal. They're in a permanent funk people might throw in the towel, so they overreact. They have to keep the lid on all the time; there are bound to be insurrections, uprisings, like Egypt and Syria. But they're always ready with their repressive State. It's not likely to happen suddenly, but over time there'll be challenge after challenge and the system can absorb only so much."

"Don't you think they might be willing to blow up the whole show rather than lose their control?"

"I'm sure they are. It's up to the people to make sure they can't."

The people. Bill was looking for the evidence his theory of impossibility of Tory victory was wrong. Corbyn's 2017 forty per cent wasn't going to be repeated. The bugbear was Starmer's EU policy. It was unreasonable by virtue of its hyper-reasonableness: please, electors, permit us to negotiate a new deal; we'll then put it to the vote; if you want it, we'll carry it through, if not we'll return to the status quo ante-2016. It was a dinner-table policy agreed by frequenters of restaurants the folk in the north who'd voted to leave couldn't afford. It was reasonable if you weren't one of those people on low wages in a run-down town who didn't know the name of your MEP, had never set eyes on them, didn't know what the function of the European Commission was and didn't care. It was so reasonable it was obviously a trick. The leavers were in no mood to accept a re-run. Why should they? They could see straight through the policy to the glib Europhilia it tried vainly to conceal.

Bill voted to leave in 1975. The big majority in favour of continued membership he saw as excessively optimistic: a Europe without borders, with ease of travel, with the right to live and work where you choose, he would have welcomed; but any fool could see the EC didn't work in the interests of the people. It was, as the vulgar propaganda put it, a "capitalist's club". All the same, his stance shifted when Jacques Delors embraced the charter of fundamental rights, including worker representation. Though he thought of it as a sop, a way of embedding workers in the capitalist mess, it could be a useful sop: if representation, why not control? The response to the Maastricht Treaty deleted his delusions: the British right was showing its teeth. Socialists were a horror, but foreign socialists? The naïve optimism of 1975 evaporated. The fight was going to get more vicious and everything European would be vilified. British capital would assert its absolute rights. Sweeping away the regulations and protections, that was the way to prosperity. He watched it happen. Thatcher began the shift of wealth upwards. Her message to the middle-classes and above, to the sharp-elbowed, the main chancers was: "We'll create more opportunity for you by forcing down the wages of those at the bottom, by shutting down on their capacity to defend themselves, by taking a scythe to their benefits. Don't look over your shoulder at those left behind. Come with us and you'll have a bigger house, a better car, more expensive holidays. Take care of yourself. Those who lose deserve to."

He watched it happen. People were given a choice and they opted for more stuff rather than better relations. Nor was it only Tories who joined the bonanza. People who called themselves socialists opened accounts in every building society to grab the two grand when they were de-mutualised. People who spouted the rhetoric of equality were buying shares in privatised companies and selling them for the biggest profit as soon as they could. People who claimed they stood for solidarity were turning their backs on those at the bottom to get two BMWs on the drive. Thatcher knew what she was doing: appeal to the most vulgar impulses and the vulgar will rally.

What chance for his sensibility? Given the choice between more money and greater inequality or less money and greater equality, he would choose the latter. So would anyone who thought it through for five minutes. What's the point of a big house if you have to live behind electric gates out of fear of those your love of lucre excludes? Only someone essentially emotionally dead would choose money over people.

Was his theory full of holes? He couldn't see how the Tories could get to a majority. They'd have the highest vote and the greatest number of seats, but how could they creep up to three hundred and twenty-six? He heard the theory that Labour was going to crumble in the little leave-voting towns, but he couldn't imagine Bolsover going blue. Corbyn could come through if the Labour vote didn't fall too badly and a coalition with the SNP, Plaid Cymru, the SDLP and Caroline Lucas might just give him the edge and let him throw down the gauntlet to the Lib Dems:

172

here's a programme, support it or line up with the Tories. Of course, they'd line up with the Tories. Predictions, they were always foolish.

The phone rang.

"Hello, mate. How are you?"

"Steve. Good to hear from you."

"What about seeing me?"

"Always good to see you."

"I'll be there tomorrow."

"Tomorrow? The two of you."

"There is no two of us."

"Oh, Christ."

"Yes, he's to blame."

"Are you okay?"

"I'm fine. I'm in the pub. See you tomorrow, mate."

"Yeah, yeah. Stay as long as you like."

"You've just got yourself a lodger for the rest of your life."

There was nothing in Steve's demeanour which suggested a crisis. He wasn't unshaven or dishevelled, there weren't bags beneath his eyes, nor was he beginning to stoop as people do when hit in late middle-age by some catastrophe which saps their energy and turns not only the ultimate, but the near future, into a cul-de-sac.

"A beer?" said Bill.

"No, coffee. Strong."

The visitor sat on the sofa in the little front room and stretched his short, heavy legs.

"What's the story, then?"

Steve savoured the coffee as if it was the first he'd drunk.

"You know, mate, this is a lovely little house."

"It's a little house."

"No, the atmosphere. It's an easy place to be."

"I'm glad."

"If Judy were here, her nose would be wrinkling."

"Well, it needs tidying."

"She'd say it stinks."

Bill sniffed.

173

"Does it?"

"Does it buggery, but she'd say it does. You'd think she has a dog's nose."

"I guess a bloke's house does smell blokey. Especially an old bloke."

"An old bloke has right to live in a house that smells like an old bloke."

"Two old blokes."

Steve shook his head.

"What a mess, Bill."

"Yeah?"

"Preamble. From my point of view. It's all from my point of view of course. Her mind has gone, Bill."

"Really?"

"Yeah. I came home, all my clothes had been thrown out of the bedroom window. My ties, why do I have ties, I never wear 'em. But my ties were cut to pieces."

"You can buy new ties."

"I can, but I won't. She'd attacked the mattress with a carving knife."

"Wow."

"It's time for me to leave, she said. I'm not going anywhere. She smashed all the crockery, played loud music in the bedroom. Kept the light on. I had to get out."

"You did. But she needs help."

"Here," said Steve, holding out his mobile, "ring her and tell her. She'll call you a fascist."

"Is there anyone she'd listen to?"

"I don't know," said Steve, shaking his head. "She's convinced she has no problem, except me, of course."

"Maybe when you're away she'll start to think differently."

"Absence and the fond heart. Fondness has been expunged from her mind, Bill. I don't know what it is, booze, religion, but there's no place for affection, towards me at least."

"All the same, three decades of marriage. It must mean something."

"Her mind has always been elsewhere."

"La vraie vie est ailleurs."

"Don't start quoting French philosophers at me."

"Poet. He was pretty bonkers, but onto something. Alienation is a terrible thing."

"What does it mean?"

"Real life is elsewhere."

"Yeah, that's how it feels."

"You can live here, Steve. Long as you like. Settle in. Get to know a few folk. People are all right here, by and large."

"They're all right everywhere, by and large."

"Sure, but in Reigate they're mostly Tories. They'd hang you from a lamppost if you said you believe co-operation should replace capitalism."

"Would I say that?"

"If you live here for very long, you will."

"You're going to indoctrinate me."

"I couldn't indoctrinate a budgie. But most people in this town would be relaxed about turning Marks and Spencer into a workers' co-op. They wouldn't blench from the idea of abolishing the employee-employer relation, and they'd be utterly comfortable with a society of equal wealth. Most of them aren't protecting their advantage because they don't have any."

"Nor do I, just now."

"You have an expensive house in London."

"Half an expensive house in London."

"That half would buy you a very nice house up here."

"Maybe I'll do that."

"Come and live among people who believe in democratic equality. But think about it, Steve. Your house in London will increase in value far faster than anything you'll buy here."

"Telling me to protect my advantage? You'll be voting Tory next."

"It's the way the system works. The middle-classes are nice folk, if you live amongst them. If you've got your nice three or four bedroomed, a garden and two BMWs. They're friendly folk. But they vote Tory because they fear a reworking of our arrangements won't mean the people at the bottom rising, but them falling. That's the horrible anxiety which besets middle-class life: that there is a lower class to fall into."

"You're all right here."

"Yeah. But the anxiety hits me too, even with no more than this. If I had to leave it and go back to a two-bedroomed terrace with no garden, I'd feel a sense of loss and decline. You have to force yourself to see property doesn't define you, but for the middle-classes it does. They feel better about themselves when they think about their roomy houses, their flashy cars and their second homes in the Dordogne."

"I feel better about myself when I think of my nice house in London."

"Judy on her own?"

"No, she's got a crate of Pinto Grigio for company."

"Shall I ring her?"

"Wasting your time, mate. And she'd resent it because you're my mucker. I think she's determined to destroy herself."

"You can't let her do that."

"I can't stop her. You know what they're like, these people. You can't tell a drunk or a druggie or a compulsive gambler or a sex addict they're heading for disaster. There's a part of them you just can't reach. It's always been like that. Some small, hidden part of her doesn't connect with the world and it drags her down, like a weight pulls you under water."

"You hungry?"

"Bloody starving."

There was a noise from the kitchen and Jasmine popped her head round the door.

"Did I hear someone say they're hungry?"

Steve craned to look. The sight of the charming, smiling face lifted his mood.

"Come in, Jasmine. This is Steve, my old mate from university."

"Not so much of the old," said the other getting up to shake hands.

"Pleased to meet you. You should open an hotel, Bill. You've always guests arriving."

176

"I landed on him by surprise," said Steve, "I'm a refugee."

"Oh my, from what?"

"The leafy London suburbs," said Bill.

"And you've come running to the north looking for our famed authenticity."

"He's the only person on earth daft enough to take me in," said Steve.

"Well, he's daft in a good way. We're sitting down to eat next door and there's far too much food. Come and help us."

Bill was glad of the relief company brought. Rakesh was at the table. Nathan wasn't slow to ask if Steve was a cricket fan and being told he preferred rugby made a sterling effort to pretend he knew about the game. As usual, Jasmine had prepared an array of deliciousness.

"I played a little bit you know, when I was at school," said Nathan, " fly-half."

"It's a good position," said Steve.

"Yes," said Nathan, "you have to be quick. Quick and nimble."

"I don't see you being quick and nimble when I ask you to paint the bedroom ceiling," said Jasmine.

"Rakesh plays too, don't you?" said Nathan.

"What?" said the boy.

"You play rugby, at school."

"Touch rugby."

"Like it?" said Steve.

"No," said the boy.

"He's too young," said Nathan. "He'll mature into it."

"It's not a pair of trousers," said Jasmine. "The boy knows his mind. If he doesn't like rugby, he doesn't. Why should he?"

Bill didn't join in. He was thinking about Steve's plight and Judy's decline. There'd always been some straining for the absolute in her, as if some purified form of selfhood were possible. It was easy to see but impossible to understand. There was a rigid and brittle quality to her personality which no one could fail to notice. We read others' minds through their behaviour and in

Judy you could sense Rimbaud's assertions: la vraie vie est ailleurs and je est un autre. Was it simply the commonplace alienation of modern life, divorced as we all are from the natural inclination to make our own decisions, run our own lives and find a way to co-operate to see all our needs met? Everybody was subject to that but not everybody was taut and arbitrary like Judy. How much of it was accounted for by what had happened and been done to her and how much by her decisions? It was impossible to know. Psychiatry, which teased out clues and attributed people to categories, was less potent in understanding than the best novelists. Yet no one could work it out. What Steve said was true: a part of her was beyond reach. Was that wilful? Would anyone deliberately cut themselves off and condemn themselves? It was impossible to know; but Steve had lived with it for more than thirty years. Listening to him talking cheerfully made Bill wonder if from the very start he'd been uneasy about Judy. Why, then, would he have married her? Maybe because one impulse outweighed another: she was attractive and intelligent. Then the idea of marriage suddenly struck him as monstrous. There were couples like Jasmine and Nathan of course who rubbed along pleasantly and brought Rakesh up well; but the burden placed on marriage was enormous: the combination of property, erotic love, companionship, child rearing, housekeeping couldn't have been better designed for failure. Of course, the rich, in whose interest it worked, paid for their kids to be looked after (which usually meant abuse), for their houses to be cleaned, took adultery and prostitution for granted and had no worries over money.

As ever, he arrived in that comfortable corner from which he surveyed the world and saw the mess we had made as in need of thoroughgoing transformation and himself as alone. It wasn't true, of course, that he was on his own. There were millions who knew the present arrangements were a dog's breakfast, but the official line, pumped out every second of every day, was intended to convince people like him no one shared their view. The polling organisations avoided the questions which would put the status quo in question: Would you be in favour of democracy in the workplace? Should compulsory school attendance be abolished? Should power be devolved to the grassroots? Would you like to be involved in deciding how your local area is planned? Given the land and the resources, would you like to build you own home? The questions posed were always within a narrow range which ensured, however they were answered, they suggested no alternative.

What was going to happen to Judy? Maybe she'd stabilize, Steve would go home, things would roll along as before and they'd Darby and Joan to the grave. On the other hand, maybe she'd be sectioned or her health would collapse. Whatever happened he couldn't help feeling it would expose the chasm in Steve's marriage.

"What does the anti-Semite think?" said Steve, as Rakesh was bidding the adults goodnight.

"Sorry?"

"Will Johnson be Prime Minister, proving once again that democracy is a system designed to ensure power never strays far from the playing fields of Eton?"

"Democracy shoves the majority onto a sinking boat with a gaping hole in the hull and then says: "You've got a choice. Go down or jump on the lifeboat which belongs to the rich and where they'll tell you what to do.""

"Too many don't vote, that's the problem," said Nathan. "The rich don't stay at home but the poor. I tell them at the Mosque, "You have to vote. It's your responsibility." But they're too depressed, you see. That's what happens, they can't see anything better so they don't bother."

"It's a Tory trick," said Steve. "The underclass keeps them in power."

"I can't believe he'll win," said Jasmine. "He's a fool, and calling Muslim women letter-boxes. How can such a man be Prime Minister?"

"You might say the same about Lord Salisbury," said Bill.

"Was he bad?" said Nathan.

"He said if our ancestors had cared for the rights of other people, the British Empire would never have been made."

"And better if it hadn't," said Steve.

"Well, there you have it," said Jasmine. "Our rights counted for nothing."

"But we got rich out of it,"said Steve

"They did," said Bill.

"We all benefit, but some benefit more than others."

"Much more," said Nathan.

"He also said he doubted we had reached the point when a British constituency would elect a black man to represent them."

"He was a racist."

"That's what the Empire was built on, and so our wealth, and so our place in the world today," said Steve.

"Not pretty when you look into it," said Bill, but no one recognised the reference.

"Surely he can't win," said Jasmine.

"He will," said Steve.

Nathan shook his head in despair rather than disagreement.

"You think so?" said Jasmine.

"Give Johnson a trampoline and Corbyn a cracked springboard. Who's going to jump higher?"

"All the same the Tories got forty-two percent of the vote in 2017. Are they going to push that much higher?" said Bill

"They won't need to. The PLP , the Labour bureaucracy, the media and Keir Starmer are ensuring the Labour vote will slump."

"But if Corbyn hangs onto most of his two hundred and sixty-two seats, the Tories can't make it. They had three hundred and eighteen in 2017. Corbyn can lose half a dozen seats to them and they can't creep over the line. If the SNP keeps its tally at about fifty. There'll have to be horse-trading and Sturgeon isn't going to get into bed with Johnson," said Bill.

"Who would?" said Nathan.

"A surprising number of women it seems," said Steve.

"Let's hope Corbyn can hang on," said Jasmine.

"They've cut the rope," said Steve. "He leads a party of bastards. They've no respect for democracy. They want the drug which inadequate people always crave: power. The anti-Semitism nonsense has been invented to damage him and worst of all, Starmer has cobbled together a policy on leaving the EU that the inmates of Bedlam would have laughed at."

"A second referendum, we could stay in," said Nathan.

"Which is exactly what Labour voters from Barrow to Grimsby don't want," said Steve. "Just look at the percentages. Barrow nearly sixty percent, Grimsby, over seventy per cent. Those people don't want another crack at a referendum, they want out. That's Corbyn's instinct which is why Starmer has headed him off from the right. In 2017 Corbyn got forty percent of the votes, but he wasn't lumbered with a daft policy cooked up by people who want to hobble the left."

"Yeah," said Bill, "but look at the Labour remain vote. It's bigger than the leave vote."

"Sure," said Steve, "but not in the places that matter. Labour voters in Cambridge might be remainers but look at Bolsover. Seventy per cent leave, and they elected Dennis for decades. Those people are socialists, but they don't like the EU and with good reason."

"There might be good reason," said Jasmine, "but it wouldn't make me side with Farage and Johnson."

"They don't care about that," said Steve. "They're cynical, and with equally good reason. They know politicians are liars who line their pockets. Look at the Labourites who ended up millionaires. The folk in Bolsover, Grimsby and Barrow are narked because they voted to leave and it hasn't happened. They'd have voted for Genghis Khan if he'd promised to take us out of the EU."

Bill was hit by a petty anxiety. His pulse raced a little and he found himself fidgeting. Was Steve right? Was Starmer part of a strategy to hobble Corbyn to ensure he lost?

"You think it's factitious," he said.

"'Course, Bill. Starmer wants to be leader. He isn't interested in standing in Corbyn's shadow, and he certainly doesn't want to be associated with the transformative left. The EU policy is designed to drag Labour to defeat. It's a feeble mess: vote for us, we'll negotiate a better deal, which they can't guarantee, we'll let you vote on it, and of course we'll work like hell for a remain

181

vote. Why should a minimum wage worker who's never set eyes on her MEP and has no idea what the EU Commission does vote for that?"

Through his little paroxysm of fret, Bill could see the logic. It was despicable, but the right's behaviour towards Corbyn had been vile since the day he was elected. The meagre flame of hope he'd been nurturing for months, the fragile possibility that Corbyn could lead a minority government and at last some simple, sensible things would be done to rectify the gross injustice of billionaires stepping over the homeless on their way to Le Gavroche, had turned cold. If Steve was right, not only was Corbyn facing a Tory Party backed by half a dozen daily newspapers but an inner cabal of anti-socialists quite willing to put Johnson in power in order to decapitate the left. Was Starmer really such a sly, crawl-on-his-belly creature? He'd always given him the benefit of having been willing to take a place in Corbyn's shadow cabinet; but now he saw that Steve might well be right. The ambitious boy from Surrey, possessor of a knighthood, ex-director of a big public body where he'd let his previous anti-State poise slide and had delivered succulent tit-bits to the ravenous right-wing media, elected to parliament no earlier than 2015; no doubt he saw Corbyn's failure as his greatest chance of leadership and being Prime Minister.

It was plausible but it was theory. He had no evidence. Perhaps Starmer was genuine and really wanted Corbyn to win. Yet on balance it seemed more likely he was honing his ambition and saving his gunpowder for the big moment. There was sense in Steve's idea: a convoluted policy on the question exercising millions of Labour voters might be a sneaky little ploy.

"You think they'll vote Tory in Bolsover?" said Bill.

"Tory or Brexit. I think Skinner will be doing his garden."

"But as you say, those people are socialists."

"Sure, when socialism looks after them. They want to leave the EU more than anything because they voted for it. They believe in democracy and Labour is telling them if they vote for something Blair and Starmer and Yvette Cooper, the entire sorry tribe of drowning-in-cash, look-at-me-mum-I'm-in-the-government, mirror-gazers don't like, there has to be a re-run. It's pitiful."

"But Bolsover," said Bill.

"They're just the common people, Bill. They don't have Bakunin or Kropotkin on their bedside table. They've accepted the deal: you vote for it, you get it and they're going to vote for it."

Henceforth, Bill listened to the news and thought about what was happening from a different perspective. He watched Starmer on the tv and couldn't help half agreeing with Steve. He found it impossible to attribute utter manipulativeness to the man and if he switched to his previous generosity in judging him to have been sincere in his support of Corbyn, he could almost project his own anarchistic egalitarianism. Yet Steve had set the dam and the water was pooling.

When his visitor received texts from Judy he shared them:

How wretched you make me. What kind of man did I marry when I took you? Don't come near me. Good riddance…

He had to agree they were self-pitying, self-aggrandizing and her wallowing in her own apparent absolute misery was obedience to some obscure impulse to topsy-turvy, perverse glory. He pictured her as he held the mobile and read: that slight lift of the chin, the mouth turning down a little at the corners or at times her bottom lip shoved forward like a sullen child's, the aura of assumed superiority which clung to her, like the phoney elevation of royalty, and what came into his head was that image of her mind as a clump, a pudding, a confection of suet, lacking fineness and finesse and the necessary separating out of impulses which is the stuff of maturity. Not that her intellect was a clod. On the contrary, in that sphere, everything was well teased-out. It was in the regions of autonomy, of individuation, of a secure limit to self which permitted the acknowledgment of other selves that the lumpishness was characteristic. Was it the effect of some quirk in the brain? If so, it was wrong to condemn her. If it partly mediated by choice, she could be reproached, at least to some extent. It was impossible to know.

Steve settled in.

Bill was glad of his company, even if it did mean his children couldn't come and stay. Their visits were rare enough anyway. The two pensioners fell into the habits they'd known as students: Bill cooked one night, Steve the next; they walked the quarter mile to the *Bull* and enjoyed a couple of drinks to end the evening; they watched and mocked stupid tv, working up a side-aching laughter. Bill was happy to see his friend relaxed and able to enjoy life and he got to know the region, joined the rugby club and gathered a coterie of acquaintances; yet there was still Judy in the background. Was he encouraging his mate to fail to deal with the crisis? What could he suggest anyway? Every day there were texts. Did she simply want to torment him? Caroline had stopped making repayments and Bill had a taut conversation on the land-line, but he couldn't be bothered with the conflict.

"Let me have what you can when you can," he said, "but in the long run, Caroline,you'll have to give me the full five thou-sand," knowing he'd be lucky to get three.

Every day, Steve shook his head as he looked at his mo-bile.

"Read that, mate."

Bill couldn't stop the thought that Judy was heading for disaster. It's precise form no one could know, but some kind of physical or mental collapse was likely. The odd idea flitted into his mind that it might be for the best: at least it might force a reso-lution; but he shoved the ill-natured thought aside.

When the inevitable news arrived, Steve took it placidly. The text from Judy's sister had a hurried, emotionally strained tenor but beneath its overblown style the simple facts were stated: Judy had been sectioned after being arrested for being drunk and disorderly. Thoroughly tanked she'd picked an argument about god and had refused to leave the pub when the landlord asked her, asserting her right to another glass of vodka. She'd complied when the police arrived but out in the street had run into the road to hail a taxi, a driver had swerved to miss her and knocked a scooter-rider into the gutter.

Steve had to go to London. Bill went with him.

The house was a wonder of disorder. Washing-up was piled in both sinks, on every surface, and ants, attracted by the mixed odours of congealed and mouldy food, marched in a military line from the corner behind the fridge to colonise the territory. Steve pulled the fridge clear and found the hole they'd made in the skirting. Prodding, the wood crumbled. He took a screwdriver and a hammer and smashed and yanked the stretch from the wall. Thousands of the tiny, diligent scavengers fled in every direction. He got to his feet and stamped, grabbed the kitchen spray and hit them with a foaming detergent stream. The plaster too had been eaten away. It crumbled between his fingers.

"Did you know they could do that?" he said.

"Super ants," said Bill.

In the living-room, an under-floor scratching made them go silent and attend.

"Rats," said Steve.

He stamped. The noise stopped. He went for a crow bar, his hammer and the big screwdriver and prised up a board. Nothing.

"Scared 'em off."

"I'll have to find where they get in and seal it. Let's hope they aren't nesting inside."

"Best get some traps and poison."

There was a hardware store half a mile away. Bill took the opportunity to stretch his legs. On his way he passed a group of young, orthodox Jews coming in the opposite direction. They were dressed in black jackets or something akin to a frockcoat, white shirts, broad-brimmed, black hats and some with the long side curls.

"Afternoon," he said as he skirted them, and they acknowledged him.

He wondered what the origin and purpose of the side curls was; and why the black hats and no shades but black and white. None of it was any odder than the way he used to dress as a teenager, his hair on his shoulder, ludicrous flared-jeans, psychedelic shirts. What was he trying to communicate? That he belonged to a particular group, listened to certain music, rejected the short hair, collars and ties and business suits of the lucre-loving world. Yet it had been less serious than that: it was simple fun. Dressing in the way you fancied and thumbing your nose at convention was just a laugh. It gave you something to share with your mates and nothing was more pleasing than if it got up the noses of stiff adults who associated hair over the collar with moral debasement.

No doubt the Hasidic dress had religious significance. In any case, he was glad the young men could walk around wearing what they fancied. The greater diversity the better. Who cares if the bridge-players walk the streets in clothes depicting the king of spades or the ace of clubs, who cares if the snooker players wear mostly red with patches of yellow, green, brown, blue, pink, black and white spot at their navel? Beneath the diversity was an incontrovertible sameness of human nature. He considered their belief in a deity foolish, but that's what beliefs were for. Everyone was permitted to believe something which had no basis in evidence. It was a relief from intellectual effort, but it consigned everyone to their own world because only what can be confirmed by every subjectivity lifts us from loneliness.

In the store, the bloke next to him in the queue said:

"Rat problem, eh?"

"Yeah."

"It's them bloody foreigners," he said. "Poles, Romanians. Dirty buggers."

"Well," said Bill, "there's plenty for them to feed on, isn't there, Fast food everywhere."

"But it was never like this before all them foreigners came here," he said. "Boris'll stop it. Get us out, eh?"

"Yeah," said Bill, putting the traps and poison on the counter.

Steve set one of the vicious, black, plastic monsetrs and poison under the board which he fitted lightly in place and one in the garden near where he'd found a gap in the brickwork.

The bedroom door wouldn't open.

"Is it locked somehow?" said Bill.

"No, there's a blockage."

Bill puzzled until Steve managed to shove it ajar just enough for them to squeeze in. The floor was covered to a depth of a couple of feet in clothes. Bill stood in amazement. A fertile array of women's clothes was beneath his feet and around him:

blouses, skirts, bras jumpers, knickers, socks, jackets, trousers, jeans, coats, hats, gloves in a marvellous abstract canvas of colours.

"You should enter it for the Turner Prize," he said.

"Tracey Emin is tidy by comparison," said Steve.

The bed was unmade, its once white sheets tinged grey and by the side nearest the door, where she slept, a small circle of floor adjacent to the bedside table on which sat three empty glasses, a bottle on its side, a packet of paracetamol and a face-down copy of the bible open, no doubt, at some indispensable wisdom, was filled with tight-balled tissues, cotton buds, empty tubes of skin creams, moisturisers, emollients.

Steve began to heap the clothes.

"There isn't room," said Bill.

"No," said Steve, "they'll have to be thrown out."

"Shouldn't you ask first?"

He got his chance to ask in the hospital. Bill declined to go with him:

"Two of us? She'll think we're ganging up."

Steve's first thought was it seemed the last place to put someone in distress. The idea of being confined with the modern, clean but obviously institutional walls could have driven him from absolute mental stability to waywardness in a week. At odds with himself he would have chosen the sea, or the top of Helvellyn or a forest. To be surprised by a doe bounding through the trees ten metres in front of you, or to see a buzzard circling or to watch a flock of oyster catchers swoop over the low tide and come to rest in a cackling horde on the sand had to be more therapeutic than any medication.

Did Judy need therapy? It's meaning was simple, like prophylaxis. Did she need to be cured? Of what? Being Judy? He fought against his cynicism as he came to the ward. They were professionals. They could surely do something for her.

The flowers he'd bought in the underground she surveyed as they might be a bomb or a drink spiked with arsenic.

"Maybe I can get a vase," he said.

"For those," she said, turning away her face.

187

Her mask-like expression and her calm demeanour were the work of the drugs. She refused to meet his eyes, raised her chin, turned her gaze on the ceiling or the wall opposite.

"Bill came down with me," said Steve.

"How nice for him."

"We're going to clean up the house."

"Don't lay a finger on my house."

"Our house, Judy."

"Oh, yes. Your house. That's you all over, isn't it. Your house. What place do I have?"

"I said our house."

"I know what you meant."

"Well, the house. We'll make it nice for you so when you get out of.."

"What right do they have to keep me in here?"

"I don't know the law, but I think they're trying to help you."

"That's what you would think. Take their side. I know you all right, mister."

"Don't you think they might be able to help you, Judy?"

"Help me? I can't even get a drink in here. What good's that to me? How can they take away my right to a glass of wine?"

"Well, I suppose, if you're taking medications…"

"I'm not taking anything. I'm having them forced on me. It's rape, that's what it is. It's an invasion of my body."

Suddenly becoming very intense and fixing him with wide eyes she said:

"How did you get here?"

"The tube."

"Order a taxi."

"A taxi?"

"Yes, do it now. Get me out of here."

"Mobile phones aren't allowed. They interfere with the equipment."

"Go outside. Get a taxi."

"Maybe I should speak to the doctors."

"Doctors? Prison warders. How long can they keep me?"

"Haven't they told you?"

"They talk gibberish."

"I don't know the law," said Steve. "I'll talk to a doctor."

"Get a taxi. We can be away before they know we've gone. We can go abroad."

"I think for the time being we have to go along with things.."

"We? You don't have to go along with anything. You can do what you like. You're on their side, of course. That's you all over," and she lapsed, switching her eyes again to inanimate things.

Steve made a few more futile efforts to engage her, but she was abrupt, brittle and high-handed. She sat staring at the wall and he at the floor. It struck him there had always been this current in her mentality. In the early days it had been a mere irritation and it ran along beneath the more in-touch layer of her mentality, like a long-buried stream beneath a building whose presence is revealed only by the odd appearance of corner damp, or at stormy times, a distant suggestion of flowing water. Now, as the richer parts of her mind had withered, this unpleasant sharpness, like the snapping of an ill-tempered dog, had become characteristic. It made him aware of how he'd always experienced a minor negativity, which he'd ignored, like we dismiss a pain which never gathers itself into fierceness.

The doctor gave him a few minutes. She was going to stay in for six months.

"Six months? I didn't think you had the right."

"Depends on the nature of the section."

"She's that bad?"

"Let's say it'll take about that length of time to do anything worthwhile."

"Is it the drink?"

"No, we have no right to section people for drinking, however chaotic it makes them."

"What's your diagnosis?"

"I haven't formulated one, definitively."

"Have you prescribed anything?"

"Anti-depressant."

Steve skipped down the steps to the exit. There were going to be many more visits. He was going to have to stay in London. Pity. He'd got used to living with Bill and the north. Maybe he could continue and jump on the train once a week. Twice a week. He could afford it. What did the money matter?

"Okay?" said Bill.

"Six months," said Steve.

"That's a stretch."

"Yeah. But if it gets her back to reality."

"She hasn't lost touch completely?"

"Don't ask me, Bill. You know, it was always there."

"What?"

"This, whatever it is. She's down my throat. She turns her nose up at the flowers. It was always there."

"But she wasn't like she is now."

"No, it's odd. As if it was slowly working its way to the surface, like bricks buried beneath a lawn."

On the way back to the house, where they had had to face the mess and try, at least, get rid of the vermin and the odours, Bill began to think about Caroline. Was what Steve said about Judy also true of her? She wasn't a bad person, just fully adjusted to her culture, whose foundation was lust for lucre. Its sentimental promise was love – erotic, parental, familial, between friends, but adjustment to lucre-seeking meant not love but power; not trust but suspicion; not generosity but grasping; not self-transcendence but self-obsession; not sharing but possession; not joy but ghoulish gleefulness; not enjoyment but strenuous acting-out; not acceptance of life but terror of its contingencies.

Consciously, Caroline wasn't a money-grubber, but her compliance operated at a level below her ratiocination. Like Judy, she was moved by a subterranean stream; like everybody in fact. He was no different. His conscious thinking wasn't powerful enough to reveal his own mind. What was the difference between him and Caroline or Steve and Judy? He couldn't help thinking it was gender. Something about being female in the mad culture of lucre-loving made life harder. It wasn't simply the obvious male precedence: it was rather the greater devastation to personality

190

caused by submission to the prevailing culture in women, but how it worked he couldn't see.

It had always been there. It was true of Caroline too. Why had he ignored it, or at least played it down? And then, what had she found disturbing about him which she'd accepted? The thought he had many times returned to him: that he should have pulled back at the first sign; but hardly anyone he'd known hadn't left him with some unease on getting to know them. There were good friends like Steve, who had been congenial from the start, but they were few; even most of the lads and men he'd known had created a negative wave in his feeling, despite relationships with his own gender being less complicated and intense than those with girls and women.

He recalled a short story by Mario Soldati: a man whose marriage has failed leaves the hotel where his wife has berated him and goes to eat in an old familiar restaurant. While there he ruminates on the girls he knew before he married. Was there one he should have chosen? The first? Who was the first? Bill flicked through the girls he'd had crushes on, been infatuated with, kissed, missed, made love to and been rejected by, as if he as looking through a photograph album. It was a sorry history.

His mind settled on his first significant meeting with Caroline. They'd been part of the same circle at university, drifting into one another's residences, lounging in kitchens in the early hours; but he'd thought of no connection with her till he was between the shelves in the library, thumbing through *Le Neveu de Rameau* when she was suddenly beside him, saying in a low, sweet, enticing voice: "Anything interesting?"

During those ten minutes of conversation, nothing of what later troubled him was present. She was charming, interested in him, pleasant, sweet, friendly, responsive: above all responsive. He could see her clearly in that iteration: her face, her demeanour. He could hear her voice, though what she said he had no hope of recalling. In those few minutes she was able to keep contained the petulance, arbitrariness, self-pity and importunity which later became commonplace. Didn't that mean she knew they were hurtful? A fleeting memory came to him of her in an unreachable mood declaring herself exactly that. Didn't that mean she was both perfectly aware that if she'd begun as she became, he wouldn't have warmed to her? Also, that she was capable of control: it couldn't be true that in those moments when she'd spoken to him like a monarch to a lackey she wasn't capable of not doing. If for quarter of an hour a person is able to recognise and employ the behaviour which will please, reassure and charm another person, why not for fifty years? All that is required is effort.

Was it true there was effort in the opposite direction? Were her unpleasant characteristics her default way-of-being or did she have to work at them? He couldn't help feeling it was the latter. It was acting-out. But why? Wasn't it because somewhere in her mind had lodged the idea that power was what everyone was seeking? Wasn't there a lurking anxiety that if she didn't join in the power game, she would be its victim?

Should he have pulled back at the first sign? No, he'd done the right thing. He'd offered her love, in the unconditional way it must be offered. It was true, he now knew, that Caroline was incapable of rising to what someone or other he'd read called the demanding ideal of erotic love. She made the effort to hook him, but once he was in the keep net, she'd let go. Love was too hard. It meant surpassing yourself. She preferred the easy path of acquaintance. Her mind lit up at all those superficial contacts which made no serious demands; the easy acquaintance of the pub, the empty chatter of the party, the apparent belonging of the group which holds together by no more than temporary ecstasy of self-abandonment – these were her arenas and they left her tormented by the sense of inadequacy which had just cost him five thousand. All the same, he'd done the right thing, made the right offer, and if it left him something to expiate it left him also at one with himself.

A PRIVATE AFFAIR

Jimmy's funeral was to take place at the crematorium, followed by food and drink at the *Joiner's Arms*, one of the pubs he'd been happy in, more or less a local, tucked between terraces, welcoming the working people of his enclave, not yet improved in pursuit of gastro identity, and whose darts team he'd played for since he was seventeen.

"But I didn't know him," said Steve.

"No one'll mind."

No one did.

The facility was out of town, at the end of a long drive lined by chestnuts and sycamores, with little monuments at intervals of two metres or so. Cars were parked the full length. Bill and Steve got off the bus and crossed the busy road.

"Good turnout," said Bill.

"Popular bloke."

"Round here, not with the Labour hierarchy."

"You don't think Tony will turn up, then?" said Steve.

"Nor Gordon. Their contempt for the common folk is visceral."

"With reason, the common folk are disrespectful of money."

"With reason," said Bill.

"I'm surprised Blair didn't privatise crematoria," said Steve. "What could be more *infra dig* than being burnt by the Council?"

"Imagine being burnt by Serco. You'd probably walk away with some other poor bugger's ashes," said Bill.

"Do you think they'll bury Blair in Westminster Abbey?"

"I hope so, while he's still alive," said Bill.

All the familiar Party and union faces were present, waiting to be admitted. Beneath the sharp sunlight, in this quiet place where nature had been permitted to assume enough of its disorder to offer solace but not enough to allow anyone to forget the work which went into keeping the locale presentable, they might have been gathered for pleasant sociability rather than to reduce to ashes the remains of one of those millions who come and go beneath

193

the unforgiving condescension of history. He was a famous figure in this tight milieu. Yet to those who controlled history, he was nobody, just like the billions who were assumed to be of lesser value than the lucre-lovers, the power-suckers, all those whose existential anxiety at the possibility of leaving the earth without a memorial made them manic for recognition.

"Do you know who Robert Burns Jenkinson was?" said Bill, as they neared the crowd.

"A Victorian poet," said Steve.

"No, had he been you'd probably not have to guess. He was Prime Minister from 1812 to 1827. No one remembers him. A stuffed shirt as they are all stuffed shirts. Two centuries from now, ask people who Boris Johnson was, or David Cameron or Theresa May or Tony Blair, they'll have no idea. These people are non-entities. Everyone knows who Shakespeare was, and Beethoven and Einstein and Picasso. They did something genuine. Everything genuine can be imitated by the phoney. That's what representative politics is: phonies pretending they're genuine."

"Jimmy was a local politico," said Steve.

"Aye, but he always believed in grassroots action."

Jimmy, Bill reflected, would be in the minds of many long into the future. Yet, in the official version of reality, he would be nobody. The world was fiercely divided into the Somebodies and the Nobodies, which was the real division underpinning all others. Was there any fear in the mind greater than insignificance? Once, surely, significance was guaranteed. Simply to exist was to enjoy it; but in societies where it was distributed like coin, specific measures granted according to rank and presumed importance, wasn't the mind haunted by the prospect of paltry receipt? Didn't that mean loneliness and humiliation? Didn't it mean invisibility to your fellow creatures?

On the periphery of the mass, Jean Shuttleworth was smoking, sucking in the smoke as if her life depended on it. She turned to them and greeted Bill with the big smile and croaky voice whose tenor and cadences had been formed over decades of speechifying in petty assemblies. The cigarette was between two fingers of her thin hand, that of woman tempting by the burning she craved the one she feared; her cheeks had sunk a little further since he last saw her. Yet she exuded that excessive confidence, that definitiveness in every question which had been the making of her decades-long career as borough and county councillor. Not lack of ambition but the funnel into which many hurled themselves and few could squeeze, the reason she'd never held a parliamentary seat. Many are called but few are chosen. Straight is the gate and few there are who enter therein. There was nothing like a sorting process to ignite the worst in the mind. Bill had long believed it ought to be a principle in all arenas that people shouldn't be permitted to put themselves forward for position (although he hated hierarchies of all kinds and believed they should be flattened) but ought to be invited by their peers, who should have the right to remove what they had granted. A system in which people advanced themselves was a factory for phoniness. Who is capable of such self-insight that they know their own capacities? Who does not flatter themselves when they judge their abilities and virtues?

"Hello...," she said, and he knew from the falling intonation she'd forgotten his name.

"Hello, Jean. This is Steve, an old friend of mine."

"Nice to meet you. Well, it's a good crowd he's got."

"Yes, he deserves it."

"He does. I was saying to Carol Oldfield, he was a stalwart. Just the kind of people the Party needs, at his level. I remember arguing with him about Tony Benn when we won in 2005. He was a great Bennite, you know, even when Tony had completely lost the plot. He was on about the Iraq War and how it would be a permanent millstone round the movement's neck. People have short memories, I told him. You can't fight the course of history. Stick to what you know, Jimmy," and she waved her finger at Bill in imitation of the gesture she'd made to the dead man. "Keep the pavements clean and the bins emptied. That's what the people in your ward are concerned about, They don't bother their heads over world affairs."

A bulky man with a paunch who Bill didn't know, looking out of place in his mourning suit, like a boy in his uniform a size too big on his first day at school, stepped from the crowd and attracted Jean's attention. She drew on her cigarette as she listened and nodded wisely.

"There speaks the authentic voice of New Labour," said Bill as they skirted the crowd.

"Whatever happened to that?" said Steve.

"It got old. Persil washed whiter and it showed, but it doesn't any more. Forms of manipulation have to be constantly renewed."

"Don't we want Watney's these days?"

"No, nor does a Mackeson do you a power of good or a Hoover beat as it sweeps as it cleans."

"Did they ever?"

"Of course not, that's why the lies have to be shunted aside and new ones introduced."

"Surely a Mars a day helps you work, rest and play," said Steve.

"Mars, like all such sweeties, rots your teeth, makes you fat and gives you diabetes. Not good for sales, is it?"

"You can't be honest and sell people stuff."

"Quite right, whether it's beer, soap powder, chocolate or a political party."

"So what's Labour's latest advertising slogan?"

"Under new management," said Bill.

"That it?"

"Start to finish. Labour is now appealing to the public entirely on the grounds that Starmer isn't called Corbyn."

A voice over Bill's shoulder said:

"Don't mention that name if you want to stay in the party."

"I'm not in the party," said Bill, turning to see Dereck Pearson, a long-serving councillor and bulwark of the stolid, unthinking right , one of those rancidly time-serving individuals who pump up their egos as they view themselves in the flattering mirror of municipal power and who recoil from ideas as from infection, convinced that all which needs to be known is already known and Labour politics is merely a matter of totting up votes, keeping the worthies in their seats and knowing when to be obsequious to power and wealth.

"Resigned when Corbyn lost did you, like all the other Trots?"

"I'm not a Trot, Dereck. I'm an anti-Semite."

"And proud of it, eh?"

"It's the definition the party imposed on me because I'm of the view that Palestinians aren't a biological aberration. They're just like you and me, Dereck. Except they never know when their houses are going to be bulldozed."

"I'm for a two-State solution. That's policy, but we can't have people in the party who offend the Jewish community."

"Can you have people in the party who offend the poor?"

"You can't help the poor unless you get elected and you can't get elected if you offend powerful people."

"Powerful? Where does the power of your so-called Jewish community come from?"

"I know what you lot say: it's always Israel that's in the wrong."

"Wouldn't you say that's about right when it comes to Gaza?"

"Israel has a right to exist."

"No nation has an absolute right to exist. Where's Czechoslovakia?"

"You lot, you're always on about it. Wanting to fly the Palestinian flag over the town hall. Who wants that?"

"Does Labour stand for democracy?" said Bill.

"Daft question."

"Not so daft if you live in Rafah, Dereck. Labour can't claim to stand for justice of any kind while it remains compliant with the racism of the Israeli State."

"Aye, well, Labour is none of your business now you're not a member, is it?"

"More my business than ever. I'm for democratic equality, and that's for everybody. No special status for those who claim god gave them property rights three millennia ago."

"Things have moved on," said Pearson. "You lost, you lot. The left is dead in my party."

"Jimmy'd be glad to hear you say that, " said Bill.

197

"Aye, well…" said the councillor whose face screwed into involuntary disgust as he moved away.

Bill spotted Jimmy's widow detaching herself from a trio of Pearson's colleagues. She dodged through to him. Her eyes were shielded behind sunglasses and she looked paler and more shrunken.

"Hello, Bill. Thanks for coming," and she gave him a peck on the cheek.

"Couldn't not have," said Bill. "This is Steve."

"Nice to meet you. Did you know, Jimmy?"

"No, only by reputation."

"Only the good side, I hope."

"There wasn't a bad, Heather," said Bill.

"Well, you weren't married to him."

He was pleased she was able to joke in her grief. She and Jimmy were like millions of others who lived in expectation of change and made the best in the meantime. They were the bedrock of Labour. What held the party together was their hope of change and the leaders' determination to prevent it. The party existed to disappointment them and simultaneously deny them any alternative. Like Jimmy, she was a radical. He would have been relaxed if all the employees in the town took their work into their own hands and shoved the employers aside. She would have been equally nonchalant about dissolving the council and parliament and letting people make their own decisions. They were the people Labour leaders exploited in pursuit of power, careers, money and glory.

"He was a good man, Heather. Not many as good."

The words were trite and inadequate, but what the thought of Jimmy aroused in him was a mixture of sorrow, nostalgia, pity, anger and disgust. It was dreadful he should have died relatively young and though he knew Heather would gird herself and cope admirably, he knew too how their life together had been unique. It was one of those marriages which required no licence. The fact they'd gone through the ceremony and had official sanction meant nothing. They'd done it for the sake of form, for others. The insouciant affection between them had always been obvious, and they had that knack of not expecting too much of each other and of laughing at one another's foibles which was absent from so many, tenser marriages.

Through all the years he'd known him, Jimmy had stayed true to his essential conviction: every human life is of equal worth. At work in him was the desire to sweep aside those distinctions of wealth, property, status, power, which divided people from one another. He was a product of the town, of the little streets of terraces the Industrial Revolution had thrown up, the vomit of the money system. He and Heather had managed to pull themselves up the greasy pole a notch or two: a house with a garden and a garage. They were amongst those stuck between the bottom twenty percent who never knew when they might fall off the ladder but knew they'd never climb it and the top ten percent who know with equal certainty being born into wealth was a guarantee of remaining well-heeled. Jimmy and Heather were part of that bulk in the middle which jiggled around a bit. Social mobility. Tush. Just another propaganda trick.

He was immensely sorry these good people were victims of a lousy system. Their lives were trammelled by the imperatives of the rich, the importunate needs of the lucre-worshippers who, in order to stack up millions prevented millions from the free fulfilment of their possibilities; and he was angry at the leaders of the movement they worked for, manipulative self-seekers like Blair and Mandelson and their sickening crew of hangers-on, and now the unimaginative Starmer, deferential to a regime of arrogance and babyish entitlement, poodle of the Israeli State, willing to compromise with racism and brutality for the sake of his place in the history books.

So long as men like Jimmy gave up their time and energy to push leaflets through letterboxes, canvas, attend dull council meetings all in the belief they were serving a movement whose aim was to reform the money-sick system out of existence, the leaders of Labour could go on showing a friendly face to the public, claiming to stand for democracy, liberty, the common folk, openness, equality, while in the dark, sinister bureaucracy which controlled the party there was nothing but disdain for the little people, for radicalism, for the cherished hope that the straight-

199

jacket of property might be removed and people be able to live as their natures dictated, rather than as the money-machine insisted.

"I saw you were chatting to Dereck Pearson," said Heather.

"Yes, I like to consort with enlightenment," said Bill.

"I'm surprised he's here. He and Jimmy were at daggers drawn."

"Well, Jimmy was a socialist."

"I know," she said. "He used to say Dereck wouldn't be happy till he'd got an MBE. He's a great royalist, you know."

"Of course. Obsequiousness before money and power is the hallmark of the regressed."

"How did we get here, Bill?" she said, shaking her head.

"Jim Callaghan."

"What?"

"He was elected on a manifesto of a fundamental shift of wealth and power to working people and their families. What did he do? Cut public spending, impose wage restraint and kiss the arse of the IMF. Then he clung to power for the sake of his ego. If he'd gone to the country with a bit of courage in late '78, we might have avoided Thatcher."

"Oh, stop. The very name gives me the creeps."

"The great philosopher Margaret," said Steve. "Alderman Roberts, touching up the girls in his corner shop on a Saturday and sitting in his mayoral chains during the week as if he was incapable of anything but public service. He was the making of her."

"And she the ruination of us," said Heather.

"Brown thought she was necessary," said Steve.

"He probably thinks herpes is necessary," said Bill.

"Bill," said Heather.

"Sorry, they bring out the worst in me, these Labour leaders who exploit people's desire for change."

"Jimmy always used to say the members will save the party."

"They tried," said Steve.

"They aren't allowed to think now," said Bill. "Commissar Evans will decide. The members are mere ants."

"When he was most frustrated with it," Heather said, "he'd talk about a new party, to the left of Labour."

"Well, I used to think so, Heather, but I've changed my mind. A new party would rehearse the old failings. We need radicalism without a party. It's the hierarchies and bureaucracies which do for us."

"Sorry, Bill, I've just got to grab my sister."

She was gone. Bill watched her back as she was ushered through the throng. These were her people. Here was the gathering of most of the significant actors from the town's left. If there was anywhere an alternative might be found, it was here. They were unexceptional folk. There were no geniuses amongst them. The town didn't harbour a native Shakespeare, a home-grown Einstein, a local Chomsky. Yet they were perfectly willing and able to change their condition. What got in the way was the party structure. Bill looked around, identifying individuals he knew well, some he'd known for decades. Would any baulk at the dissolution of the employer-employee relation? Would they object to real equality, a social guarantee of basic needs provided for? Would any shed a tear at the disappearance of billionaires?

If real potency remained at local level, most of the serious problems would evaporate. It was the sucking out of potency which did the damage and as it was passed upwards the people's potency became the politicians' power. Viewed objectively, the system was absurd: forty-odd million people vote, six hundred get to parliament, a few dozen form the government and an inner circle of four or five makes the decisions. Forty-odd million intelligences, imaginations, energies, and a tiny cabal, usually of people from privileged backgrounds, exercise real power. From any reasonable perspective it was insane. It was characteristic of people to make their own decisions, to be in control of their own behaviour. What kind of demented mind would elaborate a system in which most people were merely carrying out orders?

"Has it ever struck you," he said, "how our society is founded on a military model?"

"Yes, sergeant."

They nudged themselves slowly towards the front of the huddle.

201

"Not surprising when it's founded on conquest. However, peaceable so-called civilian life may look, the State is armed like a psychopath on amphetamines and the entire caboodle is on the *qui vive* for war."

"When you've furnished your house by robbing your neighbours you have to keep a loaded shotgun by your bed," said Steve.

A hand placed on Bill's right shoulder made him turn. Looking down at him was the face of Mark Rogers smiling in that curiously self-regarding manner which had always disturbed Bill: the little tug down at the corners of his mouth, a greediness in the cast of his eyes, like a child ogling a chocolate birthday cake. His smile was almost a snigger and sniggering was Rogers's characteristic attitude. He was one of those people who see in politics an alternative to earning a living. At university he got himself elected as Entertainment Secretary which fulfilled his narcissistic love of ingratiating himself with the rich and famous. Buying takeaway curry for Kurt Cobain, having his picture taken with Anthony Kiedis, sharing a beer with Damon Albarn or a brandy with Rod Stewart elevated him into that territory of fame and wealth which floated above the rest of society, like the State itself, sucking its blood. These were people who'd performed the trick of playing on needs in order to enrich and free themselves. They didn't need to work. They didn't share the social, or even the geographical space of the ordinary folk. They inhabited a bubble apart. They were, as they dubbed themselves, "rock royalty" and like the real thing they assumed their right to pre-eminence. They had been raised by those who buckled beneath them. Rogers thought of the fans as dupes. They were punters who had to be sold a product and the essence of the product was themselves. They were in search of identity and they craved it because their lives, like his, were empty.

As a teenager, Rogers had dreamed of rock fame. Having no gift for music, finding the guitar impossibly complex and the rules of harmony baffling, he gave up after three chords and turned to the drums in the belief they required no particular musicality: Ringo Starr, after all, had conquered the world without being able to execute a decent drum roll. He assembled his *Pearl*

202

kit in the garage and thrashed every day after school. When he approached a lad who played guitar and sang in a band which had won a local competition, he came and listened. Rogers took his advice and bought himself a book, but following the steps to slow accumulation of competence, each stage of progress nothing but a tiny nudge forward, left him impatient. He tried to follow the patterns but his feet couldn't co-ordinate with his hands. It was all too formal. He was convinced Keith Moon had never bothered with such mincing nonsense. Surely it was simply a matter of thrashing in rhythm.

He played a couple of gigs in village halls with a band led by a bass player from school who filled himself with canned lager before they went on stage and twanged in ecstatic ignorance of what his fellow cacophonists were doing. They got no more bookings. The drums fell silent. There must be some other way to fabulous wealth and out of the need to get a job.

He'd hoped the Ents Sec position would make him an impresario but the bands he promoted remained small and local and resented paying him for getting work they could get themselves. Forced to take a job and armed with nothing more than the pass degree in Business Studies which was the result of putting all his effort into becoming the next Brian Epstein, he did clerical work for the County Council until in conversation with one of his colleagues he found out that the Council Leader pulled in expenses of thirty thousand.

The Labour Party seemed the appropriate vehicle, as he was more or less skint. He had a genuine sympathy for their rhetoric. It was in keeping with what he'd known. Like rock and pop, Labour politics was about inveigling the masses to believe in what kept them in their place and enriched and empowered a few. The Tories were too blankly for the rich. There was something more satisfying about waving the flag of egalitarianism while conspiring to great riches and pre-eminence.

Rogers was proof of the ingrained tendency of political parties to swallow their own rhetoric, to let it catch fast in their gullet and to wriggle and writhe in pain rather than admit their own bait is killing them. His enthusiastic recycling of the cliches of the day convinced his compatriots he was of the true faith, like those who pray loudest and with the greatest display of self-abnegation fool their fellow kneelers they are truly selfless while their egos swell with pride at their pre-eminence. Together with his manic *networking* and meticulous flattery of the people who mattered, this soon won him the nomination for a council seat which he stood on to reach a little higher convincing the group to *elect* him Cabinet Member for Leisure. While working for the council he'd been proclaimed secretary of his branch of Unison (he was the only candidate) a position in which he used his wiles to wring as many expenses as he could from the subs of members who had no idea their money was replenishing his petrol once a fortnight.

"How are you, Bill?"

Bill was tempted to reply:

"I was fine till I met you."

Charles Péguy came into his head: *tout commence en mystique, tout finit en politique.* For a second, he saw the bald head and bulbous face of the ageing communist who'd tutored his Péguy seminar in the first term at university. Rogers was a breathing example of the corruption of an ideal. In the days before the common folk had the vote, when organising and battling for betterment were hard and risky, he would have been nowhere to be seen. It always struck Bill that the creation of a political party to represent the common people was the beginning of the decline: why couldn't they represent themselves? Their party had been born from their movement and that was rooted in the workplace. Parliament was nothing to do with them. It had been created to look after landed interests, had been forced to admit the capitalist one, but gave no voice to those who had no property. Once the franchise began to be extended to working men and in its wake the Labour Party assumed the role of speaking for them, the power-hungry, the greedy, the status hunters, those who believed they might occupy a paragraph or even a footnote in some future historical tome, or who relished the notion of their dull speechifying being recorded for posterity in *Hansard*, came running like ants to a fallen sugar cube.

The parliamentary career was the death of radicalism. It didn't take long for the number of working people elected on the

Labour ticket to start to diminish. Now there was abroad the theory that decades of erosion of the vote in the heartlands was the
result of a more or less natural process of transformation from
heavy industry to post-industrial jobs. Why, Bill asked himself,
should people working in a call centre for eight pounds an hour
be less likely to vote Labour than a coal miner? Why should a
woman scurrying from job to job in the gig economy be less likely to vote for equality than a ship builder? It wasn't the change in
employment which was shaving votes from Labour, it was the
party's cowardly and calculating abandonment of its transformative policies. The process was very old. Ramsay McDonald had
shown the way; but who could trust a party which peddled the
rhetoric of justice, equality and democracy while supporting the
war in Iraq? What did academy schools and PFI hospitals have to
do with egalitarianism? It seemed to him the essence was simple:
solidarity was the key value. People had to pull together for the
common aims of peace and justice; but Labour's leadership facili-
tated atomisation .It conspired in conflating political with consumer choices, as if choosing a government was no different from
choosing a washing machine, as if it wasn't a matter of acute
moral urgency. Finally, the leaders liked injustice, because it was
the ground of their elevation. Power and corruption. The people,
he mused, should put faith in themselves.
   "I'm okay."
   "Pity about Jimmy," said Rogers.
   "Yes," said Bill, "he was a good man and a good social-
ist. Not many left."
   "You're right. Still, Keir will pull us through."
   "A hedge backwards," said Steve.
   "Not persuaded to stand?" said Rogers.
   "I can't even be persuaded to vote," said Bill.
   "Hey, now," said Rogers, "the vote was hard won."
   "Very good of them to give us the right to choose those
who rule over and manipulate us, wasn't it ?" said Bill.
   "Corbyn is gone," said Rogers. "Get over it."
   The formula made Bill wince inwardly, being one of
those condensations of received wisdom which replaced the effort
of thinking and articulation. It was a product of the era's will to

forgetfulness which in itself was an alienation. Proust's phrase came back to him: *Reality takes shape in the memory alone.* Of course, pedants could quibble over the meaning of reality, but it seemed to him the insight was astute: only in the effort to retrieve and make sense of the past do we begin to perceive how things are. Wasn't even physics, in a sense, a matter of grasping the past? Didn't we have to go back nearly fourteen billion years to understand why the sun rises?

"If he'd won, it would have been a great gift for Jimmy," said Bill.

"He couldn't win. People don't want that left-wing stuff."

"And he was an anti-Semite," said Steve.

"It didn't help," said Rogers.

"You agree with the wisdom of Margaret Hodge then?" said Steve.

"She's a feisty woman."

"Didn't she make a tidy pile from investments in South Africa?"

"No point digging up the past," said Rogers.

"No," said Steve, "just as the Zionists say. Let sleeping genocides lie."

"She's a living insult to people like Jimmy," said Bill. "Giving his life to local politics, wearing himself out canvassing, leafletting, attending meetings five nights a week, and all in the belief Labour is committed to peace, equality and democracy. While at the top you get Machiavellian cabalists like her, who learn their lines, speak like angels and act like devils. People like Jimmy are duped and the voters are cat's-paws."

"Nothing wrong with doing well for yourself. That's what we want for our people isn't it?"

"Is that the new Jerusalem, Mark? Everyone their little bit of property, standard class hegemony, the rich drowning in pelf and the poor imitating their Maseratis on the drive by parking their battered Nissan two wheels on the pavement?"

"Everybody wants to get on, it's human nature."

"Human nature is to choose your own behaviour," said Bill. "Nature gave no man the right to order others."

206

"People can vote. No one has power unless they elect them."

"Who elected Richard Branson?" said Bill.

"He doesn't have power," said Rogers.

"He has more power then all the votes of the folk of this town combined," said Bill. "Do you think if he phones Downing Street he'll be rebuffed? Do you think these people don't have access. The votes of the entire country wield less power than the opinions of a dozen billionaires. That's how democracy is suborned, that and the fact the public has no idea what's going on."

"No one stops 'em knowing," said Rogers.

"Except the *Sun*, the *Daily Mail*, the *Daily Express*, the *Telegraph*, the *Times*, *Sky News*, the *Spectator*.." said Steve.

"You have to learn to live with media," said Rogers. "Blair did."

"Tell that to the dead of Iraq," said Bill.

"Yeah, but he won three elections."

"Of course. The Establishment let him. He was safe. He was a Tory. He joined Labour because he loathed socialism. Just like Gaitskell, Jenkins, Callaghan, Healy, Owen, Williams. They all loathed the idea of doing away with the employee-employer relation. They all believed fervently in capitalism and their own success within it. Look at the loathing Corbyn evoked in the PLP. They try to claim it's because he was a flawed character but it's because he was radical. Labour has been full of flawed characters. George Brown couldn't stand up most of the time. Bevan was expelled for radicalism. The Labour Party loathes socialism, it hates the possibility of equality, it wants capitalism to last forever. It celebrates inequality and that makes it far more dangerous than the Tories."

"Labour wants the economy to work for everyone."

"What does that mean?" said Bill. "The rich man in his castle, the poor man at his gate?"

"People want to get on with their lives. They don't want to change the world."

"They can't get on with their lives unless they change the world," said Bill. "They're just going through the motions unless they make the decisions that matter for themselves."

"Anyway, said Rogers, "you can't take it away from Blair. He won three times. Corbyn got us the worst result since 1935."

"In 2017," said Bill, "the fourth best result in terms of vote share since 1966."

"It's seats that count."

"Yeah," said Steve, "and he'd've won ten more if the PLP and the bureaucracy hadn't been against him."

"You can't turn the party into a sect," said Rogers.

"And the right isn't pursuing schism?" said Bill. "From the day Corbyn was elected the PLP disdained and snubbed him. So much for democracy. So much for the famed broad church. It's the right that insists on faction. Corbyn brought centrists into his shadow cabinet and they resigned one after another in an organised wrecking action. It's simple, Mark. The one thing we aren't allowed is radical change. You can have any system you want, so long as it's capitalism."

"People want politicians who get stuff done. Left, right, it's old fashioned."

"That's what Rupert Murdoch says, anyway," said Steve.

"Get stuff done?" said Bill. "Like making peaceful protest virtually impossible. You're missing the essential point. Liberty. Why do we need employers?"

Rogers laughed.

"So people have jobs."

"Why were slave-owners once necessary? If you'd asked them, don't you think you'd've got the same answer. Without the slave owners the slaves wouldn't have had work. Without feudal lords, the peasants wouldn't have had work. Slavery, feudalism, employment, they're morally outrageous because they rest on exploitation which is curtailment of liberty," said Bill.

"That's all theory."

"And your position is what exactly?" said Steve.

The congregation began to move inside.

Quiet descended as if something in the walls turned off speech. Reverence gathered and forbade any breach. Without command, everyone knew how to behave. Even children who couldn't hold back a question delivered them into parental ears in a whisper. Bill's irritation at Rogers's intrusion, and he did experience it as such, began to subside. It was odd how the man was able to approach people he knew disdained him as if they were friends. Bill's antipathy wasn't principally to Rogers's politics: he could have met and spoken to people who thought voting Tory was as natural as breathing and felt sympathetic and generous. Political affiliation was usually superficially mediated especially given the lack of principle in political parties. What affronted him in Rogers was his amorality. He could have given expression to the most left-wing notions and he would still have been despicable because nothing was more important to him than his own interest and his capacity to see others as a means to his ends was limitless.

Would he have been capable of expressing the ideas Bill believed in? Could he have argued for the dissolution of the employer-employee relation and the replacement of the State by socialisation? Or was there a point at which political ideas ran up against moral values and made it impossible for engrained self-seekers to embrace what might defeat them? Bill couldn't imagine Rogers comfortable with egalitarian, non-hierarchical relations. Yet it might have been possible for him to utter what was required to convince while nurturing the opposite in his heart.

The coffin stood to the left, adorned with wreaths. Bill half listened to the sincere speeches whose maudlin tone was inevitable. Wasn't it best to leave it to an uninvolved third party? He thought of the vicar who spoke at his mother's funeral, a young woman who had come to visit him one morning and chatted for two hours, turning their conversation into an informed, well-judged celebration. Heather couldn't finish for her tears. The children choked. Bill fixed his eyes on the wicker crib. Inside was his old acquaintance. The cheerful eyes which faced him over a pub table and a pint, the bustling, sturdy walk, the insistence in his voice as he made a point in a meeting: alive only in memory. But all his memories of Jimmy were positive. He was one of those people of whom you'd say, if all the folk in the world were like him, what a life we would have.

Among the many people he knew were many he didn't. Across the aisle which divided the pews he noticed an elegant

woman of fifty in a black dress which hung on the edge of her
shoulders, her back exposed to his gaze as her upper chest would
be from the front. Her brimmed hat was as funereally devoid of
colour as her mourning frock, but around its bun was a broad purple ribbon and its rightward tilt suggested mischief the occasion
couldn't supress. Her exposed skin was very white, but her hair,
cut abrupt just below her ear, was as dark as her weeds. He found
himself noodling his head, like the joystick on Liam's controller,
to bring her left hand into his line of vision. She smoothed the
fabric along her left thigh (oh, the turgid life in that upper leg).
No ring. Her hand was long and her fingers slender, reminding
him of his sister and mother and their swift, apparently effortless
capacity with needles. In profile her face seemed handsome, but it
was only when she turned, no doubt preternaturally sensitive to
the fixity of his eyes, that he could take in both the beauty and the
kindness in her features. Her dark eyes connected and the corners
of her mouth stretched, like a tiny rubber band in a child's fingers, in an incipient smile, before she turned away.

Bill came to himself. What would Jimmy have said? Funerals are for the living, no doubt. He'd've wanted no concentrated misery at his send off and he'd've been glad if people enjoyed
one another's company and had a good time; and even if Bill had
met a pleasant woman to bring a little comfort to his bachelor-
hood.

Every contribution was inadequate. He wondered what, if
he'd been asked to speak, he would have said. There were no
words. In the face of death, language guttered. Once there had
been a lively, friendly, generous, energetic bloke. Now there was
just food for bacteria. A person was alive one moment and in the
next they were gone and the difference was ineffable. He was an
atheist, yet what was needed here was ritual; something which
lifted from those who'd known and loved Jimmy, the impossible
task of articulating the meaning of his death. Death had no meaning. It annulled all significance. Jimmy lived on through those
who remembered him. The meaning of his life hadn't ended. It
would endure for centuries, for as long as the species, because
memory goes on for thousands of years and though his name
might be lost, somewhere, even ten centuries from now, someone

would be alive whose life had been changed in perhaps only the most minute particular by his existence. That was true for all of us. Our great illusion, ground of the need for an after-life, was that the significance of our lives perished with our bodies. The meaning of our lives was always meaning for others and nothing could stop that meaning being carried forward. Men who had ruled the world were viewed with disdain centuries later, their names in thousands of books but always inspiring disgust and dismay. Such was the foolishness of the time-serving Jimmy had avoided.

The Joiner's Arms stood alone, flattered by rubble on two flanks. On the opposite side of little Gray Street which ran from the main road to a cluster of small houses with tiny front gardens and a corner shop next to the boarded up Methodist Church, were small homes, some flats, now thirty years old.

"At least there's plenty of room for cars" said Steve.

"Yes," said Bill, "demolish the houses, make way for the motors. Cut down the trees, drive people into underpasses. I think it's called progress."

The little pub was divided into a snug and a lounge. The former could hold no more than a dozen and sported two circular tables, well stained and unstable, at either side of the fireplace whose wooden surround at whose centre was an oval mirror was of the kind the houses which once neighboured the pub would have had in their front rooms. The lounge was set out with tables around its periphery so the centre was a great void in which sat the blue, grey-white, tassle-edged carpet, threadbare in its areas of greatest use. Against the farthest wall, a long trestle table was shoved, paper plates piled at one end, and beyond them, platters of egg and cress, ham salad, beef, tuna, cheese and pickle followed by sausage rolls, doll's house pork pies sliced into quarters, and lastly, chocolate gateau awaiting surgery.

Behind the bar were a stout, vigorous woman of fifty and a slender, dark, bearded lad of eighteen, the two of them valiantly trying to serve the needs of the crowd, thirsty for release from intense solemnity.

"What you having?" said Steve.

"Best hang on a minute," said Bill, "you'll get crushed."

"I like a good scrum. Non-alcoholic beer?"

"You'll be lucky. Anything without alcohol."

Bill hung back at the opposite side from the array of food still under its forbidding cling-film. The woman in the black dress emerged from the swarm and smiled in the tiny elastic band manner.

"All right?" he said.

"Yes, are you?"

"Fine."

He offered her his hand.

"Bill George."

"Jo Lane."

"How did you know Jimmy?" he said.

"Through my husband. Jimmy fought his case when they tried to sack him."

"Ah. Did he win?"

"Yeah. Got him a package."

"Good. Your husband here?"

"No. I've been a widow for nearly two years."

"I'm sorry."

"These things happen. Fit as a flea. Used to do the iron man and that kind of thing. Oesophageal cancer."

"That was bad luck."

"Yes."

"So did you get to know Jimmy?"

"Oh yes, we used to go out with them. I meet up with Heather now and again."

"He was a good man."

"He was. I liked him." She paused and looked Bill in the eye. "Didn't agree with his politics though."

"No?"

"No. I think Mrs Thatcher turned this country round."

"She certainly did," he said.

"He was a nice man though, and Heather is lovely."

"Do you need a drink? My mate is fighting his way through."

"No, someone's getting me one."

Her face had very definite features: a strong nose, thick lips and big brown eyes, and her demeanour was calm and easy, as if she was utterly at home in her skin. He often wasn't. In fact, the tenor of his life was that he wasn't. She was a physically lovely woman and he sensed in her that capacity for responsiveness which he'd known but which Caroline had controlled, as she tried to control everything. Barring what he thought of as the crass remark, he would have been eager to get to know her; but in that comment opened an unbreachable gulf. It wasn't mere disagreement about nuances of policy but a fundamental difference. To him Thatcher's sensibility was denatured. She was kitsch made flesh: phoney, sentimental, cheap, vulgar, appealing to everything base and unrefined while posing as the ultimate in refinement. In her was expressed the culture's distorted view of human nature, the denial of the simple truth that our biological inheritance has made choosing how to act characteristic. Her stiff authoritarianism, copied from a hypocritical father whose marriage was cold, was the gutter stock-in-trade of every glib absorber of manufactured opinion. She oozed the need for control of those who, subjected to control, have failed to attain autonomy. Rabelais's motto swam into his mind: *Do what you will* was the opposite of the message Thatcher communicated in every gesture: *Do what you're told*. And who does the telling? Always the rich. And what has made them rich? Violence.

"So what do you do when you're not attending funerals of inveterate lefties?" he said.

She laughed in a charmingly loose way, like a flower that bends in a gentle breeze.

"I'm a social worker."

He was about to say, "Just the kind of person Mrs Thatcher admired", but restrained himself.

"That must be interesting."

"It's not the easiest job in the world but I like to feel I can make a difference. What about you?"

"I was a teacher."

"What did you teach?"

"Children, mostly."

"That must've been interesting too."

213

"Yes, the geniuses in Westminster worked wonders. It was like trying to build a wall and each time you laid a brick someone knocked it off and if you tried to stop them, you were told it was your fault: if you built the wall well enough, they wouldn't want to knock it down."

"I know. You hear such stories. People have no respect for teachers anymore."

"The public sector has taken a hammering," he said.

"There's not enough discipline, in my opinion. I heard on the radio about a school in London where the children aren't allowed to talk in the corridors. I think that's a good idea."

Bill pretended to look for Steve as he held back what he was burning to say:

"Maybe we should have barbed wire, Alsatians and search lights. Maybe if the kids try to sneak off to the chippy at lunchtime, they should be shot by snipers in watchtowers."

It was bad enough already. The secondary school he attended was now enclosed by a seven-foot, green, metal fence. Where once there'd been easy access to the woods behind, now there were gates and padlocks and a long detour. The field where in the evening and at weekends he'd kicked a ball with his mates and the girls had set up a make-shift high-jump bar and straddled and flopped into the sand, was now guarded by forbidding signs. All this in the name of rolling back the State and individual liberty.

It was bizarre how the tightrope conformism of Thatcher could be mistaken for a love of freedom. She who apparently loathed the State, used its power to fight for the Falklands and against the miners. How did people make the mistake? How did they think cutting the budgets for schools or hospitals, or imposing a National Curriculum were examples of a beneficent retreat by the State, while sending gunboats three thousand miles to fight for a piece of land taken by force whose invaders could be sent packing by sanctions anyway, was an expression of individual freedom? The confusions were astounding: as if the headlines in the right-wing press read: PROOF:THE EARTH IS FLAT or THERE IS NO SUCH THING AS GRAVITY.

214

In the eschatology of this attractive, charming woman, freedom was identification with wealth and power. The State was a monster if it took your appendix out or taught you how to calculate the volume of a sphere but a liberator if it stacked up nuclear weapons, installed cameras to watch your every move, passed laws to stop you withdrawing your labour (as if it belonged to someone else) and dressed soldiers as policemen to beat coal miners over the head when they tried to protect their jobs and communities.

Now, some of the most hard-up folk in the land had helped elect an ex-Etonian who blamed the Liverpool fans for Hillsborough, called people with   skin pigmentation different from his own picaninnies, belong to a club of entitled young vandals who thought smashing up restaurants a jape, invented stories when he was a journalist, and was reputed by almost everyone who knew him well to be an inveterate liar. Yet worse, was that some of those areas which had been most starved of funds during the unnecessary austerity were now most heavily in his favour. Here were people lashing themselves in an orgy of self-abasement because of flimsy rhetoric of "taking back" a control they never had.

Of course, the last thing their elected leader believed in was control in their hands. How did this nefarious miracle come about; why was it that granted democracy, having the power to free themselves from poverty or dull routine or submission to the will of a handful of intellectually and mentally chaotic time-and-self-servers, people used their liberty to punish themselves?

The clue was control of opinion but that in itself was puzzling. He'd been subject to the control. He read the papers, watched and listened to the news. He was subjected to the conformist message delivered by school, parents, churches, but he hadn't succumbed. Was it because the *Daily Herald* came through the letterbox when he was a lad or because his grandad had been a trade unionist and his parents Labour voters? But people in Barrow and Grimsby, in Leigh and Sedgefield from equally non-conformist backgrounds had voted Tory. What had been removed was the possibility of an alternative. A steady imposition of hopelessness in anything but the status quo, combined with a concerted spread of stupefaction which made particularly astute use of popular culture hadn't merely changed people's opinions, but had altered their sensibility. There had once been a lived experience of solidarity. His grandfather had known it: the men and women in the union were part of something bigger than their subjectivity; the people he lived amongst in the terrace streets the same. There was equality amongst them because it was hard to break out of the imposed wage limits. In their shared condition they experienced the possibility of new social relations; didn't just think about it but experienced it. His mother and father too, growing up in the mean streets where income and wealth existed between very narrow limits.

The glib argument was: changing economic conditions had eroded loyalties. Coal mining, ship-building, heavy industry were no more and in turn people were more isolated and atomised, sensing their condition as theirs alone: the minimum-wage bloke unable to pay the bills without benefits, didn't conjoin with others in the same plight, but felt himself lonely and ashamed and was easy prey for the political predators who turned his sense of grievance against foreigners and immigrants.

Bill wondered why call centre workers should be less inclined to solidarity than coal miners. They were for the most part low-paid and their conditions were far from comfortable and generous. It was convenient to paint it all as a flow of inevitable events. Yet Labour had been in power for thirteen years during which solidarity and a belief in a different life had eroded. How could those administrations bear no responsibility? How could it be true that the shift from a majority of over twenty-five thousand in 1997 to a loss by more than four thousand in Sedgefield had nothing to do with Blair? There was a terrible, deliberate confusion in the belief. Wasn't it true rather that the New Labour relaxation about people being "filthy rich", its resolute anti-left stance, its elimination of the very word socialism from its lexicon, its enthusiasm for go-getting and its vacuous belief in "whatever works" had done enormous damage? Bill saw it as the culmination of a long process intended to drive socialism from the political landscape. What was Gaitskell fighting and fighting again for if not the defeat of socialism? Why did the shabby Gang of Four leave the party if not to defeat socialism?

If there was one cause of the dislocation of the common folk from Labour, it was the resolute insistence by its leaders on being immovably right of centre. Their promotion of themselves as better managers of capitalism than the Tories was the short route to erosion of support: if you're going to vote for a Tory, it might as well be a real one. It seemed to Bill, people would tolerate mistakes and setbacks if they understood there was a sincere effort at change in the direction which would bring what they craved. The Tories could get away with blistering incompetence and woeful corruption because their supporters knew they stood for property. The monied, and not only the extravagantly so, were willing to vote for blunderers, throwbacks, profligates, freebooters, shysters to defend their economic and social advantage; but why should Labour voters tolerate the least backsliding or venality if what they were voting for was managerialism?

The slick, media-compliant, look-at-me-I-wear-a-business-suit demeanour of Blair and his cohort communicated complete absence of irreverence toward the status quo. It was easy to get weary of such compliance. A movement with endurance needed to have the uplift of young love which brings a couple together and sustains them through years and difficulties because it begins at such a high point of idealism. Cynical seduction and emotional manipulation brought quick disaffection and recoil, but the beauty of real love was sustaining. A movement for change needed the same lofty intoxication, the very vertiginous soaring the managers feared and hated. Steady as she goes was their motto as they steered their outboard-motor, boating-lake skiff past the floating ducks when what was needed was an Atlantic class speedster which could ride the waves and effect daring rescue.

It was the entrenched right-wing leadership which had sucked dry the common folk's idealism, their hope for equality, their belief the mutual helpfulness they knew in their streets could become the ruling tenor of life; it was the low, conniving, wilfully ambiguous, power-and-money-hungry drive of the elite which believed it had the right to lead and which responded to the warn-

217

ings of disaffection with "they've no one else to vote for" that had desiccated the innards of the party, turned it into a mere vote-gathering machine with no vision of transformation. Bill knew the folk in his town would have accepted without demur and with gladness a co-operative economy and direct democracy. They were anarchists in their hearts, gregarious, loving to meet in equality, happy to be of help to a friend or neighbour in trouble.

What they knew from their ordinary experience was countermanded daily by the media. That was the clue. Yet, in spite of the daily bombardment of conformist messages and the absolute exclusion of anything which spoke of the possibility of real reform, they stuck to their view. They voted Labour. In doing so they weren't saying: "Oh, please don't change anything. Heaven forbid that the chasm between the super-rich and us should be narrowed, let alone closed. Oh, don't give us any choice over our own lives. Please pursue your marvellous careers and don't mind us, we're just voting fodder after all." What Labour meant to them, he knew, was: "We're as good as the next man or woman. We don't kiss the arse of the rich and we don't accept being pushed around. We want a world in which we're free to live out our natures to the full, and this isn't it."

It was remarkable in a society where six daily newspapers pumped out Tory propaganda as efficiently as the sewage system gurgled waste, that a Labour government was ever elected, even one as right-wing as Blair's. Yet he knew well enough the difference between the delivery and receipt of a message. What encouraged him was the cynicism of the common folk, their irreverent capacity to make a joke of everything, their instinctive understanding that though they might have to make the best of their lives in the interstices of a system run for the rich, there was a tense balance between their freedom and the licence of the wealthy. Women were willing to get on with their lives if they could feed their kids, get out for a good time once a week, go to the bingo for a laugh, have a holiday in the summer, join a dance class or a badminton club, and not be too pinched at the end of the month; but they nurtured a quiet resilience and incipient rebellion. The spark wouldn't need to be great that would start a conflagration. They made a calculation: they weren't going to risk what

218

they had, but if it was taken away, there'd be cataclysm. Their assumption was the rich knew as much. They'd always be on the lookout for an opportunity to fill their pockets at the common folk's expense, but they had to look over their shoulders. Social peace was bought at the cost of the perpetual possibility of its breakdown. That was how it must be in a system of essential injustice.

Steve arrived with the drinks.

"Steve," said Bill, "this is Jo. A social worker. If you'll excuse me I've just spotted someone I haven't seen for a bit."

He slid through the huddle to the spread and arranged two egg and cress on brown, a cheese and pickle on white and a tiny quarter of pork pie on his paper plate. He stood running his eyes over the offerings again and again, as if something appetising, something confected with imagination or even love might materialise and make him want to savour. Why was there not at least a bowl of coleslaw, a mixed salad, some grated carrots with a little dressing; why no smoked salmon; why not a complete fish lying in freshwater splendour its muscular body which had once fought upstream to spawn, cooked to tender seductiveness and slit open awaiting an intrusive knife; why no triangular packets of vegetarian deliciousness like those Jasmine produced; why no gorgeous beef tomatoes sliced to reveal their lovely red innards and frogspawn seeds doused in a blended vinaigrette?

What would Jimmy have made of it? No doubt some subversive quip would have accompanied his piling his plate and making the best:

"The leftovers from the privatisation of British Rail party by the look of it."

Bill bit into the egg and cress relieved at the freshness of the bread.

"So they've kicked you out then, Bill."

He lifted his eyes to see a little man whose thick silver hair was topped by a denim cap bearing a badge showing the head of Karl Marx. His face was florid and slightly puffy and his shoulders seemed to be raised a little, as if in defence. His sartorial concession to the occasion was a black tie loosely knotted and a clean pair of well-ironed jeans.

"Suspended," said Bill.

"Told you long ago you were wasting your time. Come and join us."

"Do I have to learn a secret handshake?" said Bill.

"I'll get you in, comrade."

"I don't want to be *in*, Kevin. I've resigned from Labour. Political parties are part of the problem."

"We're different, Bill. We don't fight elections, we foment revolution."

"People have just elected Johnson because they want a socialist revolution, eh?"

"A small cadre is enough."

"Ever the democrat, Kevin."

"Bourgeois democracy is a sham, Bill. The workers' State makes it unnecessary."

"Who will run the workers' State?"

"We will."

"Bakunin was right after all."

"Anarchism is just a form of bourgeois individualism, Bill. Only the organised working-class has the power to overthrow capitalism."

"And they're just itching to do that so your half dozen mates can run the country on their behalf."

"The workers' State is for the workers."

"I know what Stalin said, Kevin. But Bakunin was right: Stalin beat the people with the people's stick."

"We'd nationalise the commanding heights..."

"You know what ?" said Bill. "That's what I heard John Prescott saying back in the late seventies. Slides off the pseudo-radical tongue like oysters gliding down the oesophagus. Look how he ended up, supporting the war in Iraq. It's not the workers' State we need, it's the erosion of the State."

"That leaves the field open to the capitalists."

"You think capitalists don't need the State? You've fallen for the free market rhetoric, Kevin. Capitalism isn't a free market system. In a free market the workers would win every time. Capitalism is State power used in the interests of property."

"All right, then we'll use State power in the interests of the workers."

"The workers don't need it. The common folk can run their own lives. That's the point, Kev. Socialisation not Statism. A society of free association. It's our nature to co-operate. Property has denatured us. Why would I join your lot to promote democratic centralism? I despise your idea that the minority must be subordinate to the majority and the entrenched hierarchy in which decisions from higher up must bind those below. The thing you do well is supporting causes. That's what you should become, a flexible pressure group. It's your forte."

The little Marxist was chomping on his ham salad. He was one of those sincere radicals who'd been seduced by the glib ventriloquism of the International Socialists, as they were when he was young, the Socialist Workers' Party in their current iteration. He was one of the duteous foot soldiers who carried out the orders of the central committee, which effectively elected itself and then permitted the members to endorse its wisdom. For nearly fifty years he'd held banners, sold newspapers, marched, manned stalls. His essential orientation was correct. He was incapable of violence or manipulation. He genuinely wanted free and equal relations; but he needed a home. The Labour Party was hopeless so he took refuge.

His little terrace was half a mile from Bill's. He lived alone, had never married or had long-term partners and twenty years earlier his brother had been killed in a motorbike accident. Was that the time when he began drinking more heavily? He'd always been convivial and Bill had enjoyed meeting him in the pub when he was home from university. He was a football fan with a taste for blues and a magpie interest in literature. A wave of pity arose, which Bill couldn't dismiss as mere sentimentalism. Jimmy, Kevin, they were good people, in spite of their many faults. They hadn't surrendered their sense of innocence. Life enchanted them in its glorious richness and prior to their intellectualising they knew equality was our natural condition.

There'd been a time when Bill would have rejected the idea, when he'd come to think that mind was entirely social; but little by little the notion had been worn away and he was im-

pressed by the power of innateness. If we didn't have a given nature, as Chomsky said, if we simply responded to environmental
stimuli, our mental life would be impoverished. Our natural condition was to be social. We had a history because our biological
endowment made us cultural, but the flexibility of culture was
possible only because of the rigidity of the given limits. As Kundera put it, there was an *anthropological scandal*: you couldn't
piss ten metres in the air, but you could murder on Stalin's orders.
No one grew to be fifteen feet tall or had a nose two feet long.
The physical boundaries, which produced the delightful variety of
human bodies, were very narrow. Why shouldn't the same be true
of cognitive boundaries?

You couldn't elaborate a culture in which people weren't
allowed to be linguistic any more than one in which people
weren't allowed to breathe; but you could create one in which
people were forcibly robbed of the right to choose their own ac-
tions. It was appalling that such a morally despicable possibility
existed but it did, because the plasticity of action could be exploited by the manipulative, the arrogant, the greedy and violence
was a permanent potential. What a pity, he thought, that biology
had wired in a capacity for aggression. It was there because our
ancestors had to kill big beasts for their dinner. Evolution didn't
prescribe its use. That was our choice.

Humanity had taken a wrong turn. Nature had provided
us with the capacity to build our culture from our endowment and
we had chosen conquest based on racism in the pursuit of lucre.
That was why the world was facing a climate crisis and there
were tendentious twerps who denied it. It was why Bill Gates was
richer than small countries; the few climbed in aeroplanes for
nothing but a jaunt while the majority had never seen an airport;
men of colour were murdered on the street by American cops;
desperate people fleeing persecution and poverty drowned in the
Mediterranean while spoilt narcissists topped up their tans in St
Tropez; Boris Johnson washed his feet in Champagne while the
poor went to food banks; why the miserable circus of rank injustice was paraded before our eyes every day and the world was
marinated in propaganda which excused it.

Kevin had done what he thought was right to try to amend the injustices, but he'd been bamboozled by an ideology which suited the needs of power-seekers, people who wanted to be right, who weren't willing to think and talk and risk that their will might not prevail. Bill admired the Socialist Workers' campaigning. He'd been active in the *Anti-Nazi League* and he thought *Rock Against Racism* an inspiration; but the central committee handing down decisions and the notion of a workers' State were risible. The State wasn't a repository of justice. For centuries it had protected the rich. Latterly, it had been used to grant benefits to the majority, but that was nothing more than a miserly protection against the harsh winds of an exploitative economy. The work to remove the exploitation was also the work to make the State redundant.

"We aren't a pressure group," said Kevin, wiping his mouth with the back of his hand, "because we oppose the system."

"I know," said Kevin, "but the system is like Hydra. You need Hercules to cut off its heads."

"Aye," said Kevin, reaching for a sausage roll, "but it's only powerful while it keeps at least one head, and we'll sever its neck."

Bill nodded and placed his hand on Kevin's shoulder.

"I hope you do. See you in a bit."

Like Jimmy, Kevin was an idealist in a world ruled by cynics, a democrat in a world ruled by violence. They were the nameless people, unrecorded and unremembered who made their small contribution through relentless effort and disappeared while *pacts and sects of great ones* strutted across the globe, dragging their ball and chain egos behind them, borne down by property and the hypocrisy needed to uphold it. They could have lived sweet, carefree, joyous lives, but the time was out of joint and it was the cursed spite of the common folk that they were born to set it right.

Kevin wouldn't sever the neck of capitalism. The rich and powerful sneered and mocked at him and Jimmy. Him too. He knew well enough how little difference he'd made, but it was true all the same that billions of little differences could change the world and the common folk had a common interest in peace and equality. How many years were left to him? His energy was diminishing. It would have been easy to close the door on the world and listen to Bach and Count Basie, read his favourite poems and novels, get on the train to the theatre when there was a Shakespeare, an Ibsen, a Sean O'Casey, an Orton, a Wycherley an Arthur Miller. Why not have a long walk each day and let the world go its mad course?

But he wouldn't. Whatever he could do, he would.

TRAGEDY AND AFTER

Steve looked up the clearance on his mobile and did the sum.

"One point three seconds," he said.

Numbers seemed to offer him comfort, as if in the swirl of experience, and particularly the distress of the news, they were the one constant.

"Hardly time to think," said Bill.

"The water would have been about fifteen centigrade. The shock would have driven the breath out of her. Her head under the water as she gasped. Gone."

Bill nodded.

"Another tea?"

"Get me a beer."

"Is that a good idea?"

"Just the one."

On the train to London, in their suits once more, Steve leaned over the table.

"You know, Bill, I don't like to say it, but it's a relief."

There was no callousness in his friend's expression or tone, but honesty at the end of the strain of living with Judy's crumbling personality. It was also a way of diminishing the sense of grief and horror. Had her heart given way or a brain haemorrhage seized her on the tube, the loss would have been as wrenching, but her deliberate self-destruction in such a dramatic manner was an added pain.

"London Bridge, of all places," said Steve looking at the backs of the houses as they neared Euston.

The afternoon of their return, Jasmine greeted them at the door.

"I knew you'd be back today," she said.

"How?" said Bill. "We didn't decide till last night."

"Feminine intuition. Come and eat. It's all ready."

"Yes," said Nathan, "come on. I've got some nice beer, Steve."

"Bill," said Rakesh, "shall we go to the duck pond?"

"Get in with you," said Jasmine. "We're going to eat."

225

"Tomorrow?" said Rakesh as his father ushered him gently indoors.

Jasmine was keen to know how Bill's dispute with Labour was faring. He explained he'd made a subject access request because he believed the party had shared his details with an outside body, had received no response, in defiance of the law; had made his complaint to the Information Commissioner's Office only to be told there was such a backlog of similar complaints, no action would be taken.

"The moral seems to be, if you break the law wholesale, you'll get away with it."

"Oh, it's outrageous," she said. "How can they break the law like that?"

"It's the way the world works," Jasmine. If the poor break the law, they get hung, drawn and quartered. But the rich and powerful can choose which laws they fancy."

There seemed little point in trying to squeeze blood from the Labour stone. The party was sunk in cowardice, hypocrisy and dishonesty. Bill laughed when he recalled one of the party hierarchy's remark on the comment which secured the removal of the whip from Corbyn: "It's true, but unacceptable." Who could expect justice from a party which found truth unacceptable?

Of course, the comment revealed the inner workings of the machine in all its miserable peace, justice and equality-shredding relentlessness. The greed for power must tread truth underfoot. The fact, incontrovertible, uncontroversial, obvious to the most cursory scrutiny that the claims of institutionalised racism were overblown, had to be buried in the mud, left to rot , to freeze and crack, sealed within the hard peaks of sun-shrunk August sculptures.

The witchcraft of language could be very concealing. For him the word "socialism" meant equal rights for all, which by definition ruled out racism, sexism, prejudice against the disabled, enabling or crippling disparities of wealth – there was no equality of rights between a billionaire and a food bank dependent. Yet behind that apparently benign term, what could be hidden? If socialism was nothing more than the effort to gain for the workers a greater share of the proceeds of colonialism, then it partook of the racism on which colonialism rested. Wasn't it true that Labour, even at its best, in the creation of the NHS and the entrenching of social welfare, had conspired with the morally repugnant view of progress which saw "lesser races" as expendable? Hadn't Crossman said as much, drawing a parallel between the US and Israel and regretting the inevitability which meant that, like the native Americans, the Palestinians would have to disappear before the advance of their superiors?

The mistake was simple but devastating. The Left had failed to grasp and push the idea of innateness: our biological inheritance imposes unity. No one chooses to be linguistic any more than they choose to have two legs or a pituitary gland. Human nature wasn't a vast, sloppy overcoat within which there was room for variation which distinguished one group from another, one individual from another in ways so fundamental it was possible to say some people belonged to one "race" and others to another; some were "entrepreneurs" and other "workers", as if natural selection itself had consigned them to categories. It was a corset whose narrowness and rigidity, ironically, guaranteed richness. But the richness fooled us: it seemed that between his miserable efforts on a tennis courts and the efficient grace of Roger Federer, there was infinite distance; in fact, the differences in hand-eye coordination, anticipation and speed around the court operated within very narrow limits. No one could hit a tennis ball at a thousand miles an hour or get from the base-line to the net in a millisecond.

The idea of the infinite flexibility of our nature gave moral licence to the exploiters and manipulators: if some were born to rule and others to serve, then who could object if the latter were made use of? But if there was one and only one human nature, if we were all essentially the same and the differences which made life so interesting superficial, then there was no moral justification for divisions of class, race, gender. Equality was not an interpretation but a fact and the culture which denied it an abuse.

There came the skirmishes in East Jerusalem. He attended carefully to the reporting which, as usual, failed to blame the Israelis. No one bothered to remark the provocation. That violence might ensue seemed as unlikely as two suns. Yet for Bill the here-we-go-againism was evident and the cause equally clear: if Net-anyahu was out of power he would almost certainly be in prison.

Israel has a right to defend itself. Seven words which hid a stinking, crawling, vermin-infested heap of cant. The right to defend illegal occupation? The right to defend apartheid? And then the distress and misery of the intemperate attacks, the hundreds dead and maimed, the necessary facilities destroyed.

The weekend after the ceasefire there was a march and rally. An e-mail arrived from one of his old union colleagues. He asked if he could speak and in the afternoon when the grey, morning clouds had transformed to huge, fluffy pillows moving quickly across the spaces of spring azure delivered his peroration to an assembled thousand on the central square:

For five centuries the world has been dominated by conquest based on racism in pursuit of lucre. Israel/Palestine is an enduring example of that phenomenon.

The relation between the State of Israel and the Palestinians is founded on racism. Here's Chaim Weizmann, hardly an insignificant figure in the history of either Israel or Zionism:

"There is a qualitative difference between a Jew and an Arab"

In 1988, Avraham Sharir, Israel's Minister of Finance, remarked:

"Arabs are liars from birth."

Ernest Bevin, Foreign Secretary in the 1945 government who banged his head against a brick wall trying to bring an agreement, said in exasperation:

"The fundamental problem of Palestine was the Jews wouldn't accept the Arabs as their equals."

Two million people are incarcerated in the Gaza Strip because they are Arabs...

The history of Israel/Palestine is a racist project, derived from the work of Theodore Herzl to establish a Jewish State in the whole of Palestine.

This is how Ben-Gurion, Israel's first Prime Minister typified it: "There is no conflict between Jewish nationalism and

228

Palestinian nationalism because the Jewish nation is not in Palestine and the Palestinians do not have a nation."

Every time there has been the possibility of an agreement two things have happened. The Israelis have used violence and the US its veto.

In January 1976, resolution was to the UN Security Council based on the internationally agreed consensus: an Israeli society and a Palestinian society on the 4th June 1967 borders..

The responsibility for everything that has happened in Israel/Palestine since 1947 lies with the US because Israel does nothing without their permission. Israel is a pipsqueak country and a nuclear armed State..

Biden is congratulating himself on "quiet diplomacy" A quiet diplomacy which has seen hundreds of Palestinians slaughtered..

Biden could have stopped the conflict at any point.

Biden is another in a long line of US presidents who have failed to face down Israeli racism and oppression...

Netanyahu says Hamas is a terrorist organisation. Well, in January 2006 Hamas fought a General Election, the first open, free and fair election in the Arab world, and won handsomely..

7th December 1987 the UN General Assembly passed Resolution 159 which made terrorism a crime. Quite right. But the resolution contained a proviso: where a people has been forcibly deprived of it self-determination, freedom and independence it has the right to fight for them...

Netanyahu says he is opposed to all terrorism.In September 1997 he ordered the assassination of Khaled Mashal, the Hamas leader, an act of international terrorism...

Israel acts in bad faith. . Remember Lebanon in 1982? They have two excuses for not negotiating: the Palestinians are terrorists and they are divided. Well, in 2014 Hamas and the Palestinian Authority signed a unity deal. What did Israel do? Bombed Gaza. Bad faith...

Seventy-three years since the Nakbah and still Israel has no defined borders...

Are we going to get a solution from Biden, from Labour? No. Where will it come from? From the common folk, all over the world....

The common folk of the world have an interest in peace and justice and we must not say to the politicians: "We will wait for you to make a gift of peace and justice to us," but "We are taking peace and justice for ourselves and if you aren't coming with us then get out of the way."

Lastly, Netanyahu has been on the television over the past days, that despicable sniggering expression on his face, as he boasts about slaughtering Palestinians. Well, why did this whole miserable affair take place? Because if Netanyahu is not in power he will almost certainly be in prison....

"Well done, mate," said Steve.

"Yes, it was very good," said Jo Lane who had tagged along with Steve. "I didn't agree with it all, but it was very good."

"No, I don't agree with all of it either," said Barbara, appearing from the crowd like the genie from the lamp. " Guess what? We got the library kept open."

"You did well," said Bill.

Steve laid his arm across Jo's shoulders.

"We'll make a social democrat of you yet," and he kissed her cheek.

The sun caught her hair and Bill was struck by how young it made her look. In the sunshine they could all gather a hint of youthfulness and the suggestion that starting again might be possible.

"No, you won't," she said. "I don't agree with it."

Bill felt a solid nudge against his shin and looked down at the black sheen of a Labrador's back, its glamour as rich as Jo's.

"Good work, sir."

Tina reached up to make Steve's peck a pair. A white on black PALESTINIAN LIVES MATTER adorned her blue zip-up.

"Didn't expect to see you here," said Bill.

"Did you expect to see me anywhere else?"

"Anyway," said Steve, "I'm parched. Let's raise a glass to the Palestinians in the *Bull*."

"Fancy it?" said Bill.

"Are they dog-friendly?" said Tina.

"Yes," said Steve, "they even let Jo in."

She gave his upper arm an affectionate punch at which he rubbed and grimaced in mock pain like a Premier League *prima donna*.

"Well, why not. I'm a free woman."

"Are you?" said Steve.

"Completely," she said, taking his arm.

www.ingramcontent.com/pod-product-compliance
Lightning Source LLC
Chambersburg PA
CBHW071151260626
47162CB00003B/1004